This book...wow. This was an amazing, spellbinding tale of faith, spirituality, love, and freedom. It was quite a ride!

T.M. Morris, author of the 11th Percent series.

This book...wow. An amazing, spellbinding tale of faith and love. ...rich in descriptive narrative. An outstanding debut novel.

M.A.R. Unger, Author of the Matti James Mystery Series

Dream of Dragons is a story that stayed with me....whimsical and light-hearted, yet with some very dark undertones. I'd recommend this baroque fairly tale to anyone who wants to escape reality and be profoundly touched

Chris H. Stevenson—Planet Janitor; Custodian of the Stars.

A Dream of Dragons, a novel by Christian authors Lauretta and Michael Kehoe, is a wonderfully original and imaginative story that will both captivate and warm your heart.

...I definitely recommend reading A DREAM OF DRAGONS.

Jeff W. Horton Author of the CYBERSP@CE Series

A Dream of Dragons

Lauretta & Michael Kehoe

Gabriel's Horn Press
2020

Contact editors@gabrielshornpress.com

Published in Minneapolis, Minnesota by Gabriel's Horn Press

Publisher's Note: This novel is a work of fiction. Names, characters, places, and incidents are either products of the author's imagination or used fictitiously. Apart from historical figures, all characters are fictional, and any similarity to people living or dead is purely coincidental.

First printing: February 20, 2020
Printed in the United States.

For sales, please visit www.gabrielshornpress.com

ISBN-13: 978-1-938990-55-7

To Kat, Cathy, Mike, James and Robbie,
our greatest creations.

ACKNOWLEDGMENTS

They say it takes a village to raise a child. It also takes almost a village to write a book. In this case it involves our beta readers; our beautiful daughter, Kat Dienethal, RN and Amy Solbach who provided medical advice in addition to story changes; Deborah Riley who prevented a cotton candy ending; our niece Christina Spaulding who in addition to editing, with her husband, Travis, helped us throw Michael out of a plane; Editors Phillip and Maria Towles; Proofreaders Shannon Kearsley, Maxime Laboy who not only beta-read once but twice, Cheryl Hoffman, Gerardine Baugh, Connie Wright, Gabrielle Higgins and Kim Huyler Defibaugh; Tina Goddard who provided psychological advice.

Also, this book wouldn't have been possible without the assistance of our author friends, established in their own right but who took the time to read the manuscript and provide their time-honored advice and edits; Chris Stevenson, author of *Wolfen Strain* and *The Girl They Sold to the Moon*; M.A.R. Unger, author of the Matti James Mystery Series; Shawn Brink, author of The Space Between Series; Chris R. Powell, author of *The Path that Shines: A Story of Life, Love and Loss*; and Laura Vosika, author of The Bluebells of Scotland Chronicles, T.M. Morris, author of The Eleventh Percent Series, Jeff W. Horton, author of several books including *Cybersp@ce, Future Schism, and The Great Collapse*, and especially, Jerry B. Jenkins, author of the Left Behind series and DiAnn Mills, author of FBI Task Force series.

Greater love has no one than this, than to lay down one's life for his friends.

John 15:13 New King James Version (NKJV)

1. DISCOVERY ON THE BEACH

Venice, Florida
Sunday, June 14

"Venice Police Department, Detective Ortega." The voice on the phone was authoritative yet distant.

"Hey Eddie, it's me, Henry. I need your help. I don't know what to do with her!"

"What? Do with who, Henry? What are you talking about, son?"

"I don't know who she is. I just found her while I was jogging on the beach. I couldn't just leave her here, so I called you."

"Oh, I see!" Ortega said. "You did the right thing by calling me. This must have been a terrible shock for you. Did you move the body at all or disturb the scene?"

"What? No, she can move on her own and there's no 'scene.' What the hell are you talking about?"

"Me? What the hell are *you* talking about?" Detective Ortega lowered his voice. "I thought you found a body."

"I did. Well, I found a girl but she's very much alive."

"Congratulations, Henry. Valentine's Day came early. Why is this a police matter?"

"Because she's naked, scared, and doesn't speak at all, and I don't want to just run off and leave her here."

Detective Ortega sighed. "Where are you? I'll head right over."

* * *

Henry Williford couldn't believe the bizarre drama unfolding before him. Bombarded by flashing red lights, a young woman lay on the sand, naked, wet and shivering, lying on her left side in a fetal position, her eyes wide open. One paramedic was talking to the girl but she didn't seem to understand what he was saying.

"We can't see any signs of injury." Another paramedic approached

Henry and Eddie. "But we're going to take her to Venice Memorial just to be sure. We'll meet you there." He returned to help his partner lift the shaking girl onto a gurney.

"Do you mind if I go with you?" Henry asked. "I just want to make sure she's okay."

"Sure," Ortega nodded. "We can take your statement there as well as anywhere else." Eddie headed over to the uniformed officers on the scene. "Check around and see if you can find anything that will help us identify her, clothes, purse, anything."

Henry headed for his car. "I'll see you there."

* * *

"You're the one who found her?" Dr. Swanson was a younger man who looked to be only a few years out of med school. "What's the story?"

"Yes." Henry said. "I don't know what happened to her or anything about her. I didn't know what else to do so I called my friend Eddie here."

"I called the paramedics," Eddie added. "I thought it would be a good idea to check her out."

Dr. Swanson shook his head. "I've done all I can but I can't see anything wrong with her. She's perfectly fine. I'm afraid there's nothing more we can do other than hold her for observation for a day or so."

"If you want," Eddie offered, "I can take her to a shelter."

"Henry!" the girl shouted suddenly, reaching out to Henry.

"Well!" Ortega smiled. "I guess she can speak." He turned to the girl. "Can you tell us your name?"

"Henry," she repeated.

"I think she's just told us what she wants," Dr. Swanson said. "Looks like she wants to go with you, Mr. Williford."

"What am *I* going to do with her?" Henry threw his hands up.

"Looks that way to me too," Ortega said closing his notebook. "She's your responsibility now."

"You'll need to pay the bill and sign a release," the nurse added.

Henry sighed and took out his wallet. "Where do I sign?"

2. AN UNWANTED GUEST

Monday, June 15

"What am I going to do with you?" Henry ran several scenarios through his mind on how he could help this woman on the way to his house. "I need to get Heidi involved," he told her as part of his continuing diatribe. "She'll know what to do." Henry hoped she would, anyway. "You'll like her. She's my sister. She's always been there when I needed help."

It was early the next morning when the car pulled into the driveway of his one-story, orange-stucco home backing onto a small lake where alligators silently waited for their next meal. "We're here." He turned off the ignition. "I'm going to call Heidi, then I'll get you out." Henry pulled out his cell phone. The girl's eyes widened at the bright screen.

"Heidi, I need your help. Can you get over here now?"

"Well hello to you too…wait, why? What the heck did you do now?"

"Nothing! I swear! I just need your help. Come over and I'll tell you why."

"Give me half an hour," Heidi said, sighing. "Let me get the kids ready." Henry had lost track of just how many times Heidi had to pull his bacon out of the fire over the years.

"Okay," Henry told his guest. "Help is on the way." He opened the passenger door and took her hand. "It's okay," he said gently, coaxing her out of the car. "Come on out." He slowly pulled her to her feet. She stood still, her eyes glued to Henry.

"Henry," she said.

Henry nodded. "Yes, that's my name. Let's get you inside." She didn't move. He picked her up and carried her into the house. "I wish you could understand what I'm saying. It would make things so much easier."

He set her on the sofa. She drew her knees up to her chin, arms wrapped around them. Henry's six cats and three dogs rushed over. The cats jumped onto the sofa, rubbing their faces against her legs, while the dogs licked her feet, wagging their tails with enthusiastic acceptance. Even Mack, a blind orange tabby, could sense her presence and was drawn to her. Flack, a red dachshund with paralyzed back legs, struggled in his doggie cart, rolling himself over to join the furry welcome party.

His strange house guest started responding to the animals. Her eyes softened and her hand reached out to each of them. Henry had never seen his pets so drawn to any other person, especially this quickly. This mysterious woman seemed to be a magnet for animal affection. The animals surrounded her, a furry blanket of comfort.

"What do we do now?" he asked the universe—who refused to provide him any direction.

A sharp knock sounded on the front door a heartbeat before Heidi and the kids burst into the house, a diaper bag on one arm, a purse on the other. Two-year-old Nattie was also in her arms, clutching her favorite "bankee" in one hand, sucking the life out of the thumb of her other. Five-year-old Robbie was glued to her side. "What's the matter now?" Heidi closed the door before anyone could escape.

"This." Henry stood by the young woman with his hand out to her. "I found her on the beach this morning. I called Eddie and we took her to the hospital but they said there was nothing they could do."

Heidi's jaw dropped in disbelief. "What the hell did you get yourself into this time, genius? Honestly, it's a miracle you survived on your own before I came along!" Heidi set her purse, diaper bag and Nattie on the floor.

"Can you help me with her? You're a girl."

"Wow, figured that one out all by yourself did ya?" Heidi quipped. "What gave me away? Popping out two kids or my boobs!"

Heidi walked over to the young woman. "Okay, I assume the hospital gave her a quick once-over." Heidi sat beside the woman. "They're right, though. With no signs of an injury or illness, there isn't much they can do."

She touched the hospital gown the girl wore. "Do you have something else she can put on? We can get her more clothes later. Then you need to figure out what to do after that. Are you going let her stay here?"

"Yeah, for now I guess. I'm not sure what else to do."

"You're an idiot, you know that, don't you?"

Henry just shrugged, then headed to his room to retrieve some clothes.

* * *

Heidi let Nattie join Robbie who was already playing with the animals. Not having any pets of their own, the kids always looked forward to going to Uncle Henry's. "That should keep you occupied while I handle your Uncle's latest crisis."

"Hi, I'm Heidi," she said, seating herself on the couch beside the girl.

"I'm a nurse. What can I do to help you?" No response. Henry returned with a white Tampa Bay Buccaneers T-shirt and a pair of shorts that tied at the waist. Heidi took the clothes, turning her attention back to the girl.

"Okay Sweetie, here are some clothes for you to wear. The bathroom is just down the hall." She pointed to the bathroom between hers and Henry's old bedrooms.

The woman blinked in bewilderment, looking back and forth between the clothes and Heidi's smiling face. Heidi tugged on the shoulder of her own shirt. "Shirt? Clothes? Dressed?" She rolled her eyes, then glared at her brother. "Oh for Heaven's sake, Henry! Leave it to you to discover the world's only Barbarian Barbie! What are ya gonna drag home next, Betty Bigfoot?"

She took the girl's hand, helping her to stand. "Come on, honey," she said, lowering her voice. "Let's get you into something more comfortable than a hospital gown." She took small slow steps, guiding the woman to the bathroom. It was almost like she didn't know how to walk. As they crossed the threshold, Heidi barked a command to Henry to watch the kids.

* * *

What the hell did I get myself into indeed? Henry wondered.

Nattie was sampling tuna flavored cat food from a bag she'd pulled from the cupboard. He grabbed the bag and picked up the loose pieces, ignoring the child screaming at the loss of her treats.

Over Nattie's screams, Henry heard his sister speaking in that caring mother voice she often used with her own children. He couldn't make out what she was saying, but he could tell she was in full mother hen mode, going on and on about something. Even though he was seven years older and a foot taller than Heidi, she made up for her short stature with attitude and tenacity.

After what seemed an eternity, the bathroom door opened and the two women emerged. Henry was relieved to see the mysterious Jane Doe finally had some regular clothes on. Heidi led her back to the sofa. Then she turned on her heels, grabbed his arm and pushed him down onto a dining room chair.

"Do you have any idea what just happened in there?" Heidi hissed.

"Of course not," Henry said in his defense. "I was out here the whole time."

"I was being rhetorical!" Heidi scolded. "She just urinated on the bathroom floor!"

"What?" Henry's brow furrowed with confusion.

"You heard me. There is something seriously wrong here. As soon as we got to the bathroom, she stopped, started shaking, and the flood gates opened. I immediately sat her on the toilet to finish. Dude, you really need to learn to put the seat down by the way!"

"It's my house."

"Whatever, the point is I had to teach her how to go to the bathroom. It was like she had never even seen a toilet before, let alone used one. I don't see any outward signs she's on something and I don't think she's mentally challenged either because she apparently can learn things really fast. After I showed her how and where to take care of her bodily functions—I'll spare you the gory details—she kept flushing the toilet over and over with a proud look on her face."

"Wow, um, thank you for that," Henry stammered. "I don't know what I'd do without you, Sis?"

"You can also thank me for cleaning up the mess." She glared at her brother. "Henry, this isn't some stray dog you picked up on the side of the road. You can't just post her picture on Facebook and hope somebody claims her. You need to think about what's best for her."

"How the hell do I know what's best for her? This wasn't my idea in the first place."

"Well, it's obviously your problem now so you'd better think of something." She bent down and picked up Nattie who had moved on to snacking on the dogs' Kibble. Heidi just stood there for a moment shaking her head. "It's a wonder she hasn't grown a tail yet."

Heidi scooped up her bags, Nattie struggling in her arms. "Who is she? Where the hell did she come from? These are all questions that need to be answered, big brother." She took another look at the girl and shook her head.

Henry shook his head. "How the heck did I get sucked into this?" He hugged his sister. "Thanks for coming by on a moment's notice." Henry kissed her cheek. "Love ya, Sis."

"I love you too," Heidi said, one hand on the door and the other around Nattie who was covered in crumbs. "I'll be back with some more suitable clothes. You need to think about what you're going to do, Henry. Whether you like it or not, she's here now. Say goodbye kids." Nattie was enjoying a post meal thumb, and little Robbie waved a tiny hand.

"Bye kids," Henry called.

Henry turned his attention back to his odd guest only to discover she was missing. He found her in the bathroom using her newly discovered toilet flushing talent. "I guess you can stay with me for a few days until we find out where you came from." His guest only responded with a smile and another flush.

3. LEARNING TO SPEAK

In the living room, the mysterious Jane Doe made sounds directed at the animals, single sounds at first, then mimicking the meows and barks with surprising accuracy.

She looked up at him and said "Henry!"

He smiled and nodded. "That's right! But what do I call you? I guess you can't tell me your name, so let me think about what name is best for you."

He thought a bit. "Let's try something easy to say. How about Anne?" He pointed to his chest and affirmed, "My name is Henry," then pointed to her, "Your name is Anne."

She rocked forward again, forcing the air out as she did with his name. "Amm." Her face brightened and for the first time, he saw her face-splitting smile showing perfect teeth.

"Close," Henry encouraged. "Let's try again. ANNe."

"ANNNNe."

"Yes, yes, very good! That's a good start!"

He helped her to her feet. "I wonder how she would react to…." Not finishing his thought, he led her to the full length mirror in the hallway. Anne kept looking back between the real Henry and his doppelganger. She jumped apparently realizing Henry's partner in the mirror was her. Henry smiled. She watched her image move whenever she did. Henry waved his hand to show her how it all worked.

While watching Anne fascinated by her own appearance, the artist in him couldn't help but notice subtle changes in the portrait of his own reflection, the slight wrinkles in the corners of his green eyes and thin worry lines starting to dig across his forehead. At thirty-two, the last few years had been rough ones and it was starting to show.

"It's okay, it's just our reflection, see? I wanted you to see what you look like." Pointing at his reflection, he said, "I'm Henry." Then he pointed at her. "And you're Anne."

"Anne!" She covered her mouth, surprised that her reflection spoke.

Henry roared with laughter.

Anne started laughing too, touching her reflection with one hand and her face with the other. Turning her attention to Henry, she grabbed his face.

"Otay...doze are my wips," Henry explained, speaking between her slender fingers. Anne explored his thin lips, caressed his square unshaven jaw to his high cheekbones. Henry explained what everything was as she moved from feature to feature. "And that's my nose," he said. She ran her index finger down the bridge stopping at the tip. Anne touched each corresponding feature on her own face, which was now beaming, finally grasping the concept.

For the first time since stumbling upon Anne on the beach, Henry was encouraged. "It's going to be okay, Anne. We're going to figure this out together, one step at a time. You're probably hungry. C'mon, let's go to the kitchen."

Henry sat her at the table and pulled several items from the fridge. Anne was playing with Groucho, the Turkish Van with a black "mustache" like his namesake. She was having a kitty conversation with the feline, answering his meows with varied versions of her own.

Henry returned with a plate of assorted indulgences and placed it on the table, sitting beside her. He gave her apples, strawberries and, especially to her delight, chocolate. "I thought you might like that," he said, smiling. She grabbed another piece of candy. "Whoa, slow down there, Sweetheart," Henry cautioned, pulling the plate closer to him. "You don't want to give yourself a tummy ache."

Anne pouted and turned away, folding her arms across her chest. A bowl of cat food on the floor caught her attention. She grabbed a handful and stuffed it into her mouth before Henry could stop her.

"No, wait!" It was too late. Anne gagged, spitting out the mistaken morsels stuck to her tongue. Henry had to suppress a laugh and quickly guided her to the kitchen sink. He grabbed a paper towel. "Stick out your tongue, like this."

Anne complied with an urgency brought on by the nasty taste in her mouth. He wiped off what he could, then turned on the cold water.

"Here, rinse out your mouth. Watch me!" Henry bent over the sink, and cupped his hands to catch the running water. No further demonstration was needed. Anne elbowed him out of the way so she could drink. Henry put one arm around her shoulders, wiping her face dry with a towel.

"I'm sorry." He smiled and offered her the plate. "How about another piece of chocolate to get rid of the bad taste?" He gave her one last piece, thinking that some lessons are best learned by experience, even if it is unpleasant.

Undaunted, Henry was determined to get through to her. They moved from room to room so he could teach her the names of different objects. She learned what a cat and dog were and each of their names. Book, sofa, lamp, and more—it was amazing how she picked up on everything.

Henry felt a bit like Annie Sullivan with his own Helen Keller, going around the room grabbing or touching items so he could teach her what they were called. They named everything in the living room, then moved to the dining room.

The front door flew open suddenly, and Heidi walked in with Robbie and Nattie trailing behind. She had a couple of SuperMart bags in her hand. "I got her some clothes, underwear and—" She stopped. Henry and Anne were picking up individual kitchen utensils spread out on the counter. "What are you two up to?"

"You won't believe it!" Henry put down a rolling pin. "She's incredibly smart. She's picking up on stuff like it's nothing. We've spent the last hour and a half learning the names of everything. It's amazing how fast she's catching on!"

"Really?" Heidi put the bags on the kitchen table. "That is amazing."

"Guess what else? She has a name." Henry didn't wait for a reply. "I call her Anne."

"Anne?"

"Yeah, I thought that would be easier to say. I didn't know what else to call her. I don't think mom would mind?"

"And she understands that's her name?"

"Yep. Anne, let me introduce you to my sister." Henry put his hand on Heidi's back. "This is—"

"Heidi!" Anne said, smiling. Both siblings' jaws dropped.

"That's right," Heidi said in disbelief. "But how?"

Anne pointed as she spoke. "Heidi, Henry, Anne."

"She must've remembered your name from before." Henry beamed like a proud parent. "I told you she was a quick study." Turning to his niece and nephew, he said, "And these two monsters are Robbie and Nattie." Henry grabbed each one in a big hug.

Robbie ran right to Anne saying, "My name is Robbie! Say my name!" Nattie hid behind her uncle's legs, peeking out and smiling at Anne from behind her pacifier, not as brave as her big brother.

Anne smiled at him and in a confident voice said, "Robbie."

"Remarkable!" Heidi said. "Have you thought about what to do with her tonight?"

"No," Henry said smiling. "Unless you want to take her."

"Ah, no." Heidi scowled. "This is your mess, brother."

Henry shrugged. "I guess I can clear out the spare bedroom." He put the utensils back in the drawer. "I'm just using the futon as a catch-all anyway. Those books can go on the floor. I guess we'll just see how tonight goes before I decide anything further. And Eddie may come back with some news that may change things. One step at a time."

"Well, I for one am glad you called him." Heidi looked at her watch. "I need to get these kids fed. You wanna watch them and I'll do a fast food run? Afterward, I can show her what I bought and see if it all fits. It will be nice to see her wearing some proper clothes."

"Sure, you know what I want. Double cheeseburger with no pickles and large fries. Get something for Anne too and get her a chocolate shake. She likes chocolate."

"Okaay, not even going to ask. Just hold down the fort and I'll get food."

Henry let Robbie take over teaching Anne. Robbie led her into Henry's studio, showing her the box of toys Henry kept for those days when he took a turn watching the kids.

Anne picked up Robbie's *Big Book of Animals*. She pointed to an animal while Robbie provided its name. She tried to repeat each name, having difficulty with a few, but seemed to enjoy the time with Robbie. Henry crossed his arms in front of him and smiled.

Half an hour later, Heidi returned with the food. "Robbie, Nattie," she called. "Come and eat. I got chicken nuggets." Robbie took Anne's hand and led her to the table to join him in his favorite fare. Henry pulled out a chair and helped Anne to sit. Heidi put a cheeseburger, small fries and a chocolate shake in front of her. Henry picked up his own double cheeseburger and took a bite.

Anne poked at the cheeseburger as if it were alive, then picked it up with both hands and brought it to her mouth. She took a small bite, smiled, then began to eat the cheeseburger with real joy in the taste. She turned her attention to the chocolate shake, staring at it for a while. After a moment watching Henry drink his soda, she took the straw into her mouth and... nothing happened. She backed away and looked pleadingly at Henry.

"What does she want," Heidi asked.

"I'm not sure." Then he smiled, realizing what the problem was. Henry removed the straws and lids from both of their beverages and handed the milkshake back to Anne. Holding his own cup to his lips, he said, "Drink."

"Drink," Anne repeated and mimicked his movements. She pulled her cup down and said "Chocolate," from beneath a big frothy foam mustache. Everyone at the table burst out with laughter.

"Yes, right. It's a chocolate shake." Henry chuckled. Anne continued enjoying her meal, oblivious to what was so funny. Like little Nattie, she was wearing almost as much as she was consuming.

Heidi took a few bites of her salad. "Have you given any thought to what you're going to do if Eddie doesn't find out where she belongs? Are you going to be able to get your work done with her here?"

"I don't know, haven't really thought that far," he said between handfuls of fries dripping with ketchup. "No need to worry about it yet. I'm also going to check for myself any missing person reports and see if anyone matches her description. What I'm not going to do is take her to a homeless shelter."

"Even if that's the best thing?"

Henry took a swig of his drink, then shook his head. "No, I don't think it is. I have a few days before my next piece is due. I can afford the time to sort this out. Hopefully, Eddie will come through with something. I'll touch base with him in a couple of days."

"Still working on the nursing manual?" Heidi said.

"Unfortunately, yes."

"Ugh, I hated that book!" Heidi put the lid back on her salad. "We can take it one day at a time."

"Agreed." Henry gulped the last of his cheeseburger down.

"Well," Heidi dusted off her hands. "Until then, let me see if she can fit into these clothes." She took Anne's hand and nodded to her, grabbing the SuperMart bags. "Kids, mind your Uncle."

* * *

In the guestroom, Heidi selected a Lilac-colored cotton blouse. "Let's start with this."

"Heidi?" Anne tugged at her T-shirt, not sure what to do.

Heidi nodded. "Oh, let me help you." She put her hands up over her head. Anne mimicked her. Heidi pulled the t-shirt off, then put the blouse on Anne, buttoning it.

"Let's get those shorts off," Heidi said. Anne pulled them down, leaving a puddle of cloth on the floor. Heidi took a pair of panties and held them out ready to help Anne step into them. Anne took the panties, studied them, then pulled them up around her waist. Purple stretchy shorts followed.

Heidi patted the futon. "Sit down. Let's do something about that hair." She brushed out Anne's long blonde hair until it shimmered.

Pulling the brush through the golden threads of Anne's hair, Heidi understood why her brother could not leave her on the sands alone, even if he was an idiot. *Maybe I'm crazy too.*

Finally, Heidi put the brush down, admiring the bright shine of Anne's locks of spun gold. "Okay, that's more like it. Let's join the others and see what disaster awaits, shall we?"

* * *

"Wow," Henry stood from where he and Robbie were playing with Legos at the same time keeping Nattie from eating them. "She really is pretty, isn't she?"

"That she is." Heidi smiled. "Okay." Heidi grabbed Nattie. "I think you've got things under control for now. Come on, Robbie."

"Bye Uncle Henry! Bye Anne!" Robbie shouted.

"Call me if you need me." Heidi said, walking out the door.

Henry took a deep breath and turned to Anne. "Now what can we do?"

* * *

Anne. She had a name. It was *Anne*. And the one who found her was *Henry*. The fear faded, replaced by excitement, especially when she learned to say words. Henry and Heidi and Robbie and Nattie and Sam and Charlie and Groucho and Baby and Mack and Flack and Bond and Elphaba and Loki...so many new names!

Anne went to the pile of toys on the floor in the studio and brought the *Big Book of Animals* to Henry.

"Okay," Henry said with a smile. "Let's see what else I can teach you."

After they finished Robbie's books, she pointed to other books on the shelf. For several hours, they looked at books on what she learned were travel, architecture, history, famous paintings, Hollywood icons, even comic books.

A book Henry said was *Fantasy Art* really caught her attention. She was mesmerized by every image. Page after page showed beautiful women, some with wings and pointed ears; others scantily clad in armor holding swords or glowing spears. These were Fairies, Elves, and Warrior Princesses. Some pages depicted strange animals like Unicorns and Griffins, and ugly creatures Henry called Trolls, Ogres, and Goblins. She wanted to say each word for every picture she saw. There were so many words! She flipped through the pages, while Henry provided the name of each picture she pointed to.

One drawing, which took up two pages, made Anne freeze and stare, the page shaking in her trembling hand.

"That scary guy is a dragon and that's fire coming out of his mouth," Henry said.

Anne couldn't reply or speak; she just stared at the book. She touched the picture as if it was a living being. Her chest hurt and her eyes filled with tears that spilled onto the page. Of all the wondrous things they had explored together that night, this picture touched something deep inside her, creating an intense yearning—for what she did not know, or even why.

"What's the matter, Anne? Why are you crying?" Henry touched her cheek and wiped the tears rolling down her face. Henry took the book and shut it, putting it on the table. "None of the things in this book are real. They're just pretend, make believe." Henry smiled at her. "You've been through a lot and it's late. You must be tired. Come on, let's get you to bed."

She picked up the book, holding it tightly to her chest.

"Okay," Henry said. "You can keep it, but you do need to get some rest. It's been a long couple of days."

He led her to the guestroom and prepared the futon into a bed. He guided Anne to lie down and covered her with a blanket. She held onto the book with both hands. The bed was soft beneath her, the blankets enveloping her in a warm cocoon.

"Get some sleep, Anne. Things will look better tomorrow." Henry turned off the light and closed the door leaving her alone in the dark.

Anne lay clutching the book of fantasy creatures like Nattie clutched her blanket. Salty tears ran down her eyes into her hair and onto the soft pillow underneath her. She could not understand what was happening, only that she could not stop crying.

She didn't know anything really, except that she was with Henry and that she was not alone. She liked learning words and making sounds. It made her feel good inside, like when she made the sound Henry called laughing.

That was until she saw the dragon. What was it about the strange picture that made her feel this way? She did not know what dragons were, only that they made her hurt inside. She couldn't tell Henry why. She didn't know herself.

Eventually, her sobbing ceased. The need for sleep took over, pushing her into a deep slumber.

I am flying!

I inhale a deep breath of sweet morning air and glide effortlessly on the strong swift current. I close my eyes and enjoy the cool wind against my face, soaring over majestic Crystal Mountains. Their sparkling summits of breathtaking colors stretch beyond the distant horizon, reaching up to a silver sky under a brilliant white sun. Far beneath me an ocean of emerald green laps at the side of the mountains, and crests white wherever the water slams against the lower outcroppings.

Sharing the sky with me is an enormous dragon with powerful, great white wings. He is the largest of all the dragons except for The Two. His massive wing span is as wide as he is long. His strong pectoral muscles flex to propel him high up into the clouds, his wings beating the air. I struggle to keep up, following him to the highest peak, which has a flattened top. Numerous multi-level structures made of bricks hewn from the crystal mountain extend out, shimmering with different colors. Each shelf leads to a dragon's lair. The higher the dwelling, the higher one's status in our world.

Dragons soar on and off their perch on the mountain. Their bodies are long and slim. Three flowing fins grace their tails, the same color as their wings. Their faces are elongated, with ears that sweep up to sharp points and turn in the direction of even the slightest sound. Their mouths are the length of their heads, with two thin slits for nostrils.

Our smooth golden skin glimmers in the sunlight, the membrane covering our wings varies in color and brightness. Some have wings of dark grey, lighter grey, silver, dark blue, light blue, yellow, red, purple, and white. My iridescent wings reflect all of the colors of the other dragons.

A deafening crack of thunder shakes the mountains! The sky is torn open with a sickening black flash. Out of the wound, several large ebony dragons come gushing through the severed jugular of the heavens. Black wings span twice the length of their bodies. They crash down. The mountain quakes under their feet. Razor sharp claws slice the pristine crystal beneath them like flesh.

I tremble from the horror before me. Fire spews from their great mouths, scorching the crystal mountain and its frightened inhabitants. Their nostrils are raised and large, emitting smoke from the deadly furnace within. Their evil eyes blaze as red as the flames they expel, mercilessly burning the golden dragons attempting to flee. I want to help, to fight the attackers but I am thrown to the ground where sharp claws hold me. I scream, helplessly witnessing this hellish genocidal inferno incinerate my kind....

4. RETURN TO THE BEACH

A loud scream ripped Henry from a deep sleep. Something was seriously wrong. The dogs were howling; all hell breaking loose. He was down the hall in a heartbeat, bursting into the guestroom, almost ripping the door off its hinges. Anne was screaming with her eyes closed and arms flailing, as if fighting off imaginary foes on top of her. "Anne," he shouted grabbing her hands. "It's alright! It's only a bad dream! I'm here! Calm down! I'm here!"

Maybe I should have let Eddie take her to the shelter!

Anne continued to fight him, even after she opened her eyes, until she realized where she was. Trembling, she tried to catch her breath.

"It's just a dream, Anne," Henry whispered. "It's alright!" She was covered in sweat, the sheets soaked. Finally she recognized him, throwing her arms around him, sobbing into his chest. She clung to him, holding tighti. Several of the animals joined her on the bed to offer their comfort.

"It's okay." Henry wiped away her tears. "It was just a bad dream." His soothing voice and the purr of a concerned kitten seemed to calm her. "Tell you what. I'll stay here with you until you fall asleep again." Sitting on the floor surrounded by his furry supporters, Henry held Anne's hand. He caressed her forehead while she settled back onto the mattress. Her breathing slowed and she eventually fell back asleep. His hand brushed her cheek. Bending down, he kissed her forehead. Silent as a cat, Henry crept out of the room, turning off the light along the way.

In the quiet of the night, Henry lay on his back, one arm tucked behind his head, staring at the ceiling, listening to every sound. The universe gave him no answers to the mystery of Anne, but thankfully, the Sandman was on duty. Eventually, Henry slipped into a restless slumber.

* * *

Tuesday, June 16

As with every morning, Henry's four-legged alarms went off before the clock had the chance to perform its task. "Why do I even bother setting it?"

As soon as he got to his feet, the tail-wagging choir broke out into their morning chorus. Before heading to the kitchen, Henry went to check on Anne. He was relieved to see her sitting on the futon, calm and awake.

"Well, good morning, Sunshine! I hope you're feeling better."

Anne replied with a smile. Despite her ordeal, she appeared no worse for wear from her nightmare mere hours before.

"Let me get these guys fed," Henry said "and then I'll make us something to eat."

Henry poured two bowls of cereal. Anne followed his lead, picking up the spoon and taking small bites. The dogs hovered nearby lapping up any flakes that landed on the floor.

Henry wiped Anne's chin, then cleared away the dishes. "I'll put the dishes in the sink in the kitchen while you wait on the sofa okay?" Henry put emphasis on key words to see if Anne remembered yesterday's teachings.

Henry poured himself a cup of hot coffee. Standing in the doorway, he inhaled its aroma before slurping down the first sip. Anne called each animal by its name like a game. Fascinated, he watched her interact with his pets, marveling at how different this girl was. He had never met anyone like her.

He finished his coffee and joined Anne. "Let's try to find out a little more about where you came from," he said. "But first, let's get you into some fresh clothes." He led her back to the guestroom.

After rummaging through the clothes Heidi had purchased the day before, he chose a pair of blue shorts and a white t-shirt with the face of a cat. "Here, put these on," he instructed, hoping she would be able to undress herself. She nodded and pulled her shirt off right in front of him. "We really need to get you a bra," he said, his eyes returning to their sockets.

He left to give her some privacy, heading for his own much-needed shower. The steamy hot water washed his concerns down the drain—until the bathroom door creaked open, startling him.

"Anne, what are you doing here?" He grabbed a towel, wrapping it around his waist.

Anne looked from the running water to Henry and back, as if trying to solve a puzzle. A moment later, she stripped off her clothes and marched into the shower, squealing under the warm water.

Henry stood dumbfounded. Here was the most beautiful girl he had ever seen, standing naked in his shower, her flawless figure glistening under the flowing water. The whole experience felt like some surreal wet day dream.

Anne pulled Henry in, snapping him out of his trance.

"Okay, that was unexpected! Now what?"

Anne ran her fingers through the streaming water rolling off his chest. Henry cleared his throat, took a deep breath, and closed his eyes. *Alright! She's oblivious to what's going on. Get a grip on yourself, man! You can get through this; just teach her how to wash herself.*

Henry locked his gaze with hers. *Just keep your eyes fixed on hers and you'll be fine.* Sighing, he held up a bar of soap. "Soap. This is soap. We use it to wash ourselves." He lathered her arm. "Then we rinse." The water washed the foam away. Placing the bar in her hand, he said, "Your turn."

"Soap." Anne took Henry's arm. "Wash."

Henry closed his eyes at her touch, then pushed her hand away.

"No, no, wash yourself." He rubbed circular motions on his chest.

Anne stared for a long moment before understanding lit her face.

Good, I think she gets it.

"Yourself," Anne chimed, reaching over and washing Henry's chest.

Henry placed his hand over hers. He didn't want things to get out of hand. His hormones, however, had kicked into overdrive and there was no denying that cold hard fact—*hard* being the operative word.

Anne grabbed him, a questioning look on her face. Modesty had not only flown out the window, it had gotten sucked into a jet engine. How was he going to explain this?

He gently took her hand away and said, "Man, Henry is a man." He put her hand on her own body. "Anne is a woman." Anne began to explore her stomach, her hips, her….

"*Okay*! That's about enough of that," Henry admonished with a smile. "We're here to wash, remember?"

Anne's gaze was drawn to Henry's right arm, which was covered by a tattoo of a large golden dragon. It was one of his favorites, his own design, with the head covering his shoulder and the body entwining down his arm. He had been haunted by the image in many dreams after his mother died. The wings wrapped around his biceps with its tail curling down his forearm. Anne traced the lines with her fingertips.

"Dragon?" she whispered.

"Yes, it's a dragon. It's a tattoo, a picture like in your book."

"Tattoo," she repeated, continuing her exploration with her fingers. "Dragon." She slowly traced the lines to the dragon's face on his shoulder, lightly drawing her hand over the open mouth of the beast.

He took a deep breath.

"That's enough for today." Henry turned off the water. He wrapped one towel around himself to conceal "Man" and held another out for her. She stepped into the over-sized towel and wrapped it around herself.

Once they were clothed—Anne dressing herself with no difficulty—

Henry led her to the car. "Come with me to the beach. Let's see if we can find anything that will help us figure out where you came from. We'll start at the beginning where I found you."

Henry fastened her seat belt. "This will keep you safe," he said. He took his place behind the wheel and fired up the engine for the trip back to Venice Beach. Anne was more comfortable in the car this time and didn't appear frightened at all. Just the opposite, she seemed to enjoy the Florida landscape passing by, asking about what she saw.

Henry parked close to the boardwalk. They walked across the wooden walkway over the tall waving grass to the bright sands beyond.

They reached the edge of the beach. Anne stopped, that same panicked look on her face when Henry first found her. She stood paralyzed, looking at the sand and the water beyond as if an unseen evil had silently crept up and seized her. She couldn't move, not even to put her foot in the sand.

Something terrible must have happened to her that was connected to this beach in some way. Henry wanted to jog her memory but hadn't stopped to consider it may cause her to relive whatever it was that had happened to her.

"It's okay," Henry assured her. "It's just sand." He stepped onto the sand, pulling her with him. He knelt down and picked up a handful, spilling it from his hands. "Sand," he repeated.

Anne blinked as if she were back in the moment. She knelt down beside him and scooped the sand in her hand, letting it fall from her fingers. "Sand." The sand sparkled in her hand, millions of minuscule pieces of crushed shells. She relaxed, as if the fear trickled out of her like the sand that flowed through her fingers.

"Water!" Anne pointed out to sea.

"That's right! Water. We called this large body of water the ocean and all of this sand is the beach. Do you remember anything?"

She stood up and walked to the ocean. Henry followed, still wearing flip flops. Anne knelt down on the wet sand and let the sparkling liquid wash over her fingers, only to rush away to come back again. Her face brightened. It was as if the horror of the previous night, triggered by her return to the beach, slipped away with each ripple of the surf. She appeared mesmerized by the movement of the water, her breath in tune with the waves washing in and out. The gentle roaring was a balm to both of their spirits.

Henry kneeled beside her. "Can you remember anything?"

She did not answer.

"Maybe it's too early yet." He took his flip flops off and sat with her, watching the waves play with the sand, splashing over their feet. A few determined shark teeth hunters walked around them with sieves on the end of sticks, dredging the sand to find millions-year-old black shark teeth and maybe an interesting shell or two. More visitors began to arrive, laying out blankets and setting up beach chairs to enjoy the Florida sun.

They sat for an hour. Henry finally stood up. "Let's give it more time," he said, helping Anne to her feet. "We can come back another day. Maybe you'll be able to tell me then." Together they walked barefoot over the sand heating up with the rising sun.

"Do you remember *anything*?" Henry asked again on the way home.

Anne shook her head. "No pictures."

Henry nodded. She was able to comprehend more than her limited vocabulary allowed her to communicate. At least he hoped that was the case. Or maybe it was just wishful thinking on his part.

"We can give it a few more days then go back and see if you remember anything. In the meantime, let's drive for a while. You had to get to that beach from somewhere. Maybe some other building or landmark will look familiar. Besides, it's a beautiful day; it would be a shame to waste it all indoors. How about some music?" Henry turned on the car's radio.

Anne started to sway, her head nodding with the beat of the music. She turned to Henry. "What?"

Henry raised an eyebrow, not sure what she meant at first. He realized it was the radio. "Music," he replied. "What you hear is music."

"Music?" She tilted her head, not understanding.

"When someone talks, you hear different tones. Sometimes the voice is higher." He demonstrated. "Or lower."

"Higher?" Anne mimicked him, speaking in a high voice. "Lower." She dropped her voice to a bass note.

"Yeah, like that." Henry nodded. "Music is the same thing, different tones, or notes, played on instruments. The voice you hear is the person singing. I guess you could say it's a special way of talking. There are many different types of music," he explained. "Too many to really learn about, but I can show you a few."

Anne nodded with that face-splitting grin. Henry smiled, pleased to see she did not seem to be suffering from the night terrors. Her smile made him feel good. He would do anything to keep it there.

Henry tapped a button on the steering wheel and gave a command. "Elvis Presley, *Love Me Tender.*" It was a simple song and Elvis's voice was slow and mellow. Anne listened, rocking to the slow beat, her eyes closed.

"That's what they call a love song or a ballad," Henry explained. "Would you like to hear more?"

She nodded, sitting up in her seat, waiting for the next new experience.

"Okay." He chose another song. "Let's ramp it up a bit. We call this rock and roll." He hit the control again. "Jailhouse Rock." Anne bounced with the fast beat of the song, lifting her hands and moving her feet.

Henry found himself rocking to the rhythm, tapping his foot. "You like that?" He grinned. "The guy singing is Elvis Presley. Those were two of his songs." The look on her face told him all he needed to know. Her eyes were bright, her smile wide. She waved her hands, eager for more.

"Elvis Presley!" she shouted.

He laughed. "Yep, that was Elvis."

They pulled into his driveway. In the house, Henry let the dogs out into the back yard and picked up his phone to call Heidi. She answered on the fourth ring.

"Nattie!" she yelled in his ear. "Put that down! Hello?"

"Hi, Heidi, it's Henry. You got some time today?"

"Henry who?"

"Come on! You know who it is!"

"Then why tell me, dufus!"

Henry grimaced, swearing under his breath. "Do you have time today?" Usually, he didn't mind Heidi's satiric wit, but he had no patience today.

"Yes, what do you need?"

"Well, I need to get Anne to talk a little more so that I can find out what happened to her. She seemed to learn quickly from Robbie's stuff. I thought maybe I could borrow some of the kids' books for her."

"Sure," Heidi said. "I'll bring some of his books. Think that'll help?"

"Can't hurt. What else can I do? I need to know what happened."

"Okay. Do you want me to bring lunch?"

"Sounds like a plan. I could go for tacos. See you in a few." He put the phone down and sat by Anne on the sofa. "Now what do you want to do?"

She pointed to some books on one of the shelves. Henry chose one of his art instruction books of models posing, and they worked on learning the words for actions rather than names of things. This model was sitting, that one standing, yet another was lying on a bed. At times he got up and physically acted out a movement, such as walking. By the time Heidi arrived with lunch, Anne knew several verbs. Taking a taco from Heidi, she announced, "Anne eat." Heidi and both kids giggled.

"That you do." Heidi laughed. "You go, girl."

After lunch, Henry cleaned the table and Heidi cleaned up Nattie. Anne had learned yet another new word, *spicy*, after sampling the hot sauce. Heidi handed over a bag containing many of the children's books, *1-2-3 Picture Books, ABC's,* and *First Time Books—First time at the Zoo, the Grocery Store,* along with many others. "Have fun, you guys," she said, packing up the kids.

Anne spent the rest of the afternoon learning to read books from preschool and very early readers up to a five-year-old level. Anne's ability to learn new things was amazing. She didn't learn the words; she absorbed book after book until they exhausted all Heidi had provided. By six o'clock that evening, Anne knew the alphabet and was able to read many words.

During their lessons, Henry got a call from his editor, Elliott Schoenfeld, reminding him his latest illustration was coming due. Henry assured him it would get done. That got him thinking about what he would do with Anne when he had to work. He could ask Heidi like he did for everything else.

I'll deal with it tomorrow.

Exhausted from the long day, Henry made a couple of sandwiches for their dinner, then turned on the television.

The screen came to life and Anne's eyes grew large. She went up to the television and tried to interact with the people flashing by. Speaking to the pictures, she repeated the greeting Henry had taught her, "Hello, I'm Anne," to no avail.

Henry sensed her frustration and joined her on the floor. Her actions were humorous and adorable at the same time. He held her hand before she could do any damage to the TV or herself.

"It's not real," he assured her. "It's pictures that move. See?" Henry tapped on the screen. "They're not really."

She scowled at the television, watching people and objects zip by in an ever-changing series of pictures and sounds. She sat on her haunches for several minutes staring at the screen before she understood what Henry meant.

"Come sit on the sofa." Henry helped her up. "We'll be more comfortable." The two of them retired to the sofa and cuddled close together. Anne watched the little people moving on a fifty-four-inch flat screen with intense concentration, listening to how they spoke and to the music in the background. Henry worried she'd be on sensory overload with so many different stimuli to process, but she seemed like she didn't want to miss any part of it.

He found a program about lions on the Serengeti plains. Anne watched the large animals, excited whenever she recognized one, shouting out each name. "Lion! Leopard! Zebra!" she squealed, at times even mimicking their roars. Henry kept it on the Animal Channel. He didn't want to frighten her with explosions, gunfire, or zombies—not to mention how hard it would be to try and explain those phenomena. Watching a wildebeest getting torn apart for dinner was upsetting enough. Anne buried her face in his chest until he sounded the all clear. They spent the rest of the evening viewing programs about difficult cats with behavior issues and a documentary of a dog show.

Anne fell asleep on his shoulder. He was nodding off himself. He carried her to the guestroom. She didn't wake at all when he laid her on the futon and tucked her in. Watching her for a few moments, he reflected on the day. It was amazing how much progress she had made learning to communicate in this strange new world. At least that's what it was from her perspective, Henry was convinced of that. How or why didn't seem important anymore. All that mattered was him being there for her. He kissed her cheek before whispering, "Sweet dreams," then headed off to bed.

I am back at the majestic Crystal Mountains. I marvel at their beauty, sparkling and shining like the gems within them. The crystals grow into flower-like shapes in colors of blue, red, yellow, green, white, and, on occasion, the precious rare purple. All of the purple crystals are reserved for Aesmay, The One, the greatest, most powerful, and wisest of all the dragons. He lives on the very top of the mountain in a purple palace trimmed in gold. The Sacred Teachings say it is the same gold the first of the golden dragons were made from before the Creator breathed life into them.

We harvest the crystals using the power of our minds, carving out lairs in the mountain's side, and shelves for landing and takeoff in front. The higher one's position is in the Golden Dragon Order, the higher one's lair is on the mountain.

I share my lair with Kenta, my guardian, protector, and closest friend. Our home is constructed of crystals hewn from the highest and oldest of all of the mountains. It is right below the purple palace where Aesmay watches over of all of us. We have lined our lair with white crystals that reflect our beautiful wings.

A ball of fire slams into the shelf outside our dwelling, shattering my serene moment! The crystal sounds like it is crying. Nearly all of the ledge outside of our home shatters and falls into countless pieces. Many of the golden dragons attempt to flee into their structures, but cannot escape the scorching missiles raining down on them from the black dragons above. Kenta wraps his enormous wings around me to protect me. His beautiful wings are hit by the fire and he screams in anguish, burning. He leaps off the jagged remains of our platform and dives down to the water far below with the black dragons in pursuit. Intense heat sears around me, burning my fellow dragons in their attempts to flee. I sense the cry of each of my brothers and sisters consumed by the white-hot flames. My heart explodes at the senseless slaughter of my kind.

Four black dragons swoop down upon me, slamming me onto the ledge, slicing me with razor sharp claws. I fight to crawl off the platform. The weight of my enemies crushes me....

5. LEARNING TO DRAW

Henry jolted awake to the sounds of screaming.

Once again, he rushed to Anne's room. She must have had another nightmare! *Two nights in a row now!* He found her as he had the night before except, this time, mixed in with the cries and screams, she was shouting "NO! NO!" and something about "Kenta!"

What's a Kenta?

His hands on her trembling shoulders, Henry called her name. He gently shook her in attempt to free her from whatever nocturnal hell she was in. "Wake up, Anne! Wake up! It's okay, Sweetheart! I'm here, everything is going to be okay!"

Anne finally settled down. She struggled to open her eyes, her face moist with tears and sweat. Her golden locks hung in wet strings down her back.

"It's okay, honey. It was just a nightmare. The pictures weren't real. Just like the television. They can't hurt you." Henry helped her sit up in bed. "I'm here now, it's okay." By this time, the bed was crowded with tail-wagging well-wishers licking her face to show their support.

Anne finally stopped shaking at the calming ministrations of the pets and Henry's soothing voice. All she could say was, "Henry" and hold onto him with the desperation of one who had just faced her darkest fears. Her tears fell on Henry's shoulder; her arms clung to him with all their strength. Henry held her tight, wishing he could do more to take away her pain. But he didn't even know the source of her torment. How could he possibly hope to eliminate it? For the moment, he just held onto her, allowing the warmth of his body and his voice to wrap around her like a comforting blanket.

What could have possibly happened to this poor girl to cause her to have such vivid nightmares? Henry himself had gone through this after his tour of duty in Iraq while in the Navy and later after the death of his fiancée. He knew what PTSD did to a person. Might she have gone through something like that?

"I'm here," Henry said. "I'm not going anywhere. I'm right here." She relaxed in his arms and settled back onto the bed. "Go to sleep, Anne. I'll stay with you." He was going to sit on the floor next to the futon but Anne would not let go. She was like a frightened child who insisted on sleeping in her parent's bed. He lay next to her. She held on tightly, only relaxing her grip to finally drift off. Henry vowed to remain vigilant the remainder of the night, determined to be there for her if the terror that haunted her dared to return. He almost made it until dawn before he nodded off.

* * *

Wednesday, June 17

"I don't know what to do," Henry told Heidi over his cellphone. "She must've really gone through something terrible to give her such horrific nightmares."

"How is she now?"

"She's fine; she's sitting on the floor with the kittens at the moment. But I've got to get some work done today."

"If you like," Heidi offered, "I can bring her over here to my house for a while. The kids love her and she's great company for them. Besides, I'd like to get to know her better myself. She and Robbie can go over some more of his books together."

"If you don't mind, I'd appreciate that," Henry agreed. "What time can you be here?"

"Let me get the kids fed and dressed and I'll come right over. See you at nine-thirty or so?"

"Perfect! That will give us just enough time to have a quick bite and clean ourselves up for the day. Thanks, Sis, see you soon."

Henry popped two sausage and egg breakfast sandwiches into the microwave. With Jimmy Dean's buns heating up, he poured a couple of glasses of fresh Florida orange juice. Anne was silent while they ate, but appeared to be okay after last night's ordeal.

With every tummy in the house full, Henry led Anne to his bathroom, after stopping at her bedroom to grab some clean clothes. He taught her how to brush her teeth with the "Monkey See, Monkey Do" method. She caught on immediately.

He demonstrated how to turn on the shower. "When you're done washing yourself," Henry said, "turn off the water like I showed you. Then get dressed. Okay?"

"Okay!" Anne took off her shirt.

Henry sighed and shook his head. *I'm never gonna win this battle, am I?* "I'm going to be right outside. If you need anything, say my name and I'll be right here." He turned to leave.

"Henry wash?" Anne looked sad and confused.

"Heidi is coming over to take you to her house today. I will wash after you leave with her. I've got to get some work done."

"Henry wash," Anne pleaded.

"You'll like it. She has a really big house with a pool. You can play with Nattie and Robbie…." Henry stopped mid-sentence. Anne was pouting and looking at him with those big blue eyes of hers. Combined with the fact she was completely naked again, Henry had to admit, she had a compelling argument. "Oh, what the hell! Why fight it?" Henry resigned, not too disappointed in his decision. "But no touching Man, okay?"

Anne smiled and nodded in reply. Then she tore his shirt off.

* * *

Dressed and ready for the day, Henry took Anne to his studio to share his art with her before Heidi got there. Once Anne was gone, he could focus on his work without distraction. Besides, it would be a nice opportunity for Anne to experience new surroundings and interact more with other people.

"Come with me," he offered, "I want to show you something very special." Anne followed him down the hall to the large corner room.

They entered his studio. She saw his latest illustration, of how to suction a tracheostomy tube, on the electronic drawing tablet and gasped. The sight of a man on his back with his throat cut open, a pair of disembodied hands inserting a menacing foreign object into the void could be unsettling to anybody. Especially when drawn by someone as talented as Henry. He didn't think she had any idea of exactly what it was she was looking at, but it upset her just the same.

Henry smiled. "Not very pretty huh? I agree. Look here." Henry made a sweeping motion toward the wall on their right. It was covered in countless doodles, sketches, and drawings in various stages of completion. Just about anything one would imagine finding in an artist's studio hung there on display. Everything from nudes to portraits, ocean scenes to landscapes, family pets to wildlife, technical drawing to architecture. There were even some sketches of cars and superheroes, some real and others straight out of Henry's vivid imagination. Some people tuck facts and ideas in the back of their mind to reference later. Henry's inspirations either ended up on his wall or in a sketchbook, or on rare occasions, napkins, scratch paper, even the back of receipts.

Henry had converted Heidi's old bedroom into his art studio because it offered the best natural light and was the second largest of the three. His drawing table was next to an old wooden desk where he kept his laptop for easy access to the internet, which he frequently used for reference material or to post photos of his work to sell. The desk also provided him extra work area, along with convenient storage for his art supplies when needed. Except for the very bottom left hand drawer. Something nasty had spilled in there so long ago, even Henry had forgotten what it was. The drawer and its fate were both sealed that fateful day, never to be opened again. Next to the desk was a small square table that held his color printer. A revolving office chair, stained with droplets of paint and smears of every art media, sat between the desk and art table, so that he could swivel back and forth as needed.

In a corner of the studio sat Henry's first art desk. The kids used it when they were there. Like the chair, it too bore the battle scars of countless hours of use from his many years of training with his father as a child. Uncle Henry kept it stocked with washable paint, markers, and crayons. Two of grandpa's old dress shirts, serving as makeshift smocks, hung on the wall nearby. It was sad they never got to meet their grandpa, but Henry liked to feel this was a way to help his dad's memory and legacy live on.

Henry credited his father for being his greatest influence in fueling his passion for the craft. His father studied, and eventually taught, at both the American Academy of Art and the Art Institute of Chicago before moving to Florida when Henry was still in grade school. He recognized Henry's natural talent early on and taught him to draw and paint while other kids were learning to ride a bike. Fortunate indeed is the man who can pursue his passions in life and make a living at it. Henry was that man.

Henry sat Anne in the chair facing the window, where he posed most of his models to take advantage of the morning light. After tilting her head into the perfect position, he swept her hair back from her face. Then he held both palms up, touching the tips of his thumbs together to frame her face. "Perfect," he said. "Hold real still for me, okay?"

Anne nodded.

"No, no, you don't need to answer me, just don't move. I promised you something special and I've been dying to do this from the moment I first saw you."

Anne smiled.

"Even better, Anne, keep smiling for me." Henry smiled back and hastily picked up his sketch pad and charcoal pencil. He still preferred working with paper, pencil, and ink over electronic media, except when necessary. He loved the feel of putting lead to paper and watching his inspiration flow from the pencil onto the page. The exhilarating sensation made him feel more connected to his work. The texture of the paper and smell the charcoal was intimate and natural. He could really bring a blank page or canvass to life, engaging all of his senses. Music or the sounds of ocean waves rushing against the shore helped create the mood or atmosphere to reflect his work.

Henry's hand danced and darted all over the page. His eyes flashed back and forth from her face to his sketch book. He was in the zone as his creation took the form of his subject. After a few last broad finishing swoops of his pencil, he dated and signed the piece, then turned it for Anne to see.

"Well, what do ya think? Do you like it? It's you, Anne!" Henry beamed.

Anne's mouth was open and her eyes were wide, sparkling with wonder. She moved in for a closer look. Henry tore the page from the book and handed it to her. "Here, this is for you. I'll do a full color portrait of you later, but you can have this for now. It shows how pretty you are."

Anne gave Henry a hug then looked back at her likeness. "Anne, picture, pretty, thank you."

"You're welcome," Henry replied. "I'm glad you like it."

As she studied her likeness, he, in turn, gazed at the real thing.

"Heidi and the kids should be along any minute now to pick you up. I'm going to get started on my work. You can watch if you want, or look at some more books." Anne nodded in reply, still mesmerized by her image.

Henry turned his attention to the drawing of the tracheostomy tube, which was nearly completed. Anne watched him intensely as he worked. A few moments later, she retrieved the sketch pad and pencil.

Henry occasionally glanced over his shoulder. Anne worked away in the sketchbook only stopping to grab another pencil from the desk when one either broke or wore down. Unlike earlier encounters where Anne was oblivious to her strange new environment, the pad and pencil didn't appear unnatural to her at all.

Amused by the sight, he asked, "Well, what are you working on so diligently? Can I have a look?" Henry grabbed the corner of the pad, turning it to inspect her work and breaking her concentration. Anne had drawn the basic overall design of the procedure, recreating the technical details.

This time it was Henry who was taken back and fascinated. He couldn't believe his eyes. He held her drawing up to his, comparing the two side by side in disbelief. "How—how did you do this?" he stuttered. "This is incredible—impossible! But incredible just the same!" Not only had Anne exactly recreated Henry's work, she had done so in a smaller scale.

Heck, there aren't even any eraser marks!

"A surgeon would give anything to have hands as steady as yours," Henry said.

Anne threw him a puzzled look.

"Never mind. I'll explain later."

"Do you like it?" Anne parroted Henry's earlier question with a smile.

"Ah, yeah, I like it, Anne, I like it a lot."

"Picture pretty?" She pressed, longing for his approval.

"No it's not pretty, it's good. You're pretty, this is good, great, amazing even..." The light in her face started to fade. "Yes, it's very pretty, Anne. You did great and I like it a lot. Thank you."

"You're welcome!" Anne replied, overflowing with joy.

Henry shook his head. The front door burst open and Heidi and her brood poured in, sparking the dogs into action and putting the cats on alert.

"We're here," Heidi called.

"In the studio," Henry yelled. Heidi and the kids came into the studio, Robbie heading straight to the little hand me down art desk. Nattie struggled to get out of Heidi's arms to join him.

As Anne joined the children, Henry took Heidi aside and shared Anne's sketch with her. "Look what Anne did," Henry said. "Pretty impressive, wouldn't you say?"

Heidi raised an eyebrow, her eyes widened in disbelief. "Wow!" She studied the drawing. "Impressive is not the word for it. How the heck did you teach her to do this so fast?"

"That's just it! I didn't teach her anything. She just picked up the sketchbook and pencil and started drawing. I mean, really drawing, and drawing well!" Henry shook his head. "Damndest thing I've ever seen! She's a natural! Even the most gifted artist would still need years of training and practice before even hoping to achieve this level of expertise."

"Well," Heidi said. "Where do we go from here? Do you still want me to take her with us?"

Henry thought about it for a moment. Having Anne drawing beside him was not a bad thing. More like a golden opportunity to help unravel the ever growing list of mysteries surrounding this unique creature. "On second thought, no. If that's ok? I'd like to explore and expand on this new phenomenon. My interest is more than piqued. I truly am sorry I made you come all the way out here." Henry begged forgiveness.

"That's okay. I was planning on heading out this way anyway to get some shopping done. I thought it might be a fun experience for Anne to tag along." Heidi let him off the hook.

"Well, at least let me buy you guys lunch and get some ice cream afterwards. I'll even throw in some quarters for the kids to ride those rides they enjoy so much." Henry removed a pair of twenty dollar bills from his wallet and handed them to his sister. His niece and nephew drew close as he rummaged through the change in his pockets.

"Deal! If it'll make you feel better." Heidi's focus shifted back into mother hen mode to rein in the kids. "Okay, kids, time to go. Say bye to Uncle Henry and Anne." After the hugs and kisses, Heidi grabbed Robbie's hand and scooped Nattie back up. "Come on Robbie, let's go to SuperMart. I need to get Nattie new flip flops."

"Flop flops!" Nattie corrected her.

"Yes, flop flops, what was I thinking?" Heidi agreed, rolling her eyes. "Call me if you need anything," she yelled, leaving the house.

"Thanks, Sis!"

"Okay, Anne." Henry stretched his arms above his head, cracking his knuckles and arching his back to relax his muscles. "Let's get to work and see what you can do." He was dying to explore the depth of her ability, or discover if this was a onetime amazing fluke. He turned his attention back to the illustration of the nursing procedure. Anne continued to flawlessly copy him. They worked side by side, Henry at his drawing tablet, Anne with the sketchbook in her lap.

By one, Henry had completed his illustration and sent it off to Elliott. Anne had completed her own drawing, perfectly replicating Henry's piece. Henry sat next to her and took the sketchbook out of her hand. "I don't know about you, but I'm hungry. Let's have some lunch, shall we?"

Anne nodded enthusiastically.

In the small kitchen with blue flowered curtains his mother had hung years ago, Henry made a couple of ham sandwiches on wheat bread with a glass of milk for each of them. He looked out to the back yard to make sure the animals were safe and behaving themselves. He had built a series of structures with shelves at varying heights where the cats perched, watching birds fly by. The dogs played with each other and with the rubber tire hanging from a bar going across the yard connecting two of the cat shelves. Henry especially kept an eye on Flack in his doggy wheelchair struggling to keep up with his brothers.

In addition to his passion for art and all things beautiful, Henry had a compassionate heart for all things with four legs. He loved all of his animals, but Mack and Flack inspired him. Mack thrived and played just like any other cat chasing balls with little bells inside them. At least he was spared the torment of the ever elusive red dot, Henry often joked. And Flack could keep up with the rest of the pack in his two-wheeled doggie cart that squeaked whenever he turned a corner too fast. His back legs had been crushed by a careless driver. Henry had saved him from being euthanized. Since coming home from the Navy, he'd found comfort in the presence of his animals rather than people.

After lunch, Henry and Anne headed back to the studio. "If you're going to do something, do it right. Let's learn how to draw!" Henry selected a fresh sketch pad from his stock and a box of artist's pencils containing over one hundred and fifty colors. "Here you go Anne, these are for you, and this will be your very own sketchbook. This way we can keep all of your work in one place and track your progress."

Henry began the lesson with graphite pencils, showing her the difference in the firmness of each, from the softer lead pencils that produced a rich darker shade to harder pencils that gave a lighter gray hue. Anne was fascinated, wanting to experience every shade of graphite. While she was intensely working on the drawing, she pursed her lips in deep concentration. She had filled up an entire sheet making different shaded blocks. Anne looked at Henry with excitement in her eyes.

"More," she demanded.

"Now that you know how to use a black pencil, let's experiment with colors!" Henry directed her attention to the vast array of colored pencils in the set. One by one, Henry selected a pencil, handing it to Anne, instructing her to repeat its name. After the individual blocks were filled in, Anne would proclaim the name of the new color, holding up the sketchbook for Henry's approval.

Henry's phone rang. The Taylor Swift *Fearless* ring tone alerted Henry that his sister was calling. "Hi, Heidi. What's up?"

"I'm planning to take the kids to the beach tomorrow. I thought you and Anne might like to come with. Are you done with your drawing?"

"As a matter of fact, I just sent it off. The next one is not due for a couple of days so I've got some time. Going to the beach for the day is a great idea. Count us in."

"Okay. Let's go to Caspersen. It's less touristy so it's usually not too crowded. Besides, Robbie wants to look for more shark teeth. I'll pack a picnic lunch. Meet me there say around nine o'clock?"

"Sounds like a plan. Do you want me to bring anything?"

"Yes, you can bring your cooler, and pick up the ice and drinks so I don't have to lug mine along. Other than that, I've got it covered. Hmm, speaking of covered, I just realized, we're gonna need a suit for Anne. You can't keep parading her around in those shorts and T-shirts I bought her."

"Yeah, you're right, I didn't think about that. Do you have one she could wear?"

Heidi let out a long sigh. "Henry, how can you be such a clever and talented artist and not be able to see size and perspective in the everyday world? Even before popping out two kids I could only dream of a having a body like hers. No, I do not have a suit she can wear," Heidi replied sarcastically. "Bring Anne to the Sun Lover's Boutique on West Venice Avenue. They open at eight thirty. Do you know where it is?"

"Of course I do. I hang out there all the time," quipped Henry, taking his turn.

"Ha, ha! Okay I probably deserved that one. I'll get her all fixed up with a suit and proper undergarments. I don't think any of us expected this to be such a long term arrangement. While I'm busy with her, you and the kids can pick up the ice and drinks at the Farm store. Be sure and get some juice and water this time, not just soda, or the kids will be hyped up on sugar and you'll be the one chasing them up and down the beach."

"Will do, see you tomorrow." Henry ended the call and smiled at Anne. "We're going to the beach tomorrow with Heidi and the kids. Won't that be fun?"

"Beach!" Anne beamed.

"Okay," Henry said, laughing. "Tomorrow, fun at the beach. For now, let's see what else you can learn today." They spent the afternoon together, with Henry teaching her to draw using proper perspective and variations of shading. Henry gathered different objects from all over the house and set them on the desk side by side. At first, he would draw the item of choice and Anne would copy him, duplicating both the sketch and his technique. She caught on fast and was quickly drawing on her own, guided only by a word or two from Henry. Soon, she had several pages full of different shapes drawn in three dimensions with the proper shadowing under them.

Henry noticed that the cats had covertly begun a silent, Navy Seal-style invasion of his art studio, inserting themselves between him and his work or rubbing themselves against his legs, meowing demands. Wow, dinner time already! "Okay Anne, I think that's enough for today. I'm going to go feed all of these guys and order us some pizza. In the meantime do you think you can remember where all this stuff goes?"

"Pizza?" Anne queried.

"Yeah, pizza. Dinner...food. I think you'll like it. If you don't like it, then I'll know you're from another planet," Henry joked.

"Huh?"

"Never mind, I'm kidding. Please just put back what you can and I'll be back to help you in a minute or two."

"Okay, I will." Anne scooped up an armful of inanimate artist models before dashing off to return them to their original resting places. Henry was momentarily stunned by her first person reference. She really was catching on.

A short while later Anne jumped. "It's just the doorbell, Anne. Everything's fine, the pizza is here," Henry said with a salivating smile. He had ordered a sausage pizza with extra cheese from Hungry Hal's Pizzeria because they were the fastest in town. "For The Best Pizza in a Hurry Call

Hungry Hal's," their jingle promised. When it came to pizza, Henry was always in a hurry.

Henry carried Italy's greatest culinary gift to mankind. The aroma filled the room and their senses as he opened the box. *If reincarnation is real, I'm coming back as a Ninja Turtle. Cowabunga!*

Anne's eyes were as big as the pie in front of her. Henry plated each of them a slice. "Okay Anne, this is very hot so we've got to be careful. Hold your slice with both hands, one on the crust at the back with the other supporting the front. Then just start with a small bite like this." Henry demonstrated, savoring the delicious morsel. Pizza is to guys what chocolate is to women. "Here let me help you try a bite of mine."

Anne took a generous bite of the proffered piece. The cheese stretched like a suspension bridge, refusing to relinquish its hold of the slice. Her eyes widened in alarm. Henry burst out laughing. She waved her hands signaling for help. He was reminded of those Chinese finger torture novelties where one gets both index fingers hopelessly trapped in either end.

"Only you could go from being an art protegee to damsel in distress in less than five seconds," he teased. "You're okay, it's just cheese. You just pinch it off like this." Henry pinched off the cheese between his fingers at Anne's lips and returned it to the top of the slice. Anne savored the mouthful she had bitten off, now that she had been saved from her perilous plight. In no time at all, they finished off the entire pie, washing it down with diet cola. As Henry had predicted, she liked pizza, and he mentally added it to the ever growing list of Anne's favorites. The jury was still out on whether she was from another planet or not.

After dinner, they sat down to watch television. Anne was more comfortable now that she knew the things she saw were not real. She paid close attention to the way the actors talked, moved and interacted with each other, sometimes repeating random words. Her language skills were quickly improving both in vocabulary and comprehension. Henry enjoyed her sitting next to him on the sofa. There was something about this strange girl that touched the dark places in his soul with little pin pricks of light.

They watched a movie about pirates and their ships, with tall masts, billowing sails, and hoisted Jolly Roger flags. Henry explained to Anne how people lived many years ago. She watched the main characters fighting with swords. "What?"

"Sword fighting," he said. "The things in their hands are called swords. It's a way for people to fight."

"Fight?"

"Yeah, um… combat, attack, the pirates try to take other people's things by force and the people fight back to stop them."

"Show me!" she demanded.

"You want to learn to fight with swords? Now?"

"Show me!"

Henry smiled, and got up to search for something to fence with. He had a few yardsticks in the garage and brought them into the living room.

"Here is your sword, my lady." He presented one to her. "Now stand like this and hold out your 'sword'." He stood in the *en guard* position, knees slightly bent and his yardstick raised in front of him. She mirrored his stance.

"When you fight, you have eight positions for your blade." He showed her each position. "Then you attack, either thrust or parry." He demonstrated each move.

"Thrust," Anne said mimicking the move.

"And parry," Henry replied, parrying her attack. He turned the movie back on and they pretended to be pirates. They "fought" across the living room, precariously climbing on top of the sofa, and even the pony wall separating the living room from the dining room, keeping up with the characters on the screen—at least in basic moves, because they really couldn't jump in spinning wheels or climb ropes. But they tried their best. The movie fight ended. Henry put his 'sword' down, both of them breathing heavy and said, "That's enough. Let's watch the rest of the movie now."

"Why do people fight?" Anne surrendered her "sword" to Henry.

Henry shrugged. "Mostly because they disagree on something or they're angry at someone."

She sat on the sofa to watch the rest of the movie. "Do you fight?"

Henry sat by her, the remote still in his hand. "I've had a few fights in my life." He stretched out his legs and sighed. "And I did see some action in the Navy."

"What is a Navy?"

Henry pointed to the screen where the pirate ships sailed on blue waters. "See those ships? The Navy is a force a country has with lots of ships. We defend our country against other countries that may attack us."

"What is a country?" She turned to him, her eyes bright with learning.

"It's the land where we live – with one government elected by the people of that land who watch over us." He turned to her. "Government is the people who are in charge of that land." He pressed the play button.

She turned back to the television. "There is so much I do not know."

"Give it time, Anne," he said smiling. "You'll get there." He pulled her closer to him, wrapping his arm around her. She put her head on his shoulder while the movie continued. Henry closed his eyes, enjoying the warmth of her body against him, as if she were a part of him.

At some point, he looked down to see that Anne had fallen asleep. Television seemed to be a good relaxing tool for her, it appeared. He picked her up and carried her to her room, tenderly covering her with the blankets. Maybe this night would be a quiet one, and the demons of her dreams would leave her alone.

I am flying over the green sparkling waters, my golden companion at my side. I am free. We rise up high into the white sky and quickly descend down close to the water. I playfully drag one clawed toe along the surface, drawing lines in my path. Silver fish jump out and I try to catch them.

I dive into the water feeling the cool liquid wash over my skin and descend deeper into the emerald oceans. The green goes from a light crystal hue to a dark rich verdant tone. The mountains under the surface reflect the darker shades of green blending into a deep blue. The silver fish descend with me, soon to be joined by the larger dragonfish. They are the ancestors of our kind, blue fish with long snouts and streaming tails like ribbons, with clawed fins which they use to catch the little silver fish.

We slow down and settle on the black sand at the bottom of the ocean. I breathe the water as easily as the air. I fall into a restful nap on the sands, my companion next to me. We are happy and peaceful curled together under the cool covering of the ocean.

I could stay here forever, but Kenta signals that it is time to depart. Following his lead, we kick off the ocean bottom and moments later, break though the surface of the water. Together we head straight to the shelf outside our dwelling, touching down effortlessly as we have countless times before. I enter first while Kenta takes a moment to stand and stretch his wings and back before following me....

I see the first fireball slam into the ledge outside. Kenta wraps his powerful wings around me in a brave attempt to protect me. I hear his heart beating before lifting my head from his chest to look into his eyes. His loving smile is soon replaced with anguish and his eyes tear in the agony of the fire that engulfs him. I choke on the intense heat and scream....

6. CASPERSEN BEACH

"Anne, wake up! I'm here!" Henry held her close. She struggled to wake from another nightmare. This was the third night in a row she'd woken up screaming. Henry felt useless. He could only hold her when she cried in the black of the night. He welcomed the opportunity to assume the mantle of protector—but how does one protect someone from a dream?

"What happened?" he asked, rocking her until she was fully awake.

As soon as she was aware of where she was, she looked around the room, searching. She grabbed the book about fantasy creatures, flipping through its pages in a frenzy until she found the picture of the dragon. She pointed to the illustration. "Dragons!" Tears streamed down her cheeks. "Dragons….fire!"

"It was only a dream, honey," he said. "There are no dragons. They're not real." Fire? Was that a clue to what happened to her? Had she been in a fire and was reliving the trauma in her dreams? He would have to check the local news for any fires in the area. But what was up with dragons? Perhaps she had a childhood fear of dragons, and the pictures in the book upset her? Yet she wanted to keep the book. These thoughts raced through Henry's mind at the first clue to the content of the nightmares she was having.

"Maybe we won't look at that book anymore," he suggested. "Come on. You can sleep in my room. Maybe we can keep the dragons away tonight." He took the blankets and spread them on the floor of his room by his bed. He encouraged her to lie down and covered her with the quilt. He lay beside her, his arm around her until, apparently, the images of fire and dragons faded, and Anne fell into a quiet sleep. Henry did not sleep for a long time, plagued by Anne's description of the nightmare, trying to figure out what it all meant.

* * *

Thursday, June 18

The next morning when the animals woke them up, Henry struggled to keep his eyes open, finding he'd fallen asleep on the floor. He stumbled to the kitchen to feed the hungry hoards. With everyone chomping loudly at their dishes, he went back to his room. Anne was already sitting on the floor.

Henry turned on the shower, handed her a fluffy blue towel and said, "I'll be here if you need me." He stepped out, leaving the door open, and flopped on the bed to grab a few more minutes of sleep. He was relieved she was able to shower and dress without help. Once she was ready, Henry took care of his own needs while Anne played with the animals. She didn't come into the bathroom this time, so he was able to relax and enjoy a leisurely shower.

They downed a quick breakfast of bagels and cream cheese and Henry's beloved coffee, which Anne really seemed to enjoy as well. Then they departed to meet Heidi and the kids on Venice Avenue.

They got to the Sun Lover's Boutique around 9:30. Heidi was waiting for them with her stand-back-kids-give-me-room-I'm-about-to-kill-your-uncle look on her face, the kids running on the sidewalk in front of the shop.

"Nice of you to show up," she snarled.

"Sorry," Henry apologized. "Another rough night."

"You couldn't call?"

Yeah, and get yelled at twice!

"It's real easy; you push one stupid button and say 'Call Heidi.' The phone does the rest."

"I was in a hurry to get here. Again I'm sorry." Henry frowned, reaching for his wallet.

Heidi shook her head. Henry barely got his credit card half way out of its slot before Heidi yanked it out of his hand. "Thank you! You take the kids and I'll take Anne shopping."

Henry put his hands out in supplication. "What do you want me to do with them?"

"Go get drinks and ice! After that, I don't care! You're in charge!" Heidi grabbed Anne's arm and marched her towards the store.

"Shopping?" Anne asked, ever curious.

"Yes, but not just any shopping. Today we're shopping for clothes. Trust me, you're gonna love it!"

Henry was left standing on the sidewalk with his niece and nephew. Both of them looked at him in eager anticipation contemplating his next move. Henry took his job as uncle very seriously, striving to be a good role model.

"Okay, kids." He took their hands. "Who wants ice cream for breakfast?"

* * *

Heidi and Anne entered the small boutique where a wall of different bathing suits hung.

"Let's see what size you are first," Heidi said. She found a saleswoman who came running with a measuring tape.

"Such a lovely girl!" the older woman with a name tag that said *Doris* exclaimed. "What is your name, dear?"

"I am Anne."

"Anne, how sweet. Now stand here, dear." She motioned to a platform in front of some mirrors at the back of the store. Anne did as instructed. "Hold out your arms, dearie," Doris crooned. Anne put her arms out to her side. Doris measured Anne's bust, waist and finally her hips. The measuring tickled and Anne couldn't help giggling.

"Be still," Doris admonished.

Heidi giggled right along with her, the two of them acting like school girls. Doris, ever the ultimate professional, continued with her work, noting the tall girl's measurements, despite her furrowed brows.

"Now, what can we help you find today?" Doris put away the tape.

"My friend needs a bathing suit and a couple of bras," Heidi said.

Doris smiled and nodded. "What kind of suit would you like? Over here," she indicated the left wall, "are our one-piece suits, and over here," she pointed to the opposite wall, "are our bikinis. Anne is a perfect size 6 and we have plenty to choose from. If you choose a bikini, I would recommend a 34D for the top. Please take your time and I'll gather up some of our brassieres for her as well." Doris trotted off to retrieve the garments as Heidi and Anne began rifling through the one-piece suits.

"What is brassiere?" Anne asked.

"It's what we women wear to hold up our breasts." Heidi pointed to her own ample top, made even more ample from breastfeeding both kids.

"Breasts?" Anne put her hands on her unhindered breasts and cradled the fullness of her bosom. She stood in front of the mirror, obviously fascinated by her appearance. "Breasts," she pronounced.

Heidi smiled. "Maybe a bikini would look good on you. Come on." She dragged her over to the bikinis.

"Bikini," Anne repeated. "What is bikini?"

"It's a swimsuit that has two pieces, one for your top, and one for your bottom." Heidi pointed to Anne's rear.

Anne put her hands on her backside and caressed the curvature of her bottom half. "Bottom."

Heidi smiled and shook her head. "You are unique, I'll give you that."

Heidi started to pull several bikinis off the rack to show them to Anne. "There are several different kinds and colors. Anything strike your fancy?"

Heidi held up a bright pink bikini with aqua highlights.

"Ooooh," Anne cried.

"Nice choice!" Heidi took Anne's hand and pulled her to the dressing room. "Try these on," she instructed.

The two girls stood for a moment taking in the beauty that was Anne. "Henry sure does have good taste," Heidi smiled. Standing behind Anne, Heidi put the bikini top on her. "Hold this," she said tying the back and neck.

"Try the bottom," Heidi said. Anne put the bottom on, turned, and posed in front of the mirror. Heidi nodded, smiling. "Henry is one lucky dude."

Anne returned the smile. "Henry is one lucky dude," she repeated.

Heidi laughed. "I think we got a winner! We'll take this one." The hot pink complimented Anne's pale skin and the cut of the suit highlighted all of her curves. "You'll need a cover up too." Heidi pulled her out of the fitting room. "Doris, we're going to take this one. She'll wear it today to the beach. I'll need a cover-up for her too."

"Very good," Doris said. "Here are some of our finest brassieres in her size." She held out six bras in various colors and styles.

"Anne, pick which ones you like, as many as you want."

"Pretty," Anne said, choosing several lace bras in pink and white, and blue and red satin as well.

Heidi took Anne to the cover-ups and picked out an aqua sheer garment.

"Excellent choice," Doris said. "And I have the perfect sandals and hat to go with that." Doris retrieved a pair of aqua sandals and a large woven floppy aqua hat, putting the hat on Anne's head. Anne took off Henry's old over-sized flip flops and put her feet into the sandals.

"Now look in the mirror, dear." Doris turned her to a large mirror in the center of the store.

Heidi and Anne gazed at the woman looking at them in the mirror. The figure reflected back was a breathtaking beauty in pink and aqua, her long golden hair flowing from under the hat.

"They're gonna have to change the name to Heartbreak Beach after you show up wearing that," Heidi said, beaming. Both girls looked at each other and giggled.

Heidi paid for the clothes with Henry's card. Anne picked up her old clothes and flip flops.

"You can put those in the bag." Heidi handed her the bag with the bras. Finalizing the transaction, she took Anne's arm. "Now let's go find that lunkhead brother of mine."

* * *

Henry was sitting on a bench outside the shop with the kids, cleaning up the ice cream Nattie had smeared all over herself. Henry slowly looked up when the girls approached. "'Bout time you two showed up. Is my card maxed ou—" He froze, dropping the napkin on the sidewalk, oblivious to Nattie hitting him, demanding that he clean her face. His mouth dropped open and his eyes grew wide at the sight of Anne standing there in her new bikini and sheer cover-up.

"Aahhh, ummm, Anne," he managed to say. "You're beautiful!"

"Henry is one lucky dude," Anne smiled back. Heidi and Anne both laughed, then Anne added, "Anne likes shopping." That made them laugh even more.

"Of course you do," Henry laughed. "It's part of the female DNA. Glad I got my credit lines increased."

Heidi corralled the kids back into her car and they all headed to the beach.

* * *

Heidi picked Caspersen Beach because it was known for the abundance of exotic shells and prehistoric shark teeth lurking in the shallow water beneath the sand. Henry parked his car and pulled out the large cooler filled with their drinks. They walked over the wooden boardwalk surrounded by palm and mangrove trees to the beach beyond. A light wind blew in over the water bringing with it the tang of the sea. Several people were in or near the water, swimming close to the shore, or bent over with little metal sieves in their search for a fossilized treasure.

Henry explained to Anne that the searchers pulled the sieves through the sand to find the shark teeth blackened over millions of years resting in the ocean. A hypnotizing whoosh of the waves on the shore mixed with calls of seagulls overhead and the din of the beach-goers enjoying the Florida coast. Washed-up seaweed lined the uncultivated sand nearer to the water. The beach was narrower than Venice Beach, left in its natural condition, and did not have the benefit of lifeguards.

Heidi spread a blanket on the sand and let the kids go to the shoreline. She sat down watching the children walk up and down the beach with their strainers looking for shark teeth. Henry put down the cooler with the drinks he had purchased, sugar free as instructed, before he and Anne sat on the blanket next to Heidi. The kids ran over, excited to show them the colorful shells they had found in the few minutes they were there. Nattie didn't have any shark teeth, but displayed the twigs and pieces of broken shells she picked up. Robbie showed them the three black shark teeth he was lucky enough to find.

"Uncle Henry! Uncle Henry! Look what I got!" the boy beamed. "I got shark teeth!"

"I got snells!" Nattie yelled, dumping her treasures on the blanket.

"Yes, I see your pretty snells. Good job." Henry examined Nattie's broken shell pieces as if they were priceless gems. Robbie pushed his strainer in front of Henry.

"Look at my shark teeth!"

"Wow, those are really cool, Robbie. Hey, do you think the Tooth Fairy visits the sharks every time they lose a tooth?" Henry teased.

"Noooo, sharks don't have pillows to leave quarters under and the Tooth Fairy can't swim," Robbie said with authority.

"How could you possibly know that the Tooth Fairy can't swim?"

"Because her wings would get all wet and she couldn't fly anymore!"

Damn, the kid has a point. Who's teasing whom here?

"Besides, sharks don't use quarters!" Robbie added confidently.

"She could bring them a fish."

"I don't think so, Uncle Henry."

"You're probably right, Robbie. After all, you are the smartest five-year-old in the world," Henry said.

Having obtained approval from Henry, the kids turned their attention to Anne, who also examined the treasures and said "pretty" to each of them. Satisfied that their finds were appreciated, the children ran back to the water's edge to keep looking. Anne got up from the blanket and followed them, bending down in the ankle-deep water to pull out handfuls of sand to see if she found anything of interest.

"She had another nightmare last night," Henry informed Heidi. "Every night. I'm not sure what to do. This time though, she was able to tell me what she dreamt about. Dragons and fire."

"Dragons and fire? Do you think she might have been involved in a fire herself recently?" Heidi asked.

"That was my guess too. I told her maybe we shouldn't be looking at the pictures of dragons in the *Fantasy Creatures* book, but she doesn't want to give it back. She seems to need it. That's the only way I can describe it." He watched Anne head deeper into the water, the kids having given up their hunt and turning their attention to chasing each other with handfuls of seaweed.

"Where is she going?" Henry got up to follow her.

"She's going deeper into the water," Heidi answered. "Do you think she'll be okay?"

"I better go with her. She didn't even know how to walk when I first found her. I doubt very much that she knows how to swim." His eyes were fixed on Anne the whole time, and he was already on his feet heading towards her. Anne was chest high in the water. He ran in to catch up with her, fighting through the waves pushing him back. With no lifeguards on Caspersen Beach, he wanted to be sure she was okay.

Suddenly, Anne disappeared under the water. Henry gasped. He called her name and dove in after her, finding it difficult to see in the murky water at first. He finally caught sight of her. She sank down to the bottom of the ocean and opened her mouth, letting the salt water rush in. Her eyes popped open wide in disbelief and her hands flew up to her throat. Henry immediately grabbed her and pulled her up to the surface, grasping her in a tight grip across her abdomen, forcing the water out of her mouth and lungs.

"What are you doing!" he shouted, pulling her back to the shore. She coughed up more water, gasping for breath with tears in her eyes. Heidi ran over to offer any help.

"Why did you do that?" Henry held her tight. Other beach-goers gathered around asking if she was okay. Heidi rounded up the kids at the same time assuring the onlookers everything was under control. The few nosey tourists who gathered soon disbursed, disappointed there would be no ambulance or TV news cameras.

"Sweetheart, why did you do that?" Henry repeated in a soft concerned tone.

Anne finally stopped coughing and said in between gasps of air. "No breathe in water!" she managed through her tears. "No breathe in water!"

"No honey, you can't breathe in water." Henry cupped her face. "Why would you think you could?" She didn't answer, her tears washing over his hand. "Please don't ever try anything like that again, okay?" Henry's heart was racing, the quick beating echoing in his ears. It had been a long time since he'd been afraid like that.

Anne stared at the water. She looked like she had just lost her best friend. She didn't want to move, but Henry insisted they return to the blanket. Heidi was calming the kids who were also crying because they were scared something had happened to Aunt Anne. Heidi assured them with hugs and cookies. Finally, with Anne back on the blanket and apparently okay, they went back to their game of seaweed tag.

"No breathe in water," Anne repeated shaking her head.

Heidi opened another bottle of water for Anne to drink to ensure she flushed out any salt water she may have consumed. "Drink this, honey." She looked at Henry. "Good thing you followed her in."

"I don't know what she was thinking." Henry pressed his lips together, shaking his head. "Why would she think she could breathe under water?"

"Maybe it's more a matter of her not knowing she couldn't. The good thing is you were there to get her out. She'll be okay. It's probably best if you stay with her for a while."

"I'm not going anywhere," Henry said. "I'm not leaving her side."

Soon, the kids grew tired of pelting each other with seaweed and came back to the blanket. Robbie sat by Anne and offered advice. "You hold your breath when you go into the water. Like this." He drew a deep breath and held it, his little cheeks blowing up like balloons. After a few seconds, he let out a long exhale and started panting until he caught his breath. "You try it."

Anne smiled, took a deep breath and held it for about thirty seconds before she let it out. "That's a long time," Robbie said. "Can you hold it a whole minute?"

"There will be no more breath-holding," Heidi said, opening the picnic basket and handing out sandwiches and little bags of chips. "Now it's time to eat." They ate their lunch in the warm Florida sun and watched the seagulls walk in the waves before taking off into the air above them. After the kids finished their food, Nattie lay down and was soon asleep. Robbie grabbed Anne's hand.

"Help me find more teeth," he begged. Anne nodded and got up to join him at the water's edge, but she did not go in farther than her knees. Henry went with them and stood on the sand watching her like a hawk, pondering the earlier events. What was it about this unusual girl? Why would she think she could breathe in water? Henry disagreed with his sister on this one. She didn't see what he saw. She tried to breathe water and was shocked at the outcome. He continued to maintain watch over Anne and Robbie walking down the beach in their search, always keeping a close distance to the pair.

After they had collected a dozen shark teeth in Robbie's basket and several small shells, they came back to the blanket. Heidi took the treasures and put them in a plastic bag to wash later when they got home. "I think we've been here long enough," she said, packing up the basket and Nattie. "Time to go."

Henry shook the sand and crumbs out of the blanket before heading back to the parking lot. The kids took advantage of one last opportunity to splash one other, stopping at the outdoor showers to wash the sand off their feet.

"Why don't you both come over on Saturday?" Heidi asked. "James is home and we can barbecue. He really wants to meet Anne."

"Okay," Henry said, holding the car door for Anne. "What time?"

"Come around lunch time. We can swim in the pool where it's a little more controlled." After everyone said their goodbyes, Heidi loaded the kids into the car and headed to her house in downtown Venice.

Both Henry and Anne were quiet on the drive home, each lost in their own thoughts. Henry contemplated the events of the day, wondering if they were connected to her nightmares in some way. Anne stared out the window and did not ask about the Florida landscape flying by. Henry would have loved to know what she was thinking about. Why did she think she could breathe under water? She seemed disappointed she couldn't do something she insisted she had done before. But how could she without proper equipment? It was impossible.

Once home, Henry led Anne to the sofa and sat beside her. "Anne," he began. "Why did you think you could breathe underwater?"

Anne hesitated, finding the words to express herself. "I see," she pointed to her head, "breathing in water. In dreams."

"Well, maybe in your dream you can breathe underwater, but in the real world you need special equipment to help you breathe." Anne looked confused, so Henry picked up a scuba diving magazine and showed her a picture of a diver under the water.

"No," she insisted. "I breathe in water long...no...help."

"Anne, honey, that's impossible. No one can breathe underwater without gear. You can't see it, but we live and breathe the air around us. Remember when Robbie taught you how to hold your breath? The two of you were breathing air. Both of us are breathing it right now. You see this thing on the diver's back? It's called an air tank, and it has air inside it for him to breathe through this tube in his mouth. He takes the air with him so he can breathe underwater. Without it, he would have the same problem you did."

Anne looked at the wooden floor of the living room. "I no breathe in water." Her eyes looked sad but she did not cry.

"I *can't*...the correct way to say it is *I can't* breathe in water. Just like I can't bear to see you sad." Henry flashed her a reassuring smile then stood up. "I have an idea! Let's draw with colored pencils some more."

She returned the smile, and together they went into the studio to amuse themselves with Henry's colored pencils. The diversion helped to lift Anne's spirit. She found joy in blending different pencils to make new colors. Henry wanted her to forget her sorrows by throwing herself into the drawing.

That night Henry had Anne sleep in his room again so that if the nightmares returned, he would be right there to help her, remembering his vow to never leave her side.

I am lying next to the largest of all the dragons: Aesmay, my father. His wings are enormous and iridescent like mine. I am safe near him and curl up comfortably near his hind legs. I shut my eyes and listen to the story of our kind.

He tells me that in the beginning The Great Creator made the First Born, including the Two; my father and Saphan, his brother. The Two were given dominion over our realm to teach them of the Creator and to live in peace with one another.

The Two assumed the form of the golden dragons, their iridescent wings rippling with the echo of all the dragon colors. Over thousands of years, the dragons grew to be in a form and mind like the Two, but none would be equal.

Saphan shines like no other dragon. His skin is like little pieces of crystal producing pinpricks of light that accentuate every pronounced muscle. He admires his form in the reflections of the crystals and the water. He is the strongest of all of the dragons and the defender of our realm.

Saphan has taken many mates from the golden dragons with whom he has many offspring. But my father does not take a mate, remaining obedient to the Creator. He longed for one that would be equal to him, one he could love, so he surrendered his own heart to create me. I am the one he loves.

But my father's brother comes before him while he is telling the story and demands that I be given to him as his mate.

"Have I not served you, my brother, for thousands of years in many realms," he says. "Have I not proven my worth?"

"You have, faithfully," my father replies. "But you know the law for our kind. You have already broken it by taking mates."

My father looks at me with love in his eyes. "I cannot command my beloved to damnation. She will not mate."

Saphan becomes angry. Kenta steps in front of him to protect me. I cannot believe my eyes! Saphan is growing in size, his eyes changing to red. How can he change his size? But Kenta does not move.

Saphan shrinks back to his normal size. "Aesmay, you are in error, my brother. Why should I not enjoy these creatures? I have seen the pleasure for so long and abstained. Why should I, or we, not partake?"

"You know why," Aesmay growls. "Aeya is bound by the same law."

Saphan approaches me. His mouth is open and dripping. "But I have never seen a female as beautiful and equal to me as she. I, and I alone, am worthy to take Aeya as mine."

He goes to the edge of my father's shelf, ready to soar to the ocean below. Just as he drops over the edge, his voice travels back to me. "And I will have her...."

The black dragons come with fire! I see Saphan come, but he does not look the same anymore. He is different! His skin is black and hard, no longer smooth like mine. His nostrils are large and round, spewing smoke from inside. His angry red eyes are focused on me. The other black dragons spit fire at our kind, burning them as they flee. He approaches me and I feel the fire of his breath....

7. TRIP TO JUNGLE GARDENS

This time, when Anne woke up screaming in the night, fighting the demons of her dreams, Henry was right there at her side. It was upsetting to witness the horror of her night terrors from the beginning. Each night Anne had to endure this torment tore at his heart, leaving him feeling helpless to stop it. He was determined he would find the cause and a way to chase the demons away.

* * *

Friday, June 19

The morning came with sunlight shining through the bedroom windows illuminating the couple curled up on the floor. Henry had intended to sleep on the floor, letting Anne take his bed, but after her nightmare, she held onto him for solace and would not let go. Henry didn't want her to, ever.

Henry rolled over to divert the sun from his eyes, his thoughts shifting from the night's ordeal to breakfast. He had a large number of mouths to feed.

Anne, however, leapt to her feet as if the terrors of the night had never happened. As if reading his thoughts, she dashed toward the kitchen, daring him to catch her. Even little Flack in his wheelchair left him in his dust. "*Et tu*, Flack?" Henry lamented.

Henry entered the kitchen. He was surprised to see Anne dishing out the pets' food. He could tell by her wrinkled nose and sour expression that she didn't much care for the pungent odor.

"Smells as bad going in as it does coming out, doesn't it?" Henry joked, before something odd caught his attention. All the animals sat quietly, waiting to be fed, tails wagging, tongues drooling, and perfectly behaved.

What the hell? Isn't that the damnedest thing I've ever seen?

With their bowls full, Anne turned and placed them on the floor two at a time, calling each pet by name. One by one they came when summoned and started chomping away.

I stand corrected! That's the damnedest thing I've ever seen. Coming from a guy who found a naked woman on the beach who didn't know how to talk or where to pee, but could draw like Di Vinci...that's saying something!

Not wanting to interrupt what had to be a filming of a new *Twilight Zone* episode, Henry maneuvered around the smaller animals aiming for the coffee pot. It didn't matter what he ate in the morning. As long as he had the mystical brown liquid to fortify him, he could face anything. Before he could reach his destination, Anne intercepted him, stopping him in his tracks.

"No, I make coffee," she said, measuring the coffee into the filter and pouring the water into the coffee machine.

As the water dripped through the grounds to the waiting pot below, Henry couldn't help but think maybe it was his turn to wake up screaming. *I have to be dreaming, it's the only logical explanation, or perhaps she really is reading my thoughts. Easy Henry, just go along, you can check the closet for seed pods later.*

"You do!" Henry smiled. "Well, that's terrific, thank you!" She poured coffee into a cup and handed it to him. "Thanks." He inhaled the aroma, hoping it might help clear his head. Holding the steaming cup to his lips, he slurped the first few sips and looked up at Anne. "I have an idea for today."

"Idea?"

"Something I want to do," he explained. "I'm going to ask Heidi to take you to see some animals while I talk to my friend at the Police Department to see if I can find any answers about what happened to you."

"Zoo?" Anne cocked her head, remembering the pictures in Robbie's books.

"Something like that. It's a place you can go and see the animals you're learning about. You can even feed some of them. You seem to have a knack for that." *I swear if I hear they all line up for her one by one, I'm having Heidi admit me.*

Anne nodded, squealing. "Zoo! Animals!"

"I'll take that as a yes," Henry said, smiling. He picked up his phone and dialed Heidi's number.

"Hello, big brother," Heidi answered.

"Hello, little sister!" Henry returned. "Can I ask you a favor?"

"Like you do every day, or is this a special favor?"

Henry smirked. "I don't ask you every day."

"Just about."

"Okay, fine, here's today's *faveur de jour* if you will! Happy?"

"Actually, yeah, I am."

Henry sighed. He could feel the smugness in her tone. "Hey, in all seriousness, can you take Anne somewhere where she can see some animals? I'm going to stop by the police department and talk to Eddie about her. I really need to find out what happened."

"It's about time," Heidi scolded. "I suppose. But you really do owe me, you know. Not for this, because the kids would love having Anne go with them, but just because I really am the greatest sister in the world!"

"You just better hope I don't find any seed pods in my closet," Henry replied, only half joking.

"What?"

"Nothing, just thanks and I'll bring her over as soon as we're dressed."

"Okey doke," Heidi replied. "We'll go to Jungle Gardens." She hung up.

Anne held a carton of eggs she had taken out of the refrigerator. "Let me help you with that," he said, getting a bowl, pan and spatula. "Time you learned to cook." They had fun cracking and scrambling the eggs, making quite the mess.

Anne wanted to wash the dishes, having observed Henry do them these past few days. Being a gracious host, he let her. Well, to be honest, he was grateful because he never enjoyed doing dishes. And he was glad she was learning her way around a kitchen.

Anne finished cleaning up, then came into the bathroom where Henry was shaving. Anne touched the shaving cream on his face. She rubbed her fingertips together, exploring the texture, then applied it to her own face.

"No, Anne." Henry took a towel and wiped the cream off her face. "You don't shave. This is one of those differences between men and women."

"I not shave?"

"Well," Henry picked up the razor, "not your face anyway. Go ahead and get in the shower. I'll take mine after you."

Anne watched him drag the razor down his cheeks, up his neck and under his nose. He rinsed his face and patted it with a towel. Anne touched his clean-shaven chin, fascinated by the change in his appearance.

Henry let her explore, then touched the hand caressing him. "Get in the shower, Anne," he said with a smile. "We have a lot to do today."

She got in slowly, her eyes still on him. Henry closed the door for her. "I'll be right outside if you need me."

Anne came out with a towel around her, letting Henry take his turn. Anne dressed in shorts, a pink t-shirt and her floppy hat. Once dry, Henry put on a pair of khaki shorts, his U.S. Navy T-shirt, and loafers.

* * *

Heidi heard Henry pull up around ten o'clock. The kids were chomping at the bit to get to the park and ran around the front door chanting, "Jungle Gardens!"

Heidi was packing up Nattie's diaper bag when he entered the house. "How long do you need?"

"Can you give me about three hours?"

"Sure! I think we can keep busy for that long, probably longer. Tell you what. I'll call you when we're ready to head home and you can meet us here."

"Sounds like a plan!" Henry kissed Anne on the cheek. "Have fun Anne. I'll see you in a little while."

"Thank you," she said.

Heidi finished packing up the diaper bag. "Let's go!"

* * *

"She's a pretty girl," Detective Ortega remarked looking at the photo of Anne. Detective Ortega was an older man in his late fifties, with greying hair that was mostly gone. He preferred black Ray Ban glasses to contacts, which made the seasoned officer look even more intelligent. He carried a few extra pounds, yet it was obvious from his muscular build that he preferred the health club over the doughnut shop.

Ortega sat at his desk at the Venice Police Department surrounded by stacks of case files piled so high, Henry couldn't see the photos in the frames peeking over the top. Assorted desk necessities and a badly chipped coffee mug with a shield and the word "Sergeant" completed the scene. Henry could only assume the cup held some sentimental value, which would explain why it had never been replaced with one depicting his current rank.

The two had met when Henry was in the Navy and Ortega an Ensign on the aircraft carrier during Henry's first sea tour. Ed was nearing retirement and the pair only worked together for about a year before Ed left the Navy and joined the police department of their home town of Venice. Years later, Henry looked him up after he returned home and they had stayed in touch, especially when Henry needed help with a speeding ticket—or the identity of the occasional naked woman washed up on the shore.

"How is she doing?"

Henry shrugged. "She seems fine during the day. It's just these nightmares she's having every night. I wish I knew what happened to her."

"Since no apparent crime was committed, there really wasn't much more we could have done at the time. Now that you took it upon yourself to take care of her, she's your problem."

"I didn't take it on! This was your idea!"

Ortega chuckled.

Henry also smiled. "It's okay really. That's also why I'm so worried about these nightmares. It's obvious she's reliving some traumatic ordeal that ended up with her all alone and naked on that beach."

"And you say she is having these nightmares every night, but the only thing she can tell you is that there was a fire involved?"

"The only things she's told me so far are that she was breathing underwater—not quite sure what to make of that—and she always sees fire. How the fire is involved is still a mystery, but my best guess is she may have been in a fire at some point, or lost someone close to her in one. Other than the nightmares, she remembers nothing about who she is or how she got there. Nothing at all!"

Ortega shook his head. "I did some digging but haven't found a report of any missing person fitting her description. She doesn't remember anything?"

"Nothing." Henry shook his head. "It's like she was just born. She didn't know how to do anything! It's amazing though how quickly she's learned though. I've never met anyone like her!"

Ortega closed his notebook. "If there are any records of her, we'll find them."

"Thanks." Henry got up to leave. "I appreciate it."

"No problem," Detective Ortega said. "Thanks for bringing me in on this. Let me know if she remembers anything at all. The smallest detail could unlock the biggest clue."

"I promise I will."

"Oh, and Henry, try not to get too attached to this girl. I don't have to be a detective to see you're sweet on her. If something serious pops up, I'm gonna have to step in in an official capacity. Do you understand?"

"I understand." Henry nodded and left, hoping he'd done the right thing.

His next step, when he got home, was to log on to the Florida Crime Information Center website and put in the information about Anne to see if there was a match. Finding nothing, he pulled up the local newspaper websites and researched recent articles about fires, especially at sea or anything about a missing woman, but nothing seemed to fit with either Anne or the area where he found her. Frustrated, he sat back and frowned. Hopefully, Eddie would have better luck.

* * *

While Henry was playing Junior Detective, Heidi and the gang were having the time of their lives at the Sarasota Jungle Gardens. Anne seemed thrilled to see the animals in the flesh instead of pictures in a book. They moved from habitat to habitat. Robbie and Anne had a contest to see who could say the name of the animal first. Then Robbie would mimic the sound the animal made, or what he thought they would make. But they were both stumped at "Putter" the Prairie Dog. Robbie, Anne, and Nattie squeaked like a Spider Monkey or squawked like a Macaw as loudly as they could, laughing with delight if they got a response. Heidi chuckled. She was used to this with Robbie and Nattie, but not with a grown woman.

They wandered the sidewalks of the park, between large willow trees and green ferns bordering ponds where flamingos stood on long thin legs. Beautiful peacocks walked un-caged, their train of feathers spread in colorful delight. They bought feed from the machines at the flamingo habitat, and Heidi recorded them on her cell phone as they fed the large pink birds. Nattie went first, courageously extending her tiny hand to a towering male. Heidi told her to think of him as Big Bird from Sesame Street with a sunburn. Her turn ended when she started eating the pellets herself. Robbie was more timid. Still, not to be shown up by his little sister, he stood stiff as a statue when it was his turn. Heidi remembered a past visit when he was Nattie's age and an overzealous flamingo had nipped his tiny fingers, proving the old adage, "Once bitten twice shy."

"Keep your hand flat, and don't curl your fingers," Heidi told him. She was proud of him facing his fear like a brave little soldier.

Anne, of course, drew the largest crowd of animals, since she was an adult and could hold more food, and partly because, well, she was Anne. Like everything and everyone she encountered, Anne immersed herself in the moment. She had a way of squeezing every drop out of a new experience and soaking it all up like a sponge. She giggled and smiled at the birds eating out of her hand. They only stopped because they ran out of quarters to buy more food. They had almost gotten out of the flamingo habitat when two of the birds began following them for a short while.

Heidi's little troupe enjoyed a picnic lunch before attending the bird show. The bird presentation showcased assorted species of exotic birds, including parrots, macaws, cockatoos, and others. All had been trained to perform tricks on tiny bird roller skates, ride little bird bicycles, and play bird basketball. Heidi watched this charming girl laughing like her children, tucking the sight away in her heart. Anne was as delighted as the kids, fascinated by the little feathered thespians and their antics.

They were all a little afraid of the crocodiles and alligators at the reptile habitat, except the fake crocodile that everyone loved to sit on for pictures. All of them were intimidated by their size and long rows of sharp teeth. Robbie was the only one in the group who enjoyed seeing the snakes. Even

Anne wasn't impressed. Snakes just don't have that warm fuzzy vibe most animals do. Robbie alone started hissing snake sounds in front of the tanks. Heidi was relieved they didn't get any response from the slithering creatures.

At the mammal habitat, they had fun saying the word *lemur*. Anne kept saying *lemur* and *flamingo*, because she said they were fun to say.

They strolled through the gardens on brick paths surrounded by a variety of trees—fruit, palm, bamboo, pine, even a bunya-bunya tree skirted by dense ferns. The kaleidoscope of nature blossomed everywhere, from the vibrant exotic birds, multicolored butterflies in the Butterfly Garden, to the many species of flowers blooming around the walkways and trees.

Anne lingered in the gardens gazing up at the trees that canopied the walkway. She touched every tree, fern and flower, feeling the texture of the plant, and leaning down to take in its scent. Heidi could see it in her eyes. They were surrounded by the rich colors of the environment and the wildlife. Anne was frozen in awe at the beauty of creation until Heidi gently took her arm, guiding her through the rest of the park.

On the way out, they stopped at the gift shop and Heidi bought them all stuffed flamingos, even Anne. The fun continued on the drive home from Sarasota on Route 75, with Anne and the kids looking for animals. Every time someone saw a herd of cows grazing in the pastures bordering the highway, the car erupted in a chorus of moos. Heidi smiled at Anne and the kids playing their cow-game, amazed at this strange girl her brother had met. Maybe having Anne in his life would finally bring Henry out of the refuge he had retreated to after the death of his fiancée, Christine, several years ago.

Halfway home, Heidi turned on the blue-tooth and called Henry. "We're almost home."

"I'll be there in a bit. Did you guys have a good time?" Henry said.

"We had a wonderful time. Not sure who enjoyed it more—Anne or the kids!"

"Happy to hear it! I'll see you soon."

Back home, Heidi ushered the kids inside, flamingos in tow, instructing Anne to gather up the diaper bag and souvenirs left in the back seat, bringing all of the bags into the house. Heidi put together some dinner for them, heating up frozen chicken nuggets and slicing up an apple. By the time she had the food on the table and Nattie in her high chair, Henry pulled up.

* * *

Henry walked in the front door. "Uncle Henry! Uncle Henry!" Robbie raced up to his uncle. "We saw alligators!"

"And lemurs," Anne added. "Leeemuuurrrrs!"

This set Nattie off on a chorus of "leeeemuuuuurrrsss" while she played with her nuggets, pretending they were lemurs climbing trees of apple slices.

"Sounds like you all had a lot of fun." Henry smiled, picking up Robbie.

"Did you find out anything?" Heidi asked.

Henry shook his head. "Not yet. Eddie is going to contact other state agencies and check missing persons, but so far, zip." He hoisted Robbie up in the air, almost hitting his head on the ceiling fan.

"Careful!" Heidi cried out.

"Sorry, he's getting so tall."

"Yes he is, and you chopping his head off will put an end to that real quick, won't it?"

"Sorry Robbie, before you know it, you'll be picking me up," Henry said. Robbie smiled and ran back towards the kitchen before all the chicken nuggets were gone

"Do you want some dinner?" Heidi offered. "It's only chicken nuggets, but I can fix you something else if you want."

"No, that's okay. I'm sure Anne's had enough fun for one day. I promise I'll bring her back on Saturday." He assured the pouting kids. Anne picked up her stuffed flamingo, kissed the children and Heidi, and went to Henry by the front door. "Thanks again, Heidi." Henry hugged the kids and his sister.

On the drive home, he was quiet, lost in thought.

"We will find." Anne put her hand on his arm.

He reached over with his left hand. "I know," he said with a smile. "I just want to help you find the right answers to make the demons go away."

"What are demons?"

"Demons are nasty things that hurt people. They're not like us, with a body, but they're more like…." Henry searched for an image to convey his thoughts, "like the bad things in your nightmares. Sometimes people refer to things that make them sad as 'demons,' which I think is more accurate. I don't think there really are evil spirits waiting to hurt us. It's just stories parents tell kids to scare them into behaving. There's no God and no Satan."

"What is God and Satan?"

Henry sighed. "Allegedly, God is this great being in the sky who supposedly made the earth and everything on it. Satan was one of his angels who got mad at God and wanted to do what he wanted to do instead of what God wanted him to do. So God made him leave the place in the sky people call Heaven. And before you ask, angels are the good spirits God created to protect us. Or so they say. You'll see pictures of them dressed in white robes with giant wings on their backs."

"They are not real? Like 'tele...vision?'"

"Yep. I think it's all just stuff someone made up to make us all feel guilty so they can keep us in line. In my experience, none of it is real. I used to believe in God and the whole religious scene. My family went to church every Sunday."

"What is church?"

"It's a place people go to be with God. I stopped going years ago." Henry didn't say anything more after that. Church meant many things. One day, as the organ played *Just as I Am*, he had gone to the front of the church to receive Christ. But there were other days; the scent of flowers in front of his mom's casket; the sound of dirt hitting the top of the vault, hiding Christine away from him forever.

After the service, he stayed at the cemetery long after everyone left, in his service dress blues, watching the workers fill in the grave. He was abandoned and betrayed. That was the day his faith finally died.

Then there was the day he held Heidi's hand, assuming the mantle of guardian after their father was laid to rest. He couldn't understand how a Loving God could allow these things to happen to someone who loved God as much as he did. What father doesn't protect his children? How much more could God take away from him? Tormented day and night, he begged for an answer to one simple question. *"Why?"*

Henry's hands tightened on the steering wheel. He shoved his anger back into a deep dark corner of his heart. *Damn it! It's been ten years! Doesn't it ever get any easier?* Glancing at the speedometer, he saw he was cruising way over the speed limit and eased back on the gas. *Get a grip, Henry. Focus on the now, on Anne. Don't let your anger at God get you both killed.*

"I'm sorry, Anne. Not a good subject to talk about." He looked over at her and forced a smile.

She put her hand on his leg, and that warm slender hand acted as a balm, helping him to relax and put his grief away.

Maybe someday he would tell Anne how he turned against God and to a life of parties, women and drink. Maybe he would tell her about the night he drank so much, he woke up in the hospital with a fractured skull, and no idea how it happened. He only remembered Heidi's distraught eyes. At that moment, he vowed to his sister he'd change. He kept that vow, stopped partying, and went back to school, earning a degree in graphic design.

Maybe someday, he would tell Anne about who he was, why he retreated into his own world filled with his animals. But not today. Having Anne beside him somehow made those memories a little bit easier. Besides, she had enough to worry about without being dragged into his private hell.

* * *

Anne didn't say anything after Henry stopped talking because he seemed to be getting upset by the conversation. She wanted to reach out to him to take away the pain she saw on his face, to see his wonderful dimples when he smiled. She felt his pain as if it were her own. She didn't even know what to say, so she just put her hand on his leg to let him know without words that she was there.

She did not understand what he was talking about with angels and demons, but in her heart, Anne somehow knew that whatever these beings were called, they were real, as real as she and Henry were. She didn't know what they were or how she knew, but she did. What she didn't understand yet was whether she should be afraid of that or relieved.

I am the most beautiful of all of the dragons and they all adore me. But one dragon loves me even more. He has great and powerful white wings and other than the Two, Kenta is the largest and mightiest of our kind. I fly across the white sky with him, watching the powerful pectoral muscles of his wings thunder pushing down the air in his path. I feel joy rise in my heart. We climb high into the air as if we will touch the white sun above us. We fly all day and never tire, stopping only to admire the beauty of our home.

But Saphan wants me and so he watches us...watches me. He is not like the other dragons. I see the evil in his eyes as he follows me wherever I go, and I am afraid....

8. AT JAMES AND HEIDI'S HOUSE

Saturday, June 20

Heidi and her husband, James Mason, lived in a two-story tan stucco home with five bedrooms and a three-car garage. James was Henry's best friend in high school, before James attended law school and Henry enlisted in the Navy. James had a successful probate and business law practice in Sarasota.

It was one of those romances where a best friend's baby sister went from pigtails and a pain in the neck, to all grown up and beautiful. They got married when Heidi was in her second year of nursing school at the University of Florida. After she graduated as a Registered Nurse, she obtained a position at Venice Regional Medical Center. She became pregnant with Robbie soon thereafter. After Nattie came along, James and Heidi made the decision that while the children were young, Heidi would be a full-time mom and resume her nursing career after the kids were both in school full time.

Heidi opened the double oak front doors with decorative glass panels to welcome Henry and Anne. The doors were mounted between two large picture windows. Beneath the windows stood manicured bushes lined with small flowers. Two large palm trees and a mature century plant adorned the lawn.

"Hi Anne," Heidi said. "I would like you to meet my husband James. James this is—"

"The beautiful and mysterious Anne I've heard so much about!" James interrupted. "It's a pleasure to meet you." He extended his hand. James was just a few inches shorter than Henry, looking every bit the lawyer, even in camp shirt and shorts.

"Hello!" Anne exclaimed, stepping past his hand and throwing her arms around him in a giant hug. "I'm Anne."

James stood there speechless with a shocked but pleasant look on his face.

Henry laughed.

"Um… Anne," Heidi started to say before Anne turned and locked her in her embrace.

"Hi, Heidi!"

"Hello, Anne." *We're going to have to talk about appropriate physical contact.* Heidi pried herself loose. "Come on, I'll show you the house."

James put his arm around Henry's shoulder, and the two of them disappeared inside the house headed toward the back yard, no doubt in search of a cold one. Heidi took Anne on a tour of their home, starting in the white marble foyer, to the raised living room with white carpet and antique Chippendale furniture. One of Henry's paintings hung over the sofa. Captured in oils, Heidi was seated holding ten-month-old Nattie in her arms, James behind her with his hands on her shoulders, and Robbie sitting on the floor at her feet. The painting was framed on either side by photographs of the family, James and Heidi's wedding, the children's baby pictures and a picture of Henry and Heidi with their parents.

Anne stared at the painting, a confused look on her face.

"You like it? Henry did that."

"I like it!" Anne said. "It is pretty but not…right. Robbie is not right. Heidi is not right." She pointed to Nattie in the painting. "Who is that?"

"That's Nattie when she was a baby. She's a toddler now. Robbie is younger too."

"Baby?"

"Yeah, remember at Jungle Gardens, we saw the baby Zebra walking with the mommy Zebra?"

"Little one?"

"Yes, the little one. Well, the little one will grow up to be like the big one and have her own babies."

"Oh."

"You don't really understand, do you?"

"No." Anne confessed.

"We'll have to have a little talk about that some other time." *Wow, I can see what Henry meant about being helpless. Not that I would ever let him know he actually got something right.* "For now, let's just finish the tour of the house."

They went through the formal dining room with a mahogany Colonial set that sat eight. On the wall between the two rooms was another large oil painting of children playing on the beach. Heidi had bought it at an estate sale.

Heidi walked Anne through the kitchen with marble counter tops and an island counter in the middle surrounded by glass and mahogany cabinets. Different plates of food waited on the island for the afternoon festivities. Off the other side of the kitchen was the den, decorated like an old ship with dark paneling, nets, and a ship's wheel on the left wall. A home theater occupied the other wall, with movie-style seats. Mounted over the book shelves was a large stuffed marlin.

"James caught that two years ago," Heidi said. "It put up quite a fight."

"Caught it?" Anne said. "Why would you want to catch it?"

Heidi gave her a strange look. "Perhaps Henry can tell you all about fishing. It's a sport guys like to do. The boys go often. Come on, let's go upstairs. I'll show you the bedrooms."

James used the downstairs bedroom as his home office, and the remaining four were upstairs. In the master bedroom was a king size bed with tall bedposts, a fireplace and French doors opening onto a balcony overlooking the back yard. The bathroom had a Jacuzzi tub big enough for two and a custom designed shower with four shower heads.

Robbie and Nattie each had their own bedroom, with a bathroom shared between them. Robbie's was themed with superheroes and Nattie's was princess bedding and paintings of ballerinas on the wall. The last bedroom was a guest room.

They concluded the tour at the back yard, where the men were seated on lounge chairs next to a large pool with a rock waterfall on one side, an attached spa on the other, and a water slide for the children. Three steps led into the shallow end on the side near the spa, with the pool going to a depth of ten feet at its deepest end. A full outdoor kitchen and patio set completed the area. The fenced-in yard had a swing set near the tall pine trees with a sandbox next to it. The kids were riding three-wheelers around the patio. Screaming Anne's name, they jumped off their bikes.

"Anne, come play with me," Robbie ordered.

"No! Play with *me*!" Nattie shouted

"Let's go!" Robbie demanded. "I want you to play with me. Do you want to see my room?"

"No, Robbie, she wants to see my room with the princesses not Ireman," Nattie insisted.

"It's *Iron* man, not Ireman," Robbie corrected. The debate continued as the two of them dragged Anne back into the house.

Heidi joined the men chatting by the pool.

"Do we have any idea yet as to who she is or where she came from?" James asked, handing Heidi a beer from a cooler between him and Henry. The coals in the barbecue were already glowing. Soon they would be ready to grill James's famous teriyaki steaks marinating in the refrigerator. He had a special sauce he called his "secret weapon" that gave it just the right flavor.

"No," Henry said. "I did talk to Eddie who's checking into it, but so far there are no matches to her description. And I've checked missing persons on the FCIC, but nothing that would fit her."

"What are you going to do for the long term?" James took a sip of his beer.

"I'm going to let her stay with me. She's not just homeless. She needs help. Ask Heidi. When I found her, she didn't know how to do anything."

"That's my point, it has to be a lot of work for you. Why bother with the burden? Just turn her over to the authorities."

"I don't think Henry wants to do that," Heidi said, sipping her own drink. "You know him."

"Yeah, I know, the knight in shining armor for lost causes."

Henry smirked. "Yeah, I guess I am. I never met a lost animal or a stray blonde I didn't like." He did his best Groucho Marks impression, complete with an invisible cigar.

James laughed, choking on his beer.

"I don't see a problem as long as Henry can get his work done," Heidi continued. "Anne seems to enjoy the art as well."

"Legally, he's taking a big risk. What if something happens to her under his care? Didn't she almost drown the other day?"

"Yes, but that's because she didn't know she couldn't breathe underwater," Henry said.

"Why would anyone think they could breathe underwater?"

"That's my point," Henry answered. "No one else is going to watch over her like I am. Turn her over to homeless shelter, she won't last a day. She's too vulnerable."

"I see your point, just be careful," James cautioned.

"Besides, she understands more and more every day," Henry said. "I'm hoping soon she might be able to tell me what happened to her. At first, I thought she might've been caught in a fire, then there's something about being in the water. My guess was that she was on a boat that caught fire and fell off. But there's no sign of physical trauma. Just emotional."

James shook his head. "Weird that no one seems to have reported her missing. You'd think someone would know her."

Heidi turned to go into the house. Nattie was screaming bloody murder at Robbie. "There are a lot of people who are alone in this world who don't have anyone to report them missing." She went to break up the kerfuffle upstairs in Nattie's room. Anne was trying to keep them apart, holding on to Nattie. Robbie had taken Nattie's doll out of her hands and used it as a hammer to bang his turtle fighters' evil nemesis into submission.

"Gimme back my dolly! Gimme!" Nattie screamed.

"No!" Robbie yelled back. "Dolly is killing the bad guy! Bam Bam!"

"Robert Alan Mason, you give your sister back her doll this instant!" Heidi yelled. Robbie looked sheepishly at her and handed the doll back to his sister. "Are you okay, Anne?"

"I am okay." She laughed. "Nattie has dolly now. The little ones do not hurt one another."

"Go on outside with Henry," Heidi said. "I'll get the kids ready to go in the pool. We'll be right out."

* * *

Anne came out the patio door to join them by the pool. Henry stood.

"Hi Anne," James said. "Are you enjoying the house?"

"Pretty house," Anne replied. She sat by Henry and took the can of lemon soda he offered her.

"Well, guess I better get the steaks started." James put his beer down and went to the kitchen to retrieve the night's main course.

"Are you okay?" Henry asked Anne. "I know the kids can be a handful sometimes."

She nodded. "Yes. I laugh with Robbie and Nattie." She put the can down and looked at Henry. "Anne go in water please? No breathe."

"Okay, we can go into the water, but you have to promise me you'll stay close and listen to everything I tell you."

"I will," Anne promised.

"I'll teach you how to swim and breathe air. We'll stay in the shallow end until I feel it's safe for you to go deeper."

"Shallow, deeper?" Anne questioned.

Henry thought for a moment. "If there is very little water, like up to your knees," Henry held his right hand to his knee, "then you're in shallow water. If the water is over your head," Henry demonstrated, "then you're in deep water. Do you understand?"

"Yes. Shallow, deep." She mimicked his movements.

"Very good," Henry said. "Are you ready to go into the water?"

"Yes, I am."

They had come prepared to swim. Anne removed her cover-up, causing James to almost drop the plate of meat seeing Anne in her bikini. He looked around to see if Heidi saw his reaction. Henry chuckled. He knew James loved his wife and would never cheat on her, but Anne's beauty caught him off guard. She was stunning and she was with Henry.

Henry went first, using the steps leading into the pool's shallow end before Robbie could jump in and splash them. They walked to the middle of the pool where it was waist deep. The kids came out of the house and followed. Robbie performed a perfect cannon ball splashing them with the cool water. Heidi was right behind them with Nattie in tow, looking adorable in her princess water wings.

"Robbie, front and center," Henry barked. Robbie torpedoed across the pool, stopping right in front of the two of them. "Yes, Uncle Henry?"

"Remember those swimming lessons I paid for last summer at the Park District, so someday I can teach you to scuba dive with me?"

"Yeah."

"Would you like to show Anne how to swim for me?"

"*Sure!*"

"Great, here's what I want you to do. Swim back and forth from side to side right in front of us. Go real slow so Anne can see how you swim, than you can show us how fast you are, okay?"

"Okay, *watch me, Anne!*" Robbie plunged forward and swam free style. Henry was impressed with the young boy's form. Either he was a natural, like his Uncle, or had been practicing on his own. Whatever the reason, this little guy could swim, and would jump at the chance to show off for Anne.

They watched Robbie pass back and forth, Henry describing what he was doing.

"Do you see how he has his head in the water and is looking straight down? That keeps his spine in line and prevents his hips from sinking." Henry gently touched each part on Anne's body as he named them. "You don't want to swim with your head up looking at what's in front of you. Also, see how he rotates—moves—from side to side, one arm stretched in front of him while he brings the other one up. That keeps his shoulder from getting hurt and lets him take a breath of air. You don't want to swim flat. Keep your legs straight and don't bend at the knees. When you breathe, remember to breathe early and keep your arms straight and fingertips pointed down so you don't pull crooked. Do you understand?"

"I understand."

"Are you ready to give it a try?"

"Yes!" Anne replied, diving into the water.

"Wait," Henry said alarmed. "I wasn't finished."

Anne skimmed across the surface of the water at a fast pace. She thrashed her legs and churned her arms like a windmill. Always the quick study, Anne was making progress and holding her own, but she expended way too much energy. She would tire out soon. He marveled at how well she was doing for her first attempt and couldn't help but notice her muscularity and power, the artist in him drawn to her anatomy. The water glistened on her skin, accentuating her form.

Henry tapped Anne's shoulder. "Anne, Anne! Stop for a minute." Anne stood up and with both hands, brushed her wet hair back away from her face.

"Anne swim, I swim," she said, smiling and dripping.

"Yes, Anne swim, I mean you swim—uh swam—now you got me doing it! Yes, you did. You swam well, but we still need to work on it. Here, watch me." Henry grabbed the edge of the pool with both hands and stretched out in a prone position floating on the surface. "Watch my legs." Henry kicked his legs, bracing himself with both arms. "See, you don't have to kick so hard. Now you try it."

Anne joined him on the ledge and kicked her legs to match Henry's movement. "That's it, you've got it. Keep kicking, but much slower. I want to try something." Anne obeyed Henry's instructions. He stood up and placed both arms under her torso. "Okay, let go of the edge but keep kicking. I'm going to hold you in one place."

Anne released her grip and Henry guided her to the middle of the pool. "Okay, now I'm going to let go and I want you to slowly swim to the end of the pool and back to me." Henry dropped his arms and watched Anne paddle off. Reaching the end of the pool, she turned around and headed back towards Henry. About two thirds of the way back, she took a deep breath and submerged below the water. Henry gasped, and for a moment felt a wave of panic. She was streaming toward him underwater, emerging right in front of him. "I no breathe," she said.

"Damn!" Henry said, impressed.

A well-aimed beach ball slammed into the back of Henry's head with a loud ping breaking the moment.

"Dinner is ready," Heidi announced. "Be sure and wash up." Robbie doubled over with laughter after witnessing the attack. Nattie continued playing with her princess ponies, oblivious to what just happened.

They all enjoyed a feast of steaks, chicken, hotdogs, corn on the cob, potato salad and a garden salad. After dinner, Heidi brought out ice cream and made sundaes for everyone. Henry added several items to Anne's ever-growing list of new foods she liked.

9. ON BEING A WOMAN

Everyone sat around the patio talking and eating. Anne jumped up, feeling something uncomfortable in her bikini bottom and ran for the bathroom near the pool. There, she pulled her bikini down. It was red with blood that trickled down her legs. *What was wrong?* Bloody images from her nightmares of dragons being ripped apart flashed in her head. The fear she had pushed down since Henry found her fought its way to the surface. She stood in the bathroom staring at the blood on her legs, her hands in the air in front of her and screamed Henry's name.

Henry banged on the door. "Anne! What's the matter?"

"I am bleeding!" she cried.

Heidi's voice came closer to the door. "Let me in, Anne. I can help!"

Anne opened the door, dripping blood on Heidi's bathroom floor, her bikini around her knees. Heidi stepped inside, closing the door behind her.

"She's started her period," Heidi called to the men on the other side of the door. "I got this."

"All yours, honey," James answered.

Henry knocked on the door. "Can I help with anything?"

"Yeah, keep an eye on the kids."

* * *

Heidi helped Anne take off her suit, sat her on the toilet, and left the bathroom, returning with fresh clothes. She brought sanitary pads, putting one on the underwear she included. "Wipe off your legs then put this on," she instructed.

Anne did as she was told, and Heidi was relieved to see her relax a little. Heidi put the lid of the toilet down and told Anne to take a seat. She leaned against the sink and put her hands on Anne's knees. "Haven't you had your period before?"

Anne didn't seem to comprehend. She looked at Heidi in confusion, and shook her head. "What is *period*?"

"You have what all women have had to go through since the beginning of time. You should have started years ago. I don't understand why you don't remember having one... Anyway, there's nothing wrong. This will happen every month. It's natural and nothing to be afraid of. When it starts, you can put a pad in your underwear like these." She grabbed a few from the package she'd brought. "Change them often, depending on how much blood there is."

Anne took the small plastic wrapped packages from Heidi's hands and stared at them as if she'd never seen them. "Women have, not men?" she asked. "Men shave, not women?"

"Well, we shave, but not our faces. But yes, this is something only women suffer with. Guys couldn't handle it. Go ahead and get dressed." Heidi took one of the small towels off the rack. "I'll take care of your suit and the bathroom. Then we'll talk more." Heidi started to clean up the blood on the floor. Anne pulled the second towel off the bar and kneeled down to help her. "Thanks," Heidi said.

Heidi couldn't get over how scared Anne was of something she should have been used to at her age. How old was Anne anyway? They didn't even know—only that she appeared to be in her early twenties, maybe the same age as Heidi—twenty five? There was no way to know. But she was certainly old enough to have been a woman for several years now.

After they cleaned up the bathroom and Anne was dressed, Heidi took her by the hand and led her into the den. "It's time to have that talk I promised you earlier." She took one of her nursing books off the bookshelf and opened it to an anatomical picture of a woman. Heidi described how each part worked, including menstruation. She pointed out the female anatomy. Anne pointed to the back yard and said, "Henry is different!"

"Yes." Heidi couldn't help smiling. "Men are different than women." She turned the page to the illustration of a man's anatomy.

Anne pointed to the evident male parts. "Man!" she exclaimed.

"I guess you've seen that, huh," Heidi said, chuckling. "Yes, that is called a penis and the things underneath are testicles. Men and women have different parts that they join together to make babies."

Anne cocked her head. Heidi nodded, put the book down and explained the birds and the bees to Anne, including intercourse and childbirth.

"Do you understand?"

"Man and woman are different. They…make love?"

"Yes, it's called intercourse."

"Is intercourse love?"

Heidi shook her head. "Not always, but when two people fall in love, they make love. It's a lot to take in, I know."

"And love makes babies? Like Robbie and Nattie?"

"Yep, like Robbie and Nattie. All of us were babies at one time. We all have a mother, the woman, and a father, the man."

"Do I have a mother and father?" Anne's eyes glistening with tears.

"Yes, you do," Heidi said, taking Anne's hands in hers. "We just have to find them. And we will. Henry's doing everything he can. Do you have any more questions?"

Anne looked at the floor and shook her head.

"Let's go join the rest of the family," Heidi said standing up.

* * *

"Everything copacetic?" James asked upon their return.

Henry went to Anne. "You okay?" He put his arm around her shoulder.

"I am okay," Anne said, smiling. "Heidi told me about man and woman." She pointed to Henry's groin and said, "You have a penis!"

Henry blushed and nodded. "Yes."

James laughed until Anne pointed to him and said, "You have a penis!" James stopped laughing at Henry, his face taking on a nice red hue as well.

Henry put his hand on Anne's elbow, guiding her to a lounge chair. "Thanks, Heidi," he said. "Wasn't ready to get into that with her yet but..." he shrugged and sat in his own chair. "Glad I dodged that bullet."

"You just dodged the opening salvo, buddy boy. You've got mood swings, cramps, and the joy of shopping in the feminine hygiene aisle to look forward to." In her chair, Heidi stretched her arms above her head, crossing her legs. "Glad to be of assistance," she said with a gloating smile.

Henry glared, knowing she was enjoying every minute of his discomfort.

They sat in the lounge chairs on the patio while the coals turned to ash and the pool lights turned on, glowing light blue under the water. They talked until the sun went down and it was time for the kids to go to bed. Henry decided it was time for them to leave as well, and kisses and hugs made the rounds, the kids heading to their rooms and Henry and Anne to home.

In their own home, Anne picked up a picture of Henry, Heidi and their parents. "Mother and Father?" she asked.

"Yes," Henry replied, coming over and taking the picture from her, staring at it. "This is my mom and dad before they died."

"I do not know mother and father," she said, a faraway look in her eyes. "Tell me."

Henry smiled. "Sit down. I'll get the photo album and show you." He took a blue album off the bookshelf and sat beside her on the sofa. "That's my mom and dad." He pointed to a picture of the couple dressed in wedding attire. The man wore a light blue tuxedo with a white ruffled shirt and dark blue bowtie. He had brown hair, blue eyes, with a sharp nose and high cheekbones, like Henry.

The woman was smaller, only up to her husband's shoulders, her veil pulled back over a diamond tiara on top of her red hair, a low cut dress revealing ample breasts highlighted by a pearl necklace above them. She had green eyes and a small mouth with full lips. There were several more pictures of the couple in different poses; at a party holding up glasses of beer, at the beach, at a birthday party for Henry's mother.

Anne spent a long time looking at each one, photos of newlyweds joining their lives together, and growing as a couple—through two children, her illness, to her death of breast cancer when Henry was eighteen.

Henry took out another album. "This is me as a baby." He pointed to a picture of a little red-headed baby in a typical hospital first photo, his little fists raised before him like a prize fighter. They went through the years of Henry's life as if watching a movie. Pictures of him in grade school, the birth of a little sister, playing little league baseball, earning belts in Tae Kwon Do, through high school, his stint in the Navy, and his life with Christine.

"Who is she?" Anne asked. The book was opened to photos of Henry and Christine, a part of his life he had thought he had safely tucked away.

"She was my fiancée," Henry replied. "She died several years ago."

"Fiancée?" Anne repeated.

"I was going to marry her, like the pictures of my parents." He put the book of his life down and picked up the album of his parents, turning to the wedding photographs once again. "I loved her and wanted to spend the rest of my life with her."

"Love," Anne repeated. "Did you make love?"

Henry was taken aback by the question. "Yes... yes, we did."

"What is love?" Anne pushed that door open a little further.

"A question for another day." He sighed, putting the books and his grief away. After Christine's death, Henry had retreated into his world with his animals, swearing off love. Having the kind of "fun," he did with Felicia and other girls was fine. One or two nights was enough. He didn't want more heartbreak. Henry wasn't ready for love again, or even ready to talk about emotions he had, to date, kept bottled up inside, locked away.

That night, Henry lay awake, memories of his parents and Christine pressing heavily on his heart, with the pain of separation and death.

* * *

While Henry struggled with his past, Anne struggled to reach the recesses of her memories, to bring up any image of a family, or even the ghost of a feeling for a connection. She *had* to have a mother and father, right? Heidi told her she did. Why couldn't she remember them? Did they look like the people in Henry's books? How could she not know her own father and mother? Were there pictures of her as a child, like Henry? Had she played games like Nattie and Robbie?

She closed her eyes, seeking something to hold on to. There was an echo of a feeling of father, but nothing she could grab hold of. She was left with only a void, like the darkness of the room. When she finally fell asleep, the void filled not with family, but with the fiery death of her nightmares.

I rejoice as another pair of dragons join in union. Dragons choose mates from among one another and once chosen, the union binds for life. The dragons wrap their necks around each other as they join together before all the others. I long for a mate but The One tells me I am forbidden. I am happy with his rule.

I am called to see my father's brother. When I enter his hall, I hear voices. Dragons make no sound when we communicate. There are two beings reflected in the crystals who do not look like the dragons. They are smaller and stand on two legs. But when I turn the corner, it is only the sparkling golden dragon.

"You know we are different than the others," I hear in my mind.

"I know what my father has told me," I reply in like fashion. "I know I was created from his heart unlike the others who are hatched from eggs."

The Other stands so close to me I feel the heat from his body. "We are special, you and I. Do you not see that?"

"I do."

"Then you know why you are the only one worthy to be my true mate. None of these others can come close to you." He rubs his head against me.

"I am forbidden to mate." I shrink back. "My father has told me this."

He moves to block the entrance, his eyes glowing bright. "Perhaps he has told you that because he wants you for himself."

My insides quiver at his words. "I do not believe that."

Saphan's tongue flickers. "Has he never told you who we really are?"

"No."

"We are unique. There are none like us. Only I am worth of you. Your father does not want to see this."

"I do not believe that." I try to leave but he presses me against the crystal walls, his large body heavy against mine.

"You will be mine." A deep growl emanates from his chest. "If you

refuse me, I will ensure you will suffer."

    I am afraid of his words and escape to the outside hoping he does not follow....

10. SHOPPING

This time after Anne's nightly episode, Henry brought her to sleep with him in his bed instead of lying on the floor with her. "No point standing on formality anymore," he told Anne. "We end up together every night anyway. We might as well be comfortable. Besides, maybe if you're with me, you'll feel more secure and won't have a nightmare at all."

Anne nodded, laying her head on his chest. Henry held her tight until he heard the soft steady sound of her breathing. The sensation of her soft body pressed against him made it difficult for him to sleep. He so wanted to caress her and give in to his building passion for her, but he would not let his own desire overrule his concern for her. His heart was taking him to a place he had closed off long ago.

Looking down at Anne's golden hair, he couldn't help but think of Christine, of her passion about her work and her intense joy in life, so much like this woman lying next to him. Christine, too, had long blonde hair and laughed at everything, even Henry's bad jokes. He had an odd sense of humor. Christine had kept him sane while he dealt with his mother's illness and death.

He listened to Anne's steady breathing and relaxed, allowing himself to unpack the memory of that day. He was on leave. His right thigh had been torn up by shrapnel during his tour in Iraq. He drove down to Orlando from the Naval Air Station in Pensacola, Florida where he was to remain stateside until the end of his enlistment, undergoing weeks of therapy to rebuild the muscles in his leg.

Henry had arranged to have two of his MP buddies interrupt their date and pretend to arrest him. During the pat down, they would discover a heart-shaped diamond ring he intended to propose to her with while in handcuffs. Odd sense of humor indeed. He only had six more months of his enlistment to go. He dreamed of settling down with Christine, making love and making babies.

Somewhere just south of Tallahassee he got a call from James telling him Christine had been hit by a drunk driver on her way to Orlando to meet him.

She had died instantly.

Henry's heart was as crushed as Christine's car. His capacity for love died with her. Henry buried his pain deep inside him.

But there was something special about this lost girl that stirred something inside him, emotions he had never felt before and a connection to her he couldn't explain. At that moment, holding her secure in his arms and whispering comforting words in her ear, his heart opened up that hidden place and his feelings for her came flooding in. Henry was falling in love.

* * *

Sunday, June 21

Henry was opening and closing the kitchen cabinets in a desperate search for his morning fix of coffee. With both his search and his cup coming up empty, he decided it was time to go to the grocery store.

Henry hustled Anne into the car and headed to the nearest Starbucks. He ordered a ham and cheddar breakfast sandwich, a tall Pike Blend for himself, and whole grain oatmeal and orange juice for Anne. He could feel order slowly return to the universe with every steamy sip. Anne stabbed at her oatmeal with a plastic spoon. Wow, I think I might have actually found something she doesn't like to eat. By the time he finished his coffee, Henry was pulling into the SuperMart parking lot. This would be a good opportunity to buy more clothes for Anne, and of course, necessary items for her female issues.

Anne stepped out of the car into the parking lot and stood in awe at the hustle of shoppers coming and going into the very large building. Big yellow letters on the side spelled SUPERMART. Henry took her elbow and guided her towards the entrance, her head turning from side to side wanting to see all the action around her.

They reached the entrance. The automatic door magically opened. Anne jumped back, staring at the door. Henry burst out laughing. Anne watched the door open and close as shoppers came and went. He pointed out the sensor above the door, and tried his best to explain to Anne how it worked. Anne kept her eyes glued to the device and craned her neck to watch it when they passed underneath into the store.

Inside, they started at the produce section. Anne stood at the first bin, her gaze taking in colorful piles of fruit and vegetables. She picked up an apple , saying, "Apple," then took a bite before Henry could stop her. Then she went to the oranges and picked one up saying, "Orange!" She brought the orange to her mouth to take a bite. Henry held her hand down.

"No, Anne," he said. "We can't eat that until we get home. We have to pay first. It's not ours until we pay for it. Just like when we bought your swim suit and went to the beach. Food at the store is no different. We can't eat it just because it's food and sitting out here."

Anne released her grip on the orange and let it fall back into the bin. She put the apple back in the stack.

"No," Henry said, "you took a bite out of it so we have to pay for it now. Finish that one and we'll put the core into the bag and pay for it when we check out. Good thing they're on sale per apple and not per pound." Anne smiled and crunched away while Henry bagged more apples. Excitement brightened her face at the variety of items before her.

She continued to each bin and picked up an item, showed it to Henry, telling him the name or asking what it was. Henry bought one of several different types of fruits and vegetables to take home for her to try.

They finally left the produce section and headed to the meat department. She picked up a package of beef and asked him the name.

"This is the meat department and that, my dear, is beef. Hamburger to be exact. Over here are ribs, and this is steak like you ate last night. It comes from a cow. All of this is meat of one kind or another. They also have chicken, pork, and fish right next to us," Henry explained pointing.

She looked at the package and said, "MOO!" Several people turned around and stared at her, smiling. It didn't answer. She frowned. "Does not look like cow."

"Well," he said, "the cow isn't alive. They cut the cow up into smaller pieces so we can eat them."

She cocked her head to the side. "Why?"

"Because we can't eat the whole cow," he said, smiling.

She smirked, picking up a package of chicken. "What is this?"

"That is chicken."

"CLUCK!" she yelled. It didn't answer either. The other store patrons who watched her laughed politely. "It does not look like chicken." She shook her head. "Chicken nuggets?" Henry nodded. She picked up a package of pork but didn't "oink" at it, understanding that even though this was an animal she knew, it wouldn't make the right sounds anymore. Henry was grateful for that.

Anne walked over to take a closer look at the piles of fish lying on a bed of ice inside a glass case.

"Dragons eat," she told him, pointing to the fish.

"No, that is not Dragons meat, it's a fish that swims in water, like you saw on TV and at Jungle Gardens."

"Noooo...dragons...eat...fish," she insisted in long drawn out words to get her point across.

"Anne, I told you, there are no such things as dragons. They're make believe, not real. They don't eat fish or anything else, except the occasional knight in shining armor in the movies."

"No! Dragons eat fish!" Anne insisted, her eyes moist and lips pressed together.

Henry was taken back by both her tone and the look on her face. She truly believed, no, somehow in her heart knew that dragons ate fish.

"Okay, okay, calm down! My mistake." Henry held both hands in front of him. "I'm sorry, I didn't mean to upset you. If there are dragons in wherever it is you come from and they like Sushi, who am I to argue?"

"Not sushi! Fish!"

Great, her first period, our first argument, this is just great.

"Sooshe, eh, Sushi *is* fish, sweetheart. I believe you okay? No reason to get riled up. Would you like to eat fish too?" he asked, changing the subject from dragons.

"Have to buy first," Anne reminded him.

"That's right, have to buy first. Thank you. Would you like me to buy you some fish and we can take it home and eat it later?" Henry had the butcher wrap up a couple of pieces of halibut, having him chop off their heads after weighing them. He hated eating or preparing anything that was looking back at him.

Noticing Anne's mood hadn't improved, he said, "Let's go look at some clothes," hoping to distract her. "We'll come back to the food."

Anne followed Henry to the Women's Department. Letting Anne push the cart seemed to brighten her disposition.

Shopping in the women's section was no easier. Anne's shopping gene kicked into high gear, and she was drawn to the racks of clothes like the proverbial moth to a flame. She darted from rack to rack snatching up several different items, asking Henry what each one was called. She seemed puzzled at several of his answers. "Expensive!" Henry finally told her to stop, picked out a few things in her size, according to Heidi's instructions, and told her to try them on. He didn't stop to think that she wouldn't know where to go to change. He quickly stopped her before she stripped down in the middle of the store.

"Anne," he said in a low voice, stopping her from removing her shirt just in time. He didn't know if he should laugh or run out of the store. "You can try them on in a fitting room."

"Fitting room?" She looked around. "With Heidi!" She remembered buying the swimsuit.

Henry took her to the middle of the clothes section, where the ladies attending the fitting rooms smiled, having watched the whole episode. "Go in here, take off your shirt and try this one on. Then come out and let me see how it fits."

Anne did as she was told, and after an hour of looking at different items and trying each and every piece on, they settled on a couple of sun dresses, more bikinis, three pairs of shorts, two pairs of jeans and six shirts in varied styles. Henry put them all in the cart. "I think we need to get you some shoes too," he said.

"Shoes?"

He pointed to the aqua sandals she had on that Heidi had bought her. "Like those."

"Flop flops!" She called them the name Nattie had given them.

"Yes, flop flops." They went to the shoe section and picked out tennis shoes, white sandals and a pair of beige flats. Henry figured these would go with all the clothes they'd bought, not seeing the need to have a pair to match every outfit.

It took them four hours to get through the store because she wanted to know the names of every single item they picked up. Several times he had to pull her along and drag her away from that moment's fixation. At one point, Henry told her not to ask about every item or they would be there all day. She sulked a little, but soon cheered up, filling the cart with brightly colored items. Henry continued letting her push the cart, hoping it would keep her mind off the impromptu "I spy with my little eye" game they were playing.

With the clothes all picked out and the few remaining foods items selected, one task remained—taking care of Anne's monthly needs. Henry sighed and took the list from his pocket his sister had prepared the night before. Anne was strangely quiet. Henry tried to shop casually and not draw attention to himself. Clearly out of his element, Henry struggled to make sense of a never-ending barrage of feminine products. Super Absorbent this, Ultra-Thin that, Super Long with Wings…Wings? What in the hell are the wings for? Deodorant, Overnight, Maxi, Douching, Yeast Infection, Vaginal Discharge. He never knew it was so tough to be a woman.

I'll never complain about jock itch again, this is seriously messed up!

Henry was about to give up and head to Sporting Goods, buy Anne some fishing waders and just hose her down in the morning. Thankfully, a store clerk stocking a nearby shelf took pity on him. "Can I help you sir?" The young girl asked politely.

"Oh, heavens yes, please!" Henry looked at her name tag. "Yes, please Darla, if you don't mind?" Henry handed her his list. "This is what I need and lots of it because I want to stock up! I mean *she*, she wants to stock up."

Darla looked at Anne. Anne smiled back, looking Darla straight in the eyes and pointed to Henry, stating, "He has a penis."

Darla didn't know what to say. She slowly uttered, "Yeah, okay."

Henry's mind was back in Sporting Goods. His thoughts were of loading the largest pistol they had and ending his misery.

"I'm sorry, you must forgive my friend. She's not from around here and she's, well, she's special."

"Oh, I see, okay, no problem," Darla replied awkwardly. "Let's get you taken care of."

Henry hated using the word "special," because Darla would take it exactly the way Darla took it. Anne, of course, really was special, but in a way only Henry understood. Darla pointed out where everything on the list was, and soon had their cart packed with enough product for an entire sorority. Henry thanked Darla over and over and made Anne push the cart out of that aisle.

Finally, they had all they had come for and headed for the registers. Henry emptied the cart onto the belt at the checkout line. Anne pointed to each newly discovered prize and announced its name loud and clear to the checker. When Anne said "Super Maxi with Wings," the poor guy did his best not to laugh and had a hard time keeping his eyes on his work and not on Anne.

Henry started to push the cart out of the store, but Anne hip-checked him out of the way and ran with the cart to the car with the excitement of a child with a new toy. Henry regretted buying her those tennis shoes, and was barely able to stop her before she hit the car. Anne watched Henry load everything into the back impatiently.

Back home, Henry unloaded the groceries and Anne dashed inside with her new clothes. Anne was in the kitchen taking stock of her haul and showing everything off to the animals gathered around her. "This is a blouse, this is a tank top, and this is an expensive."

Henry just shook his head and smiled, marveling at this special girl.

All the food was put away and the "Super Maxi with Wings" products were piled high on the counter. *We'll find a place for all that later.* He was embarrassed just looking at them. Henry would have to make room for all of Anne's things.

They had a late lunch, which they made into dinner, and spent much of the evening cleaning out the closet in the master bedroom Anne's new clothes. Henry emptied out several drawers in a long oak dresser with a mirror topped by a curved wooden shelf. A second taller oak dresser was on the wall opposite his bed. He piled all the clothes from the closet and the dresser in a stack on a red easy chair in the corner of his room. Henry showed Anne how to fold her clothes and put them into the dresser. She examined each piece, feeling the fabric and holding it up to admire it before putting the piece away either in a drawer or on a hanger. Henry finally put away the stack of clothes on the red chair, finding he had enough room for all his clothes between the closet and the taller dresser. He just needed to put them all away neatly.

They had finished making room for Anne's things, including the feminine products, which Henry tucked away deep inside a bathroom cabinet. Henry went to the kitchen and scooped out a generous portion of ice cream into two bowls to make sundaes. He smothered both bowls with lots of chocolate syrup and whipped cream. He was about to clean up when Loki the cat leapt onto the counter and began the task for him. He left the Norse Cat of Mischief the hell alone and opted instead to join Anne on the sofa to watch a superhero movie, content to feel her lean against him.

Anne loved *Superman, The Movie* starring Christopher Reeve, and Henry never grew tired of watching it either. So far, there wasn't a movie they watched together that Anne didn't like, but they had yet to watch anything from the Horror genre. Henry was afraid it would be like pouring gasoline on a fire for the girl who had nightmares each and every night. Instead he preferred to quietly observe Anne watching the film, believing a man could really fly.

Her ability to so easily believe in the impossible was refreshing on one hand—and unsettling on the other. To accept this strange new world Henry was slowly introducing her to on blind faith alone reminded him of how gullible he had been himself, when he was younger.

As a child, there had been a time Henry believed in the impossible, before the harsh realities of life tore his world apart and his heart turned against God. Now, with the joy and happiness Anne brought to his life, little tugs of hope began to pull at his heart, threatening to make him confront those long suppressed aspirations of a child who once looked at the world as an exciting and never-ending adventure.

Her simple trust, like believing a man could fly, reminded Henry of that time, and part of him longed for that peace again. His heart was at the brink of opening him to the possibility of falling again into the arms of a faceless God, knowing He would be there to hold him. Henry was fighting a battle inside between the light he basked in as a child who once believed, and the darkness that consumed the man who now refused to. Maybe this moment with Anne, combined with looking at the old photographs with her, was freeing the child Henry had locked away deep inside.

But the man refused to surrender.

Henry took care of the needs of their paralyzed dog, scooped the four litter boxes and took the garbage out. On his way back to the house, the yard light was blocked for a moment, causing Henry to stop, turn, and scan the area. The search coming up empty, Henry shrugged it off and went back inside.

I watch the little dragons learn to fly for the very first time from my shelf high up on the mountain. Soon after the golden dragons mate, the female lays her eggs at the bottom of the ocean. The eggs are watched by all of the dragons until they hatch and the dragonets are brought up to the Crystal Mountains and kept under the warm bodies of the larger dragons.

The little ones are learning to live above the water. They chase each other, flapping their wings and briefly rise off the ground in an effort to fly. Their wings are not yet fully developed and they come crashing back to the ground. But that does not stop their games, each one of them insistent to be the first one to stay in the air. Tired out, the adult dragons take them back to their shelves to eat the silver fish they had collected for them and then rest. Some of the little ones have just hatched and are trying to walk, bravely venturing out from their warm refuge under the wings of the large dragons....

The sky bursts open with a loud thunderous crack! The terrified little dragons cry out, scrambling to hide under their parents. The enemy cuts through the sky, blotting out the white sun like a black cloud of evil spreading across the sky. They spit fire from their mouths consuming everything in their path. The little ones cry and cling to their mothers and fathers, then succumb to the intense flames engulfing them.

The black dragons form into a group like a flock of birds and fly straight down, plunging headfirst into the sea. One by one, they take turns scooping up all of the eggs from the shelter of the bottom of the ocean bringing them to the surface. There they slam them into the side of the crystal mountain and crush them beneath their feet. The remaining golden dragons cry out in their attempts to rescue the fragile eggs, only to be scorched by the breath of the monsters killing their babies. The blood of the little ones pools around their tiny bodies in the broken shells. The black dragons search for any hidden ones. I try to reach them but I cannot help them....

11. WATERCOLORS

Anne shuddered in his protective embrace. Henry moved closer to her, spooning around her while she fought off the dragons in her nightmare, which were now a part of their nightly routine. He was thankful that his presence, combined with the fact that Anne now knew what a nightmare was, allowed her to actually sleep most nights, although she was still restless. Would they ever stop? He would seek professional help in the light of the morning.

* * *

Monday, June 22

The morning came and the nightly fires burned out. Henry decided today was a good day to pull out his watercolor supplies to teach Anne how to paint in a new medium. To start with, he built a still life set of an apple, an orange and a banana. He also put on a CD collection of classical pieces, part of his efforts to introduce her to different types of music.

They started by drawing the objects, which Anne already knew how to do. Once the drawing was complete, he demonstrated how to prepare the pages.

"Now choose your colors. Remember what we learned about making different colors?"

She nodded.

Henry mixed an orange shade, then brushed it over the wet page to make a soft splash of color on the pencil sketch. He added a bit of burnt sienna and a dab of purple to pick up the color of the cloth on which the fruit was placed.

Anne watched for a little while, then sprayed her own sheet with water. She mixed up her colors and put the brush to her own painting.

Henry sat back and smiled at Anne. She had paint all over her, but was smiling with an open mouth that threatened to split her face. "More!" she said.

Henry watched Anne learn the basics of watercolors. She's found her medium. She seemed to enjoy it so much, they completed two more paintings. They spread the wet paper all over the room, making sure the door to the studio was shut to keep from getting paw prints on the paintings.

Then Anne started to draw something that wasn't set up. She drew what started out as a serpentine-like creature, but soon emerged as a dragon with wide wings in the sky above a mountain.

Henry sat up, his heart jumping. Was she re-creating what she saw in her dreams? She sprayed the page after drawing the creatures, then dipped her brush in yellow and a little brown to create a golden hue for the creature.

Henry stood behind her, watching a picture emerge of a dragon flying in the sky over mountains that reflected many colors. The dragon had small thin upper arms and longer rear legs, with four toes ending in sharp claws. Its face was elongated but smooth, unlike traditional visages of dragons, on a stretched thin neck. The eyes were white with no pupils, and the nostrils more like slits at the end of the lengthened snout, almost like a cat. The wings were twice the size of the dragon's body with small bony supports covered by a membrane yet to be painted.

With a thin brush, Anne made small lines of color in the membrane of the wings that were quickly absorbed into the water. She did this with several different colors, making the wings look like the rainbow of oil on water. She left the sun in the sky unpainted, the white of the paper as its color.

She stared at the finished drawing, transfixed by the image. Henry reached down, taking the brush from her and put it in the jar of water. He put his hands on her shoulder, running them down her arm and back up to her neck. "Is this your dream?"

"Yes," she said, coming out of her almost trance-like state. "This is good part before the fire."

Henry wasn't sure what to say. He didn't want to push her to talk about the fires, but was encouraged that she was able to put something from her dreams into a visible representation. "It's beautiful, Anne. Very pretty."

She reached up and touched his arm. "Like the dragon tattoo."

"Yes," he said, smiling, "like my tattoo."

Anne turned around in her seat and picked up her brush. "I do more!"

"Hold your horses, there ma'am," he said, chuckling. "We need to take a break and get some food inside you. We've been painting for five hours now!" They went to the kitchen where Henry, with the help of Anne, who decided she wanted to learn to prepare food, made turkey sandwiches on multigrain bread. Chips, bottled water, and some of the fruit Henry had used for the still life completed their lunch.

"Tell me about the dragon tattoo," she asked him while they were eating.

He took a drink from his water. "I saw it in a dream after my mom died and somehow it made dealing with her loss easier. For some reason, the image gave me peace. I decided to make it permanent after that."

"I like the dragon on your arm," she said.

Henry looked down at the tattoo on his bare arm as if seeing it for the first time. Then he shrugged and took a bite of his sandwich.

Henry's phone rang, flashing Heidi's name on the caller ID. He answered it, chewing in Heidi's ear a moment before he got out a muffled, "Hullo."

"Are you eating?" Heidi demanded.

"Yeth." Henry swallowed. "Yes. What's up?"

"You're a pig, you know that, right?"

Henry gave a loud belch in reply.

"Oh gross! Can you watch the kids tonight without teaching them any of your bad habits? James and I want to go to a movie."

"Are his folks still in North Carolina?"

"Yes, otherwise I'd ask them. So," Heidi paused. "You going to watch them or not?"

"Of course! But no promises on my behavior." Henry looked at the clock. "What time?"

"Can I bring them around six? I'll bring some movies Nattie wants to watch and pick up burgers for everyone."

"Make it pizza and you've got a babysitter," Henry countered, pressing his advantage.

"What is it with you and pizza?"

"The only thing I like better than pizza is pizza that somebody else is paying for. It's especially tasty when that somebody is you."

"Fine, I'll get your stupid pizza."

"Don't forget the extra cheese," Henry reminded.

"Don't you forget to cut it up into small pieces so Nattie can eat it. The last time you fed her pizza, she ended up wearing more of it than she ate."

"Actually, I think the dogs got most of it," Henry corrected.

"*Whatever*," Heidi replied, exasperated. "The point is, she has to eat. That's why I was going to get burgers and fries. At least she has a fighting chance."

"I'll make sure she eats. Will this be overnight?"

"If you don't mind."

"Oh, what do you two love birds have in mind?" Henry teased. "Late night skinny dipping in the pool? Kinky sex in front of a raging fire in the fireplace. Naughty role playing in the bedroom?"

"You need serious help, big brother, you know that, don't you? And, since you asked, the answer to your question is all of the above."

"*What!*"

"None of your damn business is what! Besides, how do you think Robbie and Nattie got here in the first place? I didn't buy them off e-bay. Is six o'clock okay or not?"

"Yeah, that's fine. We'll see you in a little while, and don't forget the pizza." He ended the call and looked at Anne. "Heidi is bringing the kids over for us to watch. They're going to stay overnight. Won't that be fun?"

Anne smiled and nodded. She loved being with the kids. Deciding there wasn't time for more painting, they spent the next hours cleaning the guest room, and setting up the playpen that would serve as Nattie's crib.

Henry wasn't worried about dividing his attention between Anne and the kids because of Charlie, his Golden Rottie. Charlie and Robbie had bonded the moment they met. Charlie always slept curled up on the floor by Robbie during overnight stays and naps, protecting him. Henry pitied anyone who attempted to get near either of the kids without his okay. Must be the Rottweiler in him, taking over the Golden Retriever, like Hyde and Jekyll.

At six o'clock, Heidi and James arrived. James had Nattie in his arms with the diaper bag on his shoulder. Heidi had a small suitcase and two pizzas from Hungry Hals. Robbie trailed behind her. Heidi brought overnight diapers just to be prepared for any eventuality during the night— or her brother was asleep at the switch, the latter being the more likely scenario. "We're here!" she announced.

Henry and Anne came out of the guestroom and greeted them with hugs and kisses. "What are you going to see?" Henry inquired.

"That new Jason Bourne movie," James said, putting Nattie down. "You know a friend of mine in Las Vegas did some extra work in that."

"Lucky S.O.B., sounds like fun." Henry smirked.

"Yeah, chase scenes, car crashes, bullets and violence, I can't wait," Heidi lamented.

"Hey, I didn't complain when you dragged me to see that Vampire movie, you remember the one where the Vamps come out in the daylight."

"Of course you didn't complain! You slept through the entire movie."

"Hey, feel free to sleep through this, you're gonna need your strength afterwar-"

"*Okay*! We'll leave it at that, shall we," Henry interjected. "You don't want to miss the previews! What time will you pick the kids up tomorrow?"

"Ten o'clock?" Heidi suggested.

"Okay." Henry took the pies from Heidi, inhaling their aroma, then turned just in time to see Robbie run to the studio door that was shut. "Wait,

Robbie!" Henry shoved the pizzas into a startled Anne's hands, then dashed over to distract Robbie from opening the door and letting the animals in to tromp all over the paintings.

Henry came back to the conversation with Robbie tucked under his arm. Heidi handed the DVD's to Anne. "Here are a couple movies for Nattie. She may not sit through the whole movie but it'll distract her for a little while."

"Okay," Henry said. "Have fun guys. We'll be fine."

Heidi and James kissed the kids and left. "Nattie's movies," Anne said, handing them to Henry. "What is this one?" She pointed to the picture of a princess sleeping on a bed.

"Sleeping Beauty," Henry replied, putting the films near the television. "Do you want to see that one?"

"Yes," she smiled.

"Everyone come eat while it's still hot," Henry called, getting plates and drinks from the kitchen. The kids ran to the dining room, followed by Anne, who placed the boxes on the table. Henry put Nattie in a highchair he kept on hand for her. He made good on his promise to cut up her food. After dinner, they retired to the living room to watch the movie.

Henry put the movie in the DVD player, at the same time unwittingly passing gas. Just as he had belched at his sister, he made no attempt at discretion, and just let 'er rip, making an all too familiar sound. Robbie looked up from his turtle figures. "What was that?" he demanded.

"That? That's a duck that's been hiding in here. We can't find him."

Robbie stood with his little hands on his hips, a scowl on his face and retorted, "Ducks don't fart!"

Henry couldn't help but laugh as he fessed up. "You got me, Robbie. That wasn't a duck."

Anne smiled and said, "Quack! Ducks say quack!"

"Yeah and they don't stink either. Eeeeewww! Uncle Henry, gross!"

No promises, he reminded himself, *just in case this got back to Heidi.*

Nattie joined, racing around the sofa shouting, "Quack! Quack! Quack!"

Henry chased her around the living room flapping his arms like wings. "I'm gonna get the duck! I found the farting duck." Nattie giggled and squealed every time her Uncle got close to catching her. Robbie decided he wanted to be a duck too, and eventually, all four of them ended up running around the room quacking like ducks.

When they tired of playing ducks, Henry started the movie. From the moment it started, Anne was enthralled. She swayed to the music, watching the Prince and Princess dance together in the forest. She laughed at the fairies, and almost cried when the Princess fell under the sleeping spell. Henry watched her instead of the movie, his eyes twinkling with the overwhelming feelings for her that were consuming his heart.

A great black dragon reared up to fight the Prince. Anne had difficulty breathing and hid in Henry's arms. He held her against him, feeling her heart beating in her chest. Henry recognized what was happening and stopped the film, reassuring her it was only a picture and not real. "It's like a drawing," he explained. "Like your paintings. It can't hurt you. It'll be defeated in the end," he promised.

She took a deep breath and watched the rest of the movie, Henry's arm securely around her, until the Prince slayed the dragon. The Prince found his way to the Princess to give her love's first kiss. The happy couple danced at the end of the movie, her dress changing colors.

"What are they doing?" Anne asked.

"Dancing," he explained.

"Show me."

Nattie had fallen asleep half way through the movie on the sofa and Robbie got bored and went to play with his turtle fighters. Henry stood up, helped her to her feet, and pushed the trunk out of the way. He put his arm around her back and took her hand.

"Put your hand on my shoulder," he instructed, "and follow what I do." He put his left foot forward. "You step back." Anne stepped back with her right foot. Then he stepped forward and to the right with his right foot. She followed, stepping back with her left. He slid his left foot to his right. Anne followed to the left. Finally, he slid his left foot back, followed by the right. She followed in corresponding steps.

"That's it, basically, but you do it to a beat. Like this, one, two, three," he counted, moving his feet. She moved with him, her steps opposite his, just as they had walked through it. The movie was rolling through the credits. They followed the beat of the music until the movie ended.

"That's dancing."

"I like dancing," she said, sinking back to the sofa.

"Why did the Prince give up his...chair?" she asked.

Henry took the movie out of the DVD player. "Throne," he corrected.

"Throne. Why did the Prince give up his throne for the Princess?"

"Princess, that's right." He sat beside her on the sofa. "He did it because he loved her and wanted her more than he wanted the throne. He didn't know she was a princess until the end of the movie. But he ended up with both the Princess and the throne. All fairy tales have a happy ending."

"Did he not want...throne?"

"Yes," Henry replied. "He did. But he was willing to sacrifice it all to be with the woman he loved."

"What is sacrifice?"

"Sacrifice," he explained, "is giving up something you want for someone else. That is true love."

"What is love?"

Henry shook his head. She hadn't forgotten about her question. "That is the big secret, my dear. What is love? Some people think it's the way you feel about someone else. Some people think it's what you do for someone else, or even what you really want. Some people believe love is sacrifice. There are many aspects to love. It depends on a lot of things." He shrugged. "It's difficult to give one answer to that."

"How do you know love?"

"Most people spend their whole lives looking for that answer. I don't know. I guess you know love when you find it. That really doesn't answer the question, but I think it's something everone has to answer for himself."

"Do you know love?" she asked.

Henry was quiet for a moment. "I did. Once." Being with Anne was chipping away at the barrier he'd put up in his heart. "With Christine." He stood up and put the disc away in Nattie's bag. "Let's put Nattie to bed and see what Robbie's up to." He didn't want to open the door any more than it had already opened. It was enough to deal with Anne's nightmares.

That night was no exception, even with the children in the house. Anne did not scream, but started thrashing and fighting with the sheets as if with the dragon in the movie, whimpering and breathing heavily, until Henry woke her up. He held onto her while she cried, thanking the stars above that the kids didn't wake up.

Henry lay awake for a long time, staring up at the black ceiling as he held Anne. He didn't like what was happening to him since he'd found her. He'd done fine for several years now, holding back his grief. But now, while he held Anne fighting the demons in her dreams, he fought his own awake.

He could still smell the chemicals of the hospital at his mother's bedside, see the drab green paint on the walls, and the overworked and understaffed doctors and nurses. She wasn't a lost cause, she was his mother, damn it! Why couldn't they do something to help her?

Helpless, he sat by her bedside, holding her hand, hoping she knew he was still there. Then came the bitter moment his world crushed in around him. His mother slipped away. Blinded by tears and crushed with sorrow, he felt a tinge of relief, knowing she was finally free of the pain, free of the waiting, free of the burden she felt she was. Real love is a gift to be cherished every moment of every day, and never a burden, and to Henry, neither was she.

Running off to join the Navy didn't ease his pain. He missed his mother every day and replayed her final moments. Was she watching him from

Heaven he wondered—back when he used to believe in such nonsense? Was she proud of him, or worried about him when he was in peril?

The demons tormented him more with Christine's death. Christine was an answer to prayer; something—*someone*—positive, loving, life changing. She had been an anchor from the time they were little kids. When he finally admitted how much he loved her, he allowed himself to care again, to feel, dream, and love again.

He would never know what her answer would have been to his proposal. Unlike his mother, he didn't even get the chance to say goodbye. He not only lost the love of his life, his soulmate, best friend and lover, he lost his future —their future—ripped away in a heartbeat by some stupid drunk driver. The future of two people and who knows how many children they might have had together. Just gone.

As the tears formed in his eyes, he clenched his lips together, determined he would not cry or let the pain slip out. If he did, he wouldn't be able to put it back; it would overwhelm him. Right now, he needed to be there for Anne. He couldn't allow his own nightmares to haunt them in the night.

Eventually, the demons of his mind grew weary of haunting him and he drifted off into a restless sleep.

While Henry and Anne fought the demons in their dreams, something much worse lurked in the shadows of the dark room, watching them sleep.

* * *

I lie on my bed on the highest level of the crystal structure, made from bricks hewn of the crystals in the mountain underneath the city. Kenta and I listen to the others of our kind who come before us with their concerns. We do not speak with audible sounds, but with thoughts and images conveyed to each other.

We hear the concerns regarding our work of cultivating the crystal, building the Crystal Mountains and shelter spaces, from our brethren. He rubs his head against mine ensuring us both that we act as one in our decisions. His massive wings cover me as we hold court under the watchful eye of my father. I am content to be with him with the heat of the white sun above us. He is close to my heart....

I try to follow Kenta fleeing into the water, his wings flaming and burning away the white membrane, but I cannot follow him. The black dragons hold me and I cannot move. Kenta rushes down, but the water does not extinguish the fire that blankets him. It shines like a flower under the water as he goes deeper, but the fire does not go out. I reach out as if I can save him by my desire but I cannot...

12. VENICE AVENUE

Tuesday, June 23

In the morning, James and Heidi picked up the kids shortly after breakfast. Uncle Henry had made their favorite pancakes and sausage. He was getting good at making them look like Mickey and Minnie Mouse. Strawberry jelly made a nice bow. He was grateful they had slept through the night oblivious to Anne's nightmares.

With the children gone, and his sister and brother-in-law content from the night before, Henry invited Anne to his studio to continue their work. He set her up with her watercolors and focused on his illustrations.

Anne worked on a series of paintings of the beautiful golden dragons in their life on the Crystal Mountains: swimming in green waters, lying on cliffs, soaring through the air. This was what she saw in her dreams, she said. He marveled at her imagination and the mastery of her work.

They worked until lunch, when Henry thought it would be nice break to take Anne to Venice Avenue to visit the unique stores.

The little shops, painted in pastels with weathered arches and glass windows, invited tourists and locals alike. Henry and Anne spent a lot of time in the Treasures of the Sea shop where Anne picked up several small shells to add to those she and Robbie had found at Caspersen, as well as a few larger ones with intricate designs and colors.

Anne wanted to know what each shell was called as she inspected every one of the dozens of bins in the shop. Henry especially enjoyed watching her grill the clerk about the names of each and every shell. The poor girl tried to keep up with Anne, who was so excited about her prizes, that even with her limited vocabulary, she chattered like a roomful of monkeys. Henry was surprised she was able to breathe through all of her questions. It was also nice that someone else was answering her never-ending queries for a change instead of him, although he did feel the girl's pain and sympathized.

They finally left Treasures of the Sea, stopping for lunch at a little place specializing in fifty varieties of over-sized stuffed baked potatoes. Henry asked Anne about her pictures while eating a potato smothered in broccoli and melted cheddar cheese. Anne was enjoying a ham and Swiss, almost as big as her head, and doing a good job devouring it.

"So you see these dragons in your dreams? What is it about them that causes your nightmares? The dragons look beautiful."

"It is not golden dragons, it is black ones, like the princess movie. I do not paint them."

"Why do the black dragons upset you so much?"

"They come...kill...with fire." She stopped eating, the spoon resting in her hand.

Henry took her other hand to comfort her. "It's okay, Anne. Take your time. Tell me what you see."

"I see dragons burn in fire.... I hear little ones crying! I feel them...they are dying!" Her eyes began to fill with tears and her hands were shaking.

"Who's dying?"

"The others, the golden dragons! All dying! I feel the fire!"

"Anne," Henry asked. "Do you think someone you loved died in a fire but maybe you escaped?"

She hesitated, seeking the strength and words to answer. "I do not know. I feel fire in my dream, but not here." She pointed to her head, frowning.

Why were her dreams about dragons and what had happened to her that caused them? He didn't want to push her and upset her more, so he stood up and said, "Let's check out some more shops. Maybe we can find some different shells, okay?"

Anne flashed a weak smile and stood up. Neither of them was able to finish lunch. They left Double Stuffed Spud Hut to continue their hunt for oddities. Henry hoped to restore their good mood along the way.

The rest of the afternoon passed pleasantly. Anne's mood improved with every shop they visited. Henry never grew tired of her amazement at everything and everyone around her. She wasn't as chatty and hardly asked any questions at all; she just watched, soaking everything in. For a while they sat on the edge of a fountain and people-watched: skateboarders, surfers, countless girls in bikinis, people on bikes, dogs, and children.

When Henry couldn't hold one more bag, and Anne couldn't take one more step, it was time to go home. He was tired and hungry from walking and shopping all afternoon. Anne had to be as well. He decided to treat her to dinner at his favorite steak house.

* * *

Henry drove up to the restaurant, telling Anne they would eat there, then helped her out of the car. Anne was confused as to why Henry let another man drive off with his car. Once inside, she was overwhelmed with the delicious aromas. Between the sight of flames flaring under turning meat, and the sizzle of fresh meat hitting the grill, her mouth was salivating.

She was about to sit at an empty table. Henry stopped her and told her they would have to wait until a lady he called the Hostess seated them. Henry said, "Party of two, please," to a nicely dressed woman standing behind a tall little table. She greeted them and led them to a table near the pit. Men dressed all in white wearing tall hats piled on slabs of meat in varying sizes. Once seated, Anne was dazzled by the elegant silverware, dishes, and glasses laid out on a beautiful white cloth.

Throughout the meal, Anne was astonished at the number of people who served them. She thanked everyone from the hostess, to the waiters, to those who took away their dishes, to the boy who kept their water glasses full, to the man who stopped by to say hello and ask if everything was satisfactory with their meal, to the tall gentleman with a towel draped over his arm who kept asking Henry if he wanted more wine. She hugged the woman in the ladies room who handed her a towel, she was so excited. It was such a treat, except when Henry limited her to only one glass of wine. He said he didn't know her tolerance and didn't want to find out tonight. As it turned out, she loved the wine, and it somehow made her feel even happier.

After dinner, Henry gave a piece of paper to the man who took his car, and he ran off and brought it back. He then dashed around the car and held the door open for Anne. Everyone was so nice!

* * *

Anne acted like she'd never been to a restaurant before, or at least none so fancy. More questions rose in Henry's mind about who the strange girl was; what kind of life she had lived to have never been in a nice restaurant. He put the questions away for now, content to enjoy her company.

On the ride home, Henry didn't bring up the dreams again. Maybe he would tomorrow, but they'd made some progress tonight, so he'd let it go. It had been a pleasant evening, and poor Anne would probably suffer another nightmare before the night was over. There was no point in sending her to bed already worked up.

Back home, Anne went through the bags from the Venice Avenue shops, mentally cataloging her new treasures. Henry distributed the bag of steak bones he got from the restaurant to some very happy dogs. Not wanting the cats to feel left out, he gave them all a generous helping of treats. "Sorry guys, restaurants only have doggie bags, not kitten bags," he said in jest.

He and Anne retired to the sofa to watch TV, digest and relax a bit until bedtime. They enjoyed being with each other and letting the worries of the night wait a while.

Hours later, Anne's nightmares did indeed return, and Henry held her tight until she stopped shaking. It was their nightly routine now, not unlike brushing their teeth or letting the dogs out. It was as if her nightly torments were a part of her. Henry was able to tell when the nightmares started by her movements, holding her tight before she started screaming, although she didn't scream out as often. There was nothing he could do to stop the nightmares from coming.

Late that night, after Anne finally fell back to sleep, Henry thought he must be dreaming. A shadow darkened the bedroom window, temporarily blocking the moonlight from shining into the room. He blinked and it vanished. He could have sworn something, or someone, was there and then gone. It was hours later before he drifted off into a very uneasy sleep.

Saphan's numerous mates bore many offspring before they succumbed to the evil he now embraces.

Some of his sons follow him in blind loyalty to their father, in part, but mainly because they share his lust for power and blood. The rest of his children are cared for by their mothers, and most of them play with the other young dragons in the cool green waters. I am the only child of Aesmay, taken straight from his heart. I am unique among our kind....

Saphan's shadow casts an inky silhouette of death as he descends from the sky, leading his army of black dragons to slaughter all in their path. He is changed, no longer beautiful and graceful as he once was. Now his outward appearance mimics the cold black heart that beats beneath his massive chest. He is colossal in height and width; much larger than any dragon ever known. His red eyes burn with the fire of hatred against all whom he once loved.

The mountain crumbles at his roar, sending shards of crystal rocks crashing down to crush the golden dragons' dwellings below, killing all inside. His sons, like all who follow him, are as black as night, but none equal in size or cruelty. They spew fire from their mouths through razor teeth. The large black dragon takes pleasure in burning his former mates, and laughs, ripping open the bellies of his inferior offspring, spilling their entrails on the ground before setting them ablaze. His mates cry out to him to stop the fire and spare the young, but his laughter drowns out their screams. With a sickening smile, he turns and takes to the skies, leaving them to suffer a slow and agonizing death. Not one shred of compassion or pity remains in this soulless beast as he hunts and destroy the golden dragons....

13. THE BLACK DRAGON

Wednesday, June 24

Everything was better in the morning's bright light, with a breakfast of bagels, cream cheese, and coffee. Afterward, Henry and Anne went straight to the studio and got to work. Henry headed to his latest illustration of how to properly insert a midline catheter. Anne took her place at the new table and chair Henry had set up for her. She started to take out her watercolors. She enjoyed that medium more than any other. There was something about the flow of colors in the water that had a soothing effect on her. She told him she also felt more connected to each piece, as if her creativity were flowing through her directly onto the paper. That bond was not as strong with a pencil.

Today however, she turned abruptly from the watercolors, to the jar of pencils, and started to sketch out a figure. Henry looked up from his work. Anne was breathing heavily from the ferocity with which she was drawing. The form of this object was beginning to emerge: dragon-like in appearance, but much larger than any of the golden dragons she had previously painted or sketched. This creature had long feet with sharp claws, and large pointed ears with hard-ridged edges.

She switched to a 9B pencil to scratch in the tone of the object—black, as black as she could make it. For the eyes she chose a blood-red pencil, making them look so evil that after she completed them, she visibly shuddered. For its large snarling mouth she selected a lighter pencil and shaded in long teeth with the gray hue. Its wings were massive and covered with a gray membrane from the same pencil she used on the teeth. She used varying shades of red, orange, and yellow to create the flames exploding from its maw.

Anne's hand was a blur, scratching back and forth, up and down on the page, tearing through the paper onto the sheet beneath. Tears formed in her eyes, and her breathing came in deep rasps, but she pushed through to complete the drawing, pressing hard with the pencils, punishing the paper.

Henry had never seen her like this before, but though he deeply concerned, he let her be while she worked through this.

She sat back panting and shaking, wiping away tears with the back of her smudged hands. Henry let her take her time to gain her composure. She thrust the finished drawing into his hands. "Fire," she said through clenched teeth. "What I see."

Henry raised his eyebrows, taking in the drawing. He took a deep breath. "Fire," he repeated. "Wow! That is one mean looking Son of a...ahem, no wonder you're having nightmares! This bad boy would keep Stephen King up at night...damn!" He put the drawing back on the table. "You still have no idea what these images mean or where they came from?"

Anne shook her head. "I do not know. I see them always when I have the bad dream."

Henry sat back in his chair and sighed. He picked up the drawing again and studied it, his thumb supporting his chin and his index finger stretched across his lips, pondering the piece. "Well, if we can ever figure that out, we may finally know what happened to you." He could tell his frustration was stressing her out even more, and certainly wasn't helping her disposition. He placed the drawing face down on the table and put his hand on her shoulder. "Let's work on something different. How is your painting of the little dragons coming?"

Anne put the sketchbook away and turned to her board, where an unfinished picture of several tiny golden dragons was tacked down. The little dragons swam on the surface of the green water, appearing to chase each other in circles. Silver fish jumped over their backs. Anne pulled the watercolors back out, sprayed the paper to refresh the water on the page and squeezed her colors onto the tray.

Henry critiqued her painting and made a few minor suggestions, but overall, had very high praise for her work. He then turned his attention back to his catheter illustration, which he needed to complete today to make his deadline. He was filled with renewed hope, knowing Anne had a breakthrough today, bridging the gap between her unconscious and conscious mind. Something opened up that might help him find the answers to who Anne was and had what happened to her, leaving her so traumatized that she had no memories at all of her life before he found her.

They worked through into late afternoon, stopping only once for a quick lunch. Anne finished the illustration of the little dragons and Henry completed and forwarded his illustration, confident Elliott would be pleased with his work. With the work done, Henry suggested they go out for an early dinner and maybe see a movie. Had Anne had ever been to a movie theater?

They enjoyed a light dinner at a small bar and grill close to the Metroplex, leaving room for popcorn and candy. Soon after, they arrived at the theater to see the latest animated feature about a princess and her sister in a frozen land with talking snowmen. Henry hoped the escape from reality would help Anne recover from reliving her black dragon nightmare. In the lobby, Anne stared and pointed at all the movie posters and displays with wide-eyed wonder. Of all the moments they had shared together, Henry cherished these the most. She was unguarded and relaxed and trusted him completely.

After securing the biggest tub of popcorn Anne had ever seen along with, of course, some chocolate, they settled into their seats and let the cares of the day slip away with every frame that flashed by. True to form, Anne immersed herself in the story that unfolded, crying and laughing with the characters as if the scenes before her were her own life.

Seeing how much Anne was enjoying the movie, Henry resolved to take her to Orlando sometime to meet some real live princesses. It dawned on him that by making that commitment, he was taking a bold step toward leaving part of his past behind. Christine's memory haunted him to this day. To take Anne to the place he had planned to propose to his former fiancée would take courage on his part—an act of love. Henry had never met anyone like Anne, and to be honest, he didn't want to meet anyone different. His feelings for her were growing stronger with every beat of his heart.

* * *

Damn it! Can't we ever get a break? Anne shrieked and thrashed from what must have been her worst nightmare yet. Henry held her in his arms and repeatedly kissed her tear-streaked face. In between, words leapt from his heart like a caged animal finally set free. "Anne, sweetheart, everything will be all right." Each kiss more passionate than the last. "I'm here Anne, I will always be here." His tears mingled with hers.

Anne began kissing him back, pressing close against him. Their mouths met and Henry's mind exploded.

"Henry," Anne whispered. "I want to make love."

Henry was taken aback. Was she ready for this? Was he ready for this?

"Honey," he said. "Are you sure?"

"Yes." She snuggled against him. "I want to know love. Please. Show me love."

He paused a moment to contemplate just how quickly their relationship was moving, but as sure as day follows night, he was powerless to stop it. Anne had just opened the floodgates.

He surrendered to the moment and allowed his body to follow his heart. Henry was lost in everything that was Anne. They caressed and explored each other. Part of him felt unworthy of such a beautiful woman, winning her trust and her heart, but somehow it was meant to be, they were meant to be. Maybe he could extinguish the fires in her dreams and ignite the fires in her heart. Henry was pleased that Anne was totally immersed in this new sensation, her body yielding to the inevitable. The two of them collapsed into each other's arms.

"Anne," he breathed, his hand warm on her leg. "Are you sure about this?"

"Yes," she whispered. "Do not stop. I want this. Please. I...need... love."

His lips followed where his hands had gone. Henry let his experience guide her. They became one, joined to one another and moving in perfect harmony. They crossed the threshold together, their passions peaked.

Afterwards, they lay silently together still locked in their embrace for a long time, enjoying the momentary reprieve from the demons that haunted them. A weight had been lifted off his shoulders, freeing him from a lingering doubt he didn't even know was there. His thoughts turned to Christine, and instead of guilt, he felt peace. He hadn't replaced his love for her with another; he simply allowed himself to move on. Their love would always be there as a memory tucked away in a special place in his heart.

He gently kissed Anne on the top of her head laying on his chest, thinking of the enormity of the step their relationship just took. Softly, he whispered, "I love you."

* * *

Somewhere around three o'clock, Henry was woken by the dogs barking, sounding the alarm. He threw off the covers, pulled his shorts on and grabbed the automatic and flashlight he kept in his nightstand drawer. He pulled the slide back on the gun with a loud snap, chambering a round, and told Anne to stay put. He rushed to the kitchen where all of the dogs were gathered, scratching at the back door. Henry joined them, patting Charlie and Sam on the head, then threw open the door. To his surprise, neither dog ran out. After sniffing the evening air, they began to whine and cower. *What the hell has gotten into them?* Taking one step outside, he closed the door. A quick examination revealed no attempt to break in.

Assuming any intruder would have been scared off by the dogs, Henry decided to walk slowly around the entire house, gun in his right hand, flashlight in his left. All the windows were intact and there were no footprints in the soft earth beneath them. He moved his search to the back fence and scanned the pond behind the yard. Everything was eerily quiet and still, as if nature itself was holding its breath waiting for something to happen. Finding nothing, he headed back to the house.

As he opened the back door, he thought he saw a shadow move out of the corner of his eye, and spun around pointing his gun…but there was no one there. Just as he shut the door behind him, he could swear he heard what sounded like the flapping of giant wings taking flight.

I sit at the feet of my father as Saphan comes before him angry. He shouts that he is the stronger of the two and will no longer obey his brother anymore. His sons shout out in agreement. No one has ever challenged Aesmay before! We live in peace, and honor each other. We do not know of the hatred he speaks of.

"Aesmay," Saphan roars. "I will no longer bow to your will. I should be ruling this world."

"Saphan," Aesmay says. "You not only rebel against me but against our Father as well."

"I have surpassed even Him." Saphan bares his teeth and leaps at Aesmay. Aesmay lashes back and they fly into the air, biting and raking at each other with their long sharp claws. The other dragons watch the control of our world being decided, some in horror, some in glee. The battle rages above, the blood of both dropping on me like rain from the wounds each inflicts on the other.

Aesmay finally throws his rebellious brother to the earth and crashes down on him, taking his neck in his teeth, ready to crush it. But Aesmay loves his brother and cannot kill him.

"Leave," he commands. "Take your rebellious sons with you. For if you remain, you will surely die."

Saphan is no longer shiny but badly wounded. He slinks away in defeat to the black mountains with his sons behind him. I fly to my father to lick his wounds, his golden blood flowing from many places....

14. LET'S WRITE A BOOK

Thursday, June 25

Henry was enjoying his new life with Anne, or his renewed life with Anne. The two of them spent their days together painting, swimming, or exploring and learning new things. Anne's insatiable thirst for knowledge, combined with her childlike enthusiasm for learning, was as infectious as it was inspirational. As intelligent as Henry was, he didn't know everything. Together they made each day count, learning or experiencing something new.

Their nights together were an entirely different matter. The time they spent in each other's arms was indescribable. The love they expressed through their passion was inexhaustible and boundless. Everything would have been perfect if not for those damn dragon dreams that terrorized his beloved each and every night. He was determined to find the meaning of these winged manifestations, and was convinced the key to that mystery was to uncover their root cause. There had to be something in Anne's past that triggered these demons haunting her dreams. He visited several online sites on psychology and dream interpretation, trying to find answers. His efforts bore little fruit.

There was one positive ray of sunshine that came out of her dreams: Anne's paintings of the golden dragons. She had created quite the body of work, and numerous paintings were piling up, each more detailed and beautiful than the last. Each painting had something different to say. Anne's subconscious mind was reaching out through her art. If he could help Anne focus on the positive, and try to get her to talk about what she had brought to life through her art, it might give them some insight to what was really troubling her.

"Anne," Henry called to get her attention, "why don't we write our own story book?"

"Write?" Anne replied, intrigued.

"Yeah, like those story books of Robbie's we read when you were first learning about, well, everything I guess; the ones with all the drawings and illustrations, remember? We could use your paintings and tell our own story. Wouldn't that be fun?"

Anne squealed and threw her arms around Henry's neck and squeezed. In between repeated kisses to his face, Henry said, "I'll take that as a yes." Prying himself loose, he retrieved his laptop and had Anne spread many of her paintings out on the floor in front of the wall that was already covered with them. Anne leaned against his side with her head on his shoulder, watching the words magically appear along the screen as Henry typed.

"Okay," Henry began. "Let's see if we can spice up the standard introduction just a tad.

"Once upon a time in a Realm far away, lived a peaceful race of golden dragons who resided on a Crystal Mountain."

Their eyes perused the vast selection of paintings on display before them. Anne pointed to one painting showing the dragons lying on various heights of shelves on the crystal structure on top of the mountain. She leapt to her feet, and scurried over to snatch it down off the wall, holding it up. Henry nodded his approval and motioned for her to bring it over. He typed the description on his laptop to later add to that painting.

Anne picked up another one where the dragons flew in the white sky.

"They flew high and soared over mountains of crystal, across a sky where a white sun shone bright."

Anne picked up one of the smaller dragons playing in the water.

"They swam in the green ocean where they dove to catch silver fish."

Dragons eat fish not *soo-she* flashed across Henry's memory. He smiled.

Next, she chose the painting with the two dragons, one with iridescent wings on the top shelf of the crystal structure. Henry got his wish. Anne was guiding the story, and he was eagerly following her bread crumbs hoping they would lead them to some answers.

"They were ruled by a good king...."

"Wait, what do we name him?"

"The king?"

"Well, yes but now that I think about it, are we just calling the dragons 'dragons'?"

"Thraekenya. That is what they are called. They are the Thraekenya."

"That's pretty," Henry said. "Now what will we call our king?"

"Aesmay."

"Where did you get that name from?"

Anne shrugged. "I do not know. I just know it."

"Okay. 'The Thraekenya were ruled by the good King Aesmay.' That's a good start anyway. Are we going to include the black dragons at some point?"

"Yes," Anne said hesitantly. "They are the story."

"Okay, what do we want to call the black dragons?"

"They are Tannen. One time, they were like Thraekenya but they did not want to stay under Aesmay, the good King."

"You have quite an imagination, Anne," Henry commented. "How do you come up with those names?"

"I feel they are the right names," she answered. "I hear them in my head but do not know them."

Good! I think we're actually making progress.

"So the black dragons are the Tannen." Henry resumed typing. "Before we get to the attack, we have to build up the story. How about let's make up a leader of the Tannen. That might help with the 'history' of our dragon world."

"Saphan. He is Saphan, brother to Aesmay."

"So, Saphan and Aesmay were brothers?"

"Yes."

"Okay, so we can use a Cain and Abel approach."

"Cain and Abel?"

"Yes. Cain and Abel were brothers, but Cain killed his brother Abel when God found Abel's sacrifice more pleasing. It's in a book called *The Holy Bible,*" Henry voiced what had to be the worst Charlton Heston impression in all recorded history.

"Why did Cain kill Abel?" Anne looked at him frowning.

"Well, Cain was jealous of his brother and got angry. A lot of the stories in the Bible are about people doing stupid things. Tell me more about Saphan and Aesmay, so I can see if I can tie them to Cain and Abel." Henry stopped typing, more interested in where the story was going.

"Aesmay was King. Saphan was his brother but did not like Aesmay to be King. He and others got angry and tried to take the mountain."

"Okay, that's good. Do we want to make Saphan a black dragon, or should he start out as a golden one?"

"He was a golden one once. Then he turned into a black dragon and killed Aesmay. His body changed."

"Changed? How did it change?" Henry was intrigued with where this story would go. "So he physically changed and then killed his brother? This is more like Cain and Abel than I thought." Henry's heart was racing. Had Anne witnessed a murder, her own father, perhaps?

"He was more like my drawings and paintings. His skin was hard with scales and his wings were dark. He had fire breath now and was bigger, stronger. His eyes were red, not white like Aesmay's."

"You know what changed about him, but do you know how he got like that?"

"No. Aesmay sent him away and he was changed when he came back."

"Anything else?"

"He could not talk with his mind anymore and had to talk like we do. And he could not make things move with his thoughts but had to use his hands."

"So the golden dragons are telepathic and telekinetic."

"What is tele...kin...etic?"

"Being able to move objects with your mind. So once the black dragons left, they lost their abilities. But why did they change shape?"

"Their body was...twisted...is that the right word? They changed."

"Okay." Henry typed up what they had just talked about. "We need to think about where we go from there. So Saphan grew angry because he was not King, and Aesmay sent him away. And the golden dragons lived their lives until what?"

"Saphan came back with the others out of the sky with the fire. Then he killed Aesmay and...." she stopped.

"Is this too hard for you, is this the nightmare?" Henry touched her leg where she was sitting next to him.

"It is hard, but I will tell you."

Henry stopped typing. This was the basis of her nightmares, and he wanted to pay close attention to every detail she told him, hoping to find out the reasons these images haunted her.

She took a couple of deep breaths for courage. "I am called Aeya in my dreams, the daughter of Aesmay."

"Wait, you're his daughter?" This might be the breakthrough he'd been looking for! She had just revealed her father and uncle. If they really existed at all, that was.

"Yes, Saphan hated Aesmay because he would not let Saphan have Aeya."

"Well, this is a children's book, so we might want to leave that part out. So there was a woman–female involved, very interesting. What happens next?"

"I see the sky open and Saphan and the others come back. They have fire breath and I see the others burn. I feel them, all of them, even the little ones, burn and die! Everything about them is different, their teeth, their claws, their size, all bigger, sharper, so the golden dragons are..."

"Powerless, helpless," Henry interjected.

"Yes, powerless. They cannot stop the black dragons. They cannot run from them, and many are ripped apart before being burned. The little ones are stomped on or even swallowed in one bite. Then there is the darkness and I scream...."

"We can stop if you want." Henry took her hand.

"No." She shook her head. "I will try." She took a few deep breaths.

"The sky opens and the black dragons come down with fire in the...." She went to the drawing of the black dragon and pointed to fire coming from its mouth. "Fire comes from their mouths. I am with another dragon called Kenta, like you and I are together, but he does not make love to Aeya. No one is allowed too. Kenta protects and watches over me. He tries to shield me from their fire breath, and I hear his cries and watch him burn. They burn all of the golden dragons until none are left but me. I see their bodies become black from the flame and hear their screams."

"Wow," Henry exclaimed.

"In my dream, Saphan comes for me. He tells me he will take me. The golden dragons are all gone. I am covered with darkness. That is when I wake. There is nothing after that."

"Wow, wow, wow," Henry was stunned. "I am so sorry, honey. I never imagined it was that bad."

Anne had never relived her dreams while awake. In fact, he believed she slammed the door in her mind shut and locked it up tight, desperately hoping it would never open again. But every night, something compelled her back across the threshold, plunging her into the world of the golden dragons and, eventually, into the nightmares. She could not hold back the tears and buried her head into Henry's chest and sobbed.

Henry held her tight, kissing the top of her head. Despite the moment, he couldn't help but smell the fragrance of her hair. His thoughts mingled with her scent and together they swirled in his head. Only time would tell if Anne facing her fears and unburdening her heart like this would help or make things worse. Either way, it was good that he had a better understanding of what she was going through.

Time to switch gears and get the day back on a more positive note.

He gently pushed her back at arm's length, kissing her forehead along the way, and brushed a tear from her cheek. Smiling, he said, "That's enough for today, don't you think? Let's do something a little more light-hearted. You get to choose. Anything you want to do?"

"Beach!" she shouted.

"Beach it is. Come on, let's pack a lunch and grab our suits."

Soon they were packed up and headed to North Jetty Park in Nokomis to watch the boats come through the channel. True to form, Anne was excited to see all the different kinds of boats, some big, some small, sailing through the rock-lined channel into the harbor beyond. The seagulls took flight every time a horn blew or a bell rang, adding to the spectacle.

Later, Henry took her down to the harbor where they met a nice older couple named Ron and Betty White, who were willing to take them out on their sailboat, for a small fee.

The sun was out, and with the wind in their sails, they were miles out on the ocean in no time. The shore became a dark line along the horizon. Anne beamed the entire time, looking as beautiful as ever with the wind blowing back her golden tresses along with her cover up. Mr. White turned a brilliant shade of red when Mrs. White caught him staring.

"Don't pay him any mind," Mrs. White said, waiving off her husband. "He still thinks he's as handsome as he was back in the day. He did look good in his Navy uniform, though."

"You were in the Navy?" Henry asked. "So was I. What did you do?"

Ron puffed up his chest, as if reliving the glory days of long ago. "I was a turret captain. I was just a young buck too bored to stay on my parent's farm. I thought I'd find adventure on the high seas." He looked at the deck. "I had enough adventure to last a lifetime."

"You must have seen a lot of action in your time," Henry said.

"I've seen a few wars."

"You still look good for such a seasoned warrior."

Ron reached for his wife, his gnarled hands grasping hers. "She keeps me young." He smiled. "If it weren't for her, I'd be long gone."

"Wow," Henry said fascinated. "What stories you must have."

"And if you let him," Betty said, "he'll talk your ear off all night."

Ron gave her a nasty look. "This young buck was a sailor too. He knows 'em all already. What did you do?"

"For most of my time, I was Flight Support," Henry said. "Then I did a 9-month tour as an Individual Augmentee in Iraq."

"Slummin' with them army boys, huh?"

Henry laughed. "We taught them how to fight with style."

"You see a lot of combat?"

"I saw my share." Henry shrugged. "I'm sure not as much as you did."

"That where you got that scar?" Ron pointed to the permanent depression on Henry's right thigh.

"Yeah," Henry rubbed the scar. "Got hit by some shrapnel when our transport was hit by mortar shell."

"Enough of the war talk!" Betty stood up. "Why don't you two enjoy the day? Go for a swim!"

Henry nodded and took Anne's hand. "Sure, we'd love to."

"Port side is lookin' pretty," Ron said.

"Port?" Anne asked.

"The port side is the left side of the boat," Henry explained. "The right side is starboard. The trick to remember is port and left both have four letters."

"But stars are in the sky, not on boards," Anne frowned.

"She sure is a funny girl," Ron said. Betty nodded.

Together Henry and Anne dove off the boat and swam in the deep ocean. Mr. and Mrs. White watched from the deck smiling, perhaps remembering their youth.

Henry took Anne out farther into the water, swimming several meters from the boat, enjoying the freedom that swimming in the open water gave him. At a certain point, they raced each other back to the boat. Somehow, Anne always won those races, and if the truth were known, it was because Henry enjoyed the view from second place. Besides, it made his girl happy, and it was the gentlemanly thing to do.

After they boarded, Mrs. White handed each of them a towel and offered them a soft drink.

"Help me with these sails, young man," Ron said to Henry.

"It would be my sincere pleasure." Henry was happy to do so and in fact made Mr. White relax while he took care of the winches to unfurl the sails, securing the furling line around the drum.

"I saw dolphins!" Anne told the older couple. "There were so many jumping all around us! I wanted to swim with them."

The joy she found in the little things made Henry smile. He breathed a silent breath of relief that his attempt to raise her spirits was working out so well. She had an unquenchable love of life that infected everyone around her. Even the Whites couldn't stop from smiling.

The gentle rocking of the boat as it neared the shore helped them both relax and allowed the cares of the day to drift away with the tide. The sun made its daily descent, leaving behind a sky filled with clouds of ever changing colors and seagulls calling out their farewells to the day. All they cared about was scanning the heavens and taking it all in. Happily, there was not a dragon in sight.

Back in their berth in the harbor, there were hugs all around as Henry and Anne said goodbye to their new friends. Henry thanked them, but only after they promised to come see the Whites again and their little sailboat. It was dark by the time they left the park, stopping on the way to pick up sandwiches.

But when they finally went to sleep, the dragon fires returned. Henry held the shaking woman tightly in his arms. Awake, she turned to him, and a different kind of fire consumed them.

There is peace on the mountain since my father's brother is banished.

But Aesmay is sad. I know he misses his brother and did not want to force him to leave our mountain. I snuggle against him to let him know I am here…

The sky explodes! Saphan returns! He is no longer a defeated golden dragon, but fills the sky with his massive wings and large nostrils that bellow smoke. The enormous black dragon lands in front of Aesmay and roars his defiance.

"Did I not tell you I alone was worthy! The Master has shown me that."

"If you have gone to the Master, then you are truly lost," Aesmay says with tears in his eyes.

Saphan has a long sharp crystal in his claws. He plunges the crystal into my father's body. I scream! My father falls to the ground, his one-time brother stabbing him over and over. Hard claws grab me, digging their sharpness into my skin, holding me, cutting me. I reach out to my father and watch him bleed golden blood that flows down to wash over my feet. With his remaining strength, he exhales his last breath toward me. I want to fly to him, but I am thrown to the ground and covered in darkness….

15. DR. RAYBACK

Friday, June 26

The next day, Henry dropped Anne off at Heidi's house while he went to talk to his psychologist friend, Dr. Susan Rayback. Henry and Susan had been friends in college, back when he returned to finish his senior year and Susan was in her second. Henry hadn't seen Susan since he graduated.

The assistant showed him to the office, where Susan greeted him with a hug.

"Hello, Henry," she said. "So nice to see you again! You're looking good." Susan was in her early thirties with shoulder length brown hair and blue eyes. "Can I get you something to drink?"

"Water would be fine," Henry said. The office was done in a nautical décor with dark paneled wood on the walls. Nautical lanterns served as the light fixtures, and the furniture was rich brown leather pieces. The antique desk was made of oak, with panels set in the side surrounded by raised frames.

All around the office were items from the sea; shells, some large, like the pink conch shell on the end table, to baskets filled with smaller, intricately designed shells. Over the couch was a framed copy of Ivan Aivazovsky's *The Ninth Wave*. Henry loved the painting, feeling like one of the survivors holding to the raft in the fury of the sea, the hope of a new day rising above the turmoil, like the sail of a ship heading in to the wind. Behind her desk stood a model of a three-masted barque ship, exquisitely made with minute details, including complete rigging and separate sails.

She's done well for herself. Henry smiled remembering the frazzled college student struggling to get through her studies after her mother died.

Susan came back and handed Henry a bottle of water, then sat behind her desk. "Now tell me about Anne."

"Well, I found her almost a couple weeks ago on Venice Beach. She was naked and scared and couldn't talk to me or understand anything I was saying to me. It was really kind of freaky. She didn't seem to know how to do anything, almost like she was a newborn baby. She didn't even know how to control her bladder!"

"Really?" Susan said.

"But," he continued, "the most amazing thing about her is her ability to pick things up quickly. She learns at an astounding rate! We only had to show her something once and she could do it. She's learned to talk, to take care of herself, even to swim. And then there's her art. I've never seen anything like it! She just watched me for a little while, then picked up a pencil and drew as if she had years of training. She's the most amazing person I've ever known!"

"Tell me about the nightmares, Henry. You seemed very concerned about that. You said they happen every night?"

"Every single night."

"And she remembers them?"

"That's the strange thing, the thing that brought me to you today. She can remember every detail about the dreams, including the names of the dragons, but she has no memory whatsoever of her life before I found her. Nothing! I don't understand how that can be."

"Well," Susan said. "Severe trauma can cause memory loss, but I've never heard of a case this severe where there is no memory at all. There is a possibility she suffered a physical injury, which may have caused some type of amnesia. I suggest you get her checked out by a physician to be sure."

"I will," Henry agreed. "I'll call Dr. Jackson and set something up." He continued. "Fire is a recurring theme in her dreams. I think she may have been in a fire at some point. And there is something about breathing underwater. My best guess is that she may have been on a boat that caught fire and was thrown into the sea. But what do the dragons in her dream represent?"

"Being in a fire can certainly qualify as a traumatic event, which can cause post-traumatic amnesia. If there was any brain injury, it could cause neurological amnesia. This could be a type of retrograde amnesia, although I would think it would have had to be a severe injury or a large tumor or swelling to cause the extent of loss we are talking about. Any of those disorders have other symptoms, often severe and very obvious. If she's not experiencing any pain, slurred speech, or loss of equilibrium, it's a safe bet we can rule that out."

Susan leaned forward, continuing. "Another rare type of amnesia is called dissociative amnesia and it stems from emotional shock or trauma, such as being the victim of a violent crime. With this disorder, a person may lose personal memories and autobiographical information, but usually only briefly." She put her hands up in surrender. "We can't even attempt a diagnosis until she has been examined by a medical doctor.

"As to why she dreams about dragons, there could be many reasons. Jung believed that dreams of dragons represented the danger of the newly acquired consciousness being swallowed up again by the instinctive psyche, the unconscious. It could be that subconsciously, her past life is fighting against her life as she perceives it now, trying to re-establish itself. Who she was before you found her could be much different than who she is now, for example.

"Freud has a slightly different outlook, believing the dragon symbolized 'the Great Mother' and that fighting the dragon could mean she is breaking away from her upbringing. There may have been things in her past so horrific she is trying to escape them. Perhaps an abusive parent, but again, the extent of her memory loss, to regress to the point of a newborn, is puzzling.

"There's yet another theory that dreams of being attacked by a dragon may be one's own basal impulses, or overcoming an unconscious need for destructive behavior that she may have engaged in before the memory loss.

"These are all popular theories about why people dream about dragons, but it's difficult to know without spending time with her to try to draw out some of those memories. The point though is that these dreams are representations of something in her past and shouldn't be taken literally. And we certainly don't want to over-analyze them. You said Anne has a vivid imagination. That may be why her mind creates such fantastic and detailed dreams to deal with whatever trauma underlies them. But I think it's clear there's something in her past making its way out, whether it be from a very traumatic event or medically based.

"I would encourage you to have her continue with the story and her pictures. Having her tell the story to you, along with creating the paintings is a way to get those repressed memories out in a constructive way. I agree, her situation is quite unique. I'm going to do some further research on the subject of dragons, and once you have her checked out by a medical doctor, we can get a clearer picture of the cause of both the memory loss and the dreams."

Henry stood up. "Are we good, Susie?"

She hugged him then stepped back holding on to his arms. "We were both at a bad time in our lives back then. You helped me deal with my mom's death. I helped you deal with yours. I never expected more than what we had—friends with benefits. We needed each other and it got us through a tough year. I'm glad you're happy."

"Thanks. I owe you one." He kissed her cheek.

"Nonsense, I still owe you from saving my ass in English Lit! Who knows where I'd be if it weren't for you!"

Henry kissed her cheek. "I'll call you once we know what Dr. Jackson says."

On the way home, Henry called Dr. John Jackson's office and was able to make an appointment for Anne for that Thursday.

He pulled up to Heidi's house. The sounds of children laughing and violent splashing came from the back yard. Heidi, Anne, and the kids were all in the pool having a wonderful time throwing water at each other.

"Uncle Henry!" Robbie called.

"Hi Henry," Heidi said. "Come on in!"

"Hi kids! Not today, Sis. Anne, please get ready, we need to go." "Awwww," Robbie whined. "Can't she stay and play some more?"

Heidi herded the kids out of the pool, carrying Nattie on the way. "No, kids. Daddy's going to be home soon. Henry, are you coming over for the Fourth of July? We'll barbecue, then go see the fireworks at the Venice Pier."

Henry picked up a blue and white striped towel from the lounge chair and wrapped it around a dripping Anne. "Sure, what time do you want us to be here?"

Anne went inside to change. Heidi put Nattie down and she followed.

"How about ten o'clock?"

"Sounds like a plan!"

Anne soon came out in dry clothes and they kissed all the faces and left.

In the car Anne asked Henry about his visit to his friend. "What did Susan say?"

"She said we should continue with our story and your art. She's very interested in meeting you, but wants you to see a doctor to make sure there isn't anything physically wrong."

"A doctor?"

"Someone who heals you when you're sick or injured. He's just going to look at your body to make sure everything is okay."

"Okay," she said.

For the remainder of the car ride home and all throughout dinner, Henry was silent and deep in thought. Between the baring of Anne's soul and Susan's insights on amnesia, he had a lot to sort out in his mind. He only wanted what was best for her, but what that was remained an enigma. One fear was that by exposing her to "the system," she would get locked up for observation and have to undergo numerous invasive tests, psychological and physical. What if she did have some horrible past? Would dredging it up help? Or would it force her to face whatever hell she had escaped? He doubted very much that she could have perpetrated any sort of crime or evil act, and therefore be wanted by the law, or worse. She was so sweet and loving: there was no way amnesia would change her entire personality too, was there?

Then there were those damned dragons added to the mix, leaving only about a bazillion different scenarios and possibilities why they came calling every friggin' night. Each possibility was more perplexing than the last. What was it exactly that Susan had said? "Don't over-analyze them." Yeah, right, that's like telling someone not to think of the color pink.

Henry's mind was on a roll. *Let me think, there was Freud and his mommy issues, nothing new there. With Freud, breathing was a mommy issue. Zo let me zee here, breathing in or ze inhaling iz like da penis going into da voman und exhaling, or breathing owt is like da voman giving birth, ya. Yeah, no I don't think so. No help there.*

That Jung fella said it was all about her "consciousness being swallowed." Sorry Jung, that's a little too hard for me to swallow. But hey, maybe the old Anne was trying to move back into her old hangout. It's a nice place to be, let me tell ya. Maybe Mr. Jung is right after all. But then why all the other dragons? And the killing of the babies, not to mention Kenta and the brothers that were her uncle and father. Hey, I just realized no mention of a mommy. In your face Freud, ha! No I don't think her consciousness being on the menu in her dreams is the answer.

Next there was the "overcoming and unconscious need for destructive behavior" crap.

I love ya, Susan, but the only destructive behavior she's capable of is all the hearts she breaks when she walks into a room hanging on my arm. There is no way in hell I am ever going to believe my Anne would harm anyone. Heck, pets and wildlife alike fall in love with her just for showing up. If a black heart beats beneath those perfect breasts, the animals would sense it and run from her, not to her. Not to mention the deep connection I felt from the moment I laid eyes on her. There was no malevolence in that moment—the exact opposite in fact. Even Aeya, her dream counterpart, was an innocent victim, with nothing but compassion and love for her people. No, there is another answer I'm sure, and one day soon I'll find it.

As the day and his roll came to an end, Henry could only hope the new path he had chosen for them was the right one. Good intentions do not guarantee good results, but he had to find a way to end these nightmares for her. They were the only dark cloud in an otherwise perfect sky. While he and Anne settled in for the evening, he could only wonder how long it would be before Saphan would rear his ugly head inside of Anne's. *Well you better watch out asshole, there's a new dragon slayer in town and you're top on my list.*

I am being carried by two black dragons, flying over the Crystal Mountains. I see fires raging below me, burning the bodies of my father and my kind. We pass over the green ocean. The sky grows dark and the waters turn black. Eventually, even the sun is swallowed by the darkness. We arrive at the Black Mountains spewing fire from their peaks, the inferno rising up from the center of the mountain.

At the highest of the Black Mountains, I am thrown to the rocky pinnacle, my escorts landing around me. I have never been in the dark and I am afraid of what will happen. My body hurts with fear and I cannot breathe either air or water. I am consumed with dread.

Saphan lands and comes near me, his red eyes blazing and his mouth open, revealing his teeth dripping with the blood of his only brother. I try to crawl away from him but I am held by the others.

He laughs as he approaches me.

"Did I not warn you, Aeya, that you will suffer for your choice? You refused my love. Now you will know what my hate feels like."

16. BREATHING UNDER WATER

Saturday, June 27

Henry decided he would show Anne how she really could breathe underwater—by taking her scuba diving. He was certified to dive from his days in the Navy, but needed to get her certified as well, so he signed her up for classes with a local dive shop.

The class was one day with a dive after, with experienced instructors. Like everything else she started, she took to the class like a natural, swimming across the pool like an Olympic swimmer, and comfortable with the equipment. Her instructor, a gentleman from Australia named Matt, commented that she picked up diving so quickly, he would sign her certification and arrange for her to dive that afternoon, as long as he went with, of course. Like everyone who met her, Matt fell under her spell. Her zest for experiencing all life had to offer was infectious. Everything was new and exciting to her, and her enthusiasm gave Henry a fresh outlook on life too.

Matt arranged for Henry and Anne to go out on one of their charter boats, a 30-foot open dive boat with a crew of six. Several other diving students and instructors joined them on the trip. They went two miles from shore to an area where people dove for the Megalodon shark teeth. Matt fitted Anne with a single tank, buoyancy control device, fins and mask, and helped her put the regulator in her mouth. Henry suited himself up without assistance, only requiring Matt to perform a safety check of his equipment. Matt told her to wait and asked Henry to go first, to show her how to jump into the water, one foot first, stepping off the boat holding onto his mask.

She followed with a splash and Henry gave her the "descend" thumb-down hand signal he had taught her, inviting her to join him. Matt came after, staying behind as they explored the deep. They swam down twenty-five feet, to the ocean floor and shifted through the sand looking for the larger shark teeth. Wide-eyed wonder peeked through Anne's mask.

Henry loved diving because it gave him the opportunity to visit another world, a beautiful and exotic world where the inhabitants of one could not survive in the other. It prompted a deep respect for this environment and creatures that lived there. They were uninvited guests after all, and he could only wonder if fish were as fascinated with him as he was with them.

Henry guided Anne along the ocean's bottom, exploring the brightly colored coral and plant life. He was thankful she had a regulator lodged in her mouth because he couldn't even come close to naming a fraction of the sea life before them. Anne was probably ready to burst at any moment from the pressure of all the questions he knew were bubbling up inside her.

But she kept her promise Henry made her swear before submerging, not to touch anything without Henry's or Matt's okay first. If she saw anything she wanted to pick up, like a shell or a tooth, she had to point first and wait for the diver's hand signal of either okay or danger. In the ocean, the prettier something was often meant the deadlier or more poisonous it was. One also had to beware of who was lurking under the surface of the sand or had taken up residence in a nook or cranny among the rocks and coral. Sea snakes and eels loved small dark holes, and deadly rock fish lay on the ocean floor invisible to the untrained eye or unsuspecting passerby.

Anne followed several schools of fish swirling around her, watching the brightly colored fish swim by, the schools switching direction. Henry pointed out an octopus he spotted and she nodded, watching the animal pulsing its way across the ocean floor. Matt found a large prehistoric Megalodon shark tooth and brought it to her. Her eyes gleamed with excitement behind the mask as she held it in her hands. The size of this tooth filling both of Anne's hands was yet another reminder that they were visitors in an alien world.

After so many nights of horrible dreams, Henry wanted Anne to feel like she was in a real dream now, living in the peaceful scenes she painted where she settled on the bottom of the green ocean to sleep. At one point, she signaled she was going back down, so the men followed her to the sand. She knelt on the ocean bottom, the sea life swimming above her, reaching out to try to touch the fish. She sat there for a long time. Maybe she was reliving her dreams, at least the peaceful parts until the nightmares cut their way into her slumber.

At one point, Matt checked their gauges and flashed Henry the low-air signal. Henry turned to Anne and signaled it was the end of the dive. Anne nodded. The three divers headed back up to the boat. Matt got on first, then helped Anne up, then Henry. She took the regulator out of her mouth, unable to contain her joy, hugging both Henry and Matt, tears forming in her eyes, her Megalodon tooth held tightly in her hands as if it were a precious jewel.

"I can breathe underwater!" she cried, tears in her eyes, her mouth wide and smiling. "I can breathe underwater! There are so many fish, so many colors! Tell me names of the fishes," she demanded. "What was the yellow one?"

"Tang," Matt replied.

"What was the long silver one?"

"Tarpon."

"What was the orange one?"

This went on for a while because she remembered every fish she saw. Then she asked the names of the coral; staghorn, elkhorn, lettuce, brain. She asked questions all the way back to the harbor. Matt and Henry answered as many as they could, but she just had too many. Henry was right: she was ready to pop from all the questions.

Off the boat, Anne was still smiling, her teeth gleaming in the sun, her eyes bright. Henry thought her face would split, her smile was so big. Henry thanked Matt and Anne kissed him on the cheek. Henry didn't mind. It was worth it for Anne to have such an amazing day.

Henry couldn't wait to show her his next surprise. He was going to take her flying!

"Bind her with chains," Saphan orders. The chains are heavy and hurt. My heart is already broken. My father and Kenta, my guardian, are gone! How much more can he hurt me? Fear grips my heart, and I cannot breathe in dread of what will happen next.

With heavy chains on all my legs, Saphan orders his sons to hold me down. He takes the black crystal sword and starts to cut into my beautiful wings! I scream! The pain is so great it blinds me! I cannot move or get away—sharp claws dig into my body. The heavy chains hold me to the floor of the mountain. Making a sound unlike anything I have ever heard before, he saws through my pectoral muscles and bone, then wrenches my wings off with his claws, my golden blood flowing to the ground in a flood. I am sick from the pain and soon unable to make any sounds, my throat raw from screaming.

There is no reason to hold me down anymore, I do not have the strength to rise...

17. FLYING

Sunday, June 28

Henry woke up as excited as a school boy on the first day of summer. Today was the day he would reveal his second surprise for Anne and take her to fly in the sky. They were going skydiving! Anne often talked about the joy of soaring through the sky, flying over the Crystal Mountains in her dreams. They were the happy moments before the black dragons came to spread death and terror upon her nocturnal counterpart and her people. He wanted to recreate that happiness as best he could to offset whatever horrors she may have endured. Maybe, just maybe, with enough positive and happy real life experiences, the bad memories would begin to fade, and new dreams would take their place.

Henry remained mysterious throughout their morning rituals and under-cooked breakfast in his rush to get them out the door. Anne had a puzzled look on her face watching him. Henry could sense she was frustrated, but he wasn't going to tell her where they were going.

"We're going to do something really special today," he said in the car.

"Diving?" she asked, a bright smile on her face.

"Well, sort of in a way, but it's not what you're thinking," he teased.

"Tell me," she begged.

"Nope."

"*Tell me!*" she said in a deep voice through clenched teeth, slugging him in the shoulder.

"Hey, behave yourself, young lady. Don't make me turn this car around."

Anne settled into her seat with silent anticipation.

"You'll see when we get there." He pulled the car out of the driveway and headed out toward their secret destination. They drove to the Sarasota Bradenton International Airport where the skydiving school was. They pulled up to the main entrance and parked. Henry turned to Anne and said, "You're going to fly today."

Anne was speechless, her mouth open for almost a full minute. "F-fly?"

she could barely speak. "Really, I'm going to fly?"

"Yes, fly. Like in your dreams, Anne."

* * *

Anne shook with anticipation. She followed Henry into the building and marveled at the pictures of past patrons on their jumps, the wind blowing their hair straight up, huge smiles on their faces. She could barely focus on the safety video before heading to the plane with her instructor. Henry helped her into her jumpsuit, along with a harness, helmet, altimeter and goggles.

Anne's jump partner was an instructor named Travis. He introduced himself, telling them about his history as a retired U.S. Air Force Officer, having served on their Wings of Blue Sky-diving Team. He said he loved jumping so much, he continued his passion for it after leaving the Air Force, and had over a thousand jumps to his credit. After going over the safety instructions one last time, they headed for the plane.

Anne smelled something in the air and asked Henry what it was. He told her it was jet fuel. They climbed the stairs and entered the plane through a wide opening with no door, then took their places side by side on two benches running parallel along opposite sides of the plane. The jumpers sat next to their instructors in pairs. The chatter amongst the group was a mixture of excitement and dread.

The plane climbed into the air. Anne's stomach flopped and her ears popped. She pointed out the window, prompting Henry to look at the Florida coast as they climbed higher into the blue sky. She asked him in a raised voice why the fields, houses, and roads below them looked so tiny. He explained it was a matter of perspective, like when she drew something far off in the distance. Immediately, she understood.

The plane leveled off at 12,000 feet. The instructors fastened themselves to their students' harnesses, tethering them to each other. The pair closest to the door made their way to the opening and knelt at the edge. Giving each other the thumbs up, together they leaned forward and disappeared from Anne's view. Then Henry and his instructor jumped. Two by two, they took their turn jumping. Everyone else scooted up advancing towards the doorway.

Most everyone else was scooting. Poor Travis was being dragged by Anne, who nearly pushed the others out of the plane so it could be her turn.

Finally, the moment arrived and Anne knelt at the threshold of her dream. There she was, gazing into the wide open sky with the wind blowing in her face, inviting her to take her rightful place among the clouds. Travis's fist appeared in front of her face with his thumb up indicating it was time. Anne didn't waste time signaling back, but plunged forward into the open sky with a squeal of delight.

She was flying! She assumed the stable position with her arms out at her side and elbows bent at a ninety degree angle, hips down and her legs bent slightly, knees apart. She closed her eyes for a minute, and could swear the muscles in her back and chest flexed as if she had wings. Then she opened her eyes and like her dreams, she was flying into the white sun with her golden companion at her side, the wind in her face. Her heart soared as she did, the smile on her face as wide as the world below her. The wind whipped around her, making her clothes billow out. She was really flying! Her heart beat wildly, her joy at the experience exploding inside her. Imaginary powerful wings on her back spread. She stretched her arms wide, letting the air lift her into a state of euphoria while she plummeted towards the earth below. The jerk of the parachute opening snapped her out of the moment.

She transitioned from soaring to floating on the air, and the sensation was amazing. This was beyond her wildest dreams! She drifted like a cloud. Slowly wafting towards the ground, she looked down at her feet dangling in the open air and playfully kicked them a bit. Then, she looked up at the parachute spread wide overhead and watched it ripple from the air passing through it. Travis asked her if she would like to drive for a while, and pointed her attention to the handles on the sides of the rigging. By grasping one in each hand and pulling down, she could turn to the left or the right. Now this was flying! Anne was really in control, and was able to soar in whichever direction she chose.

The ground was rapidly approaching and her flight was about to end. Travis instructed her to hold her feet up so his would be the first to touch the ground. Anne saw Henry waiting for her at the edge of the landing sight. He had retrieved his phone before she landed and was holding it in front of him with both hands, smiling. She waved at him a heartbeat before landing and would have run immediately over to him, if not for the hundred and seventy pounds of instructor strapped to her back. Travis detached his harness from hers. He asked her if she enjoyed her first skydive. She was jumping with joy and nearly snapped his neck hugging him saying, "Thank you!"

Henry joined them. "Well? What did you think?" Anne jumped into his arms, wrapping her legs around his waist and squeezed his neck.

"I was flying!" She replied, screaming in his ear.

"Yes, you were, I saw. I'm so proud of you."

"I was flying!" She repeated.

She gave Henry a big kiss and climbed down, only to start bouncing up and down again with joy.

"How did she do?" Henry turned to Travis.

"Oh, she did great, most enthusiastic student I've ever had." He nodded in Anne's direction. "It was also the first time a student dragged me out of the plane. I've had eager students before, but I never had one that made me feel like I was the one just along for the ride. She's a natural. You should think about signing her up for certification."

"Maybe some other time. Thank you for taking such good care of her." Henry shook Travis's hand and gave him a nice tip.

"My pleasure, drop in anytime."

"Yes, thank you, Travis. *I was flying!*" Anne added.

"Yes, I know, and you did great. Good-bye, and I really do hope to see you again. If you ever come back, please ask for me."

"We will," Henry promised.

"*I was flying!*" Anne reminded him one more time.

The jump lasted seven minutes, but for Anne, it was a lifetime of ultimate joy that brought tears to her eyes, along with a very large dose of adrenalin. On the way through the gift shop to pick up her photos, she repeated to everyone she saw that she was flying! Henry told them it was her first time. She showed everyone who was waiting for their own jump the pictures they gave her, and anyone else who came within five feet of her, exclaiming to each, "I was flying!"

* * *

"How are you feeling," Henry asked her on the way home once she finally stopped talking about the experience.

She turned to him, the smile still wide on her face. "I cannot find words to say! I was flying! I could feel the wings on my back like they were really there! I did not think such a thing could happen. I want to go again!"

"We will," he said, smiling. "That's a promise."

"Thank you," she whispered, barely able to get the words out. "Thank you!"

"You are welcome, my lady."

In the house, Anne took the pictures and showed each one of the animals, telling them about her flight. They simply sniffed the pictures and went back to whatever mischief they were into. Henry had to recharge his cellphone, Anne had watched the video over and over on the car ride home.

Henry wasn't done yet. "I have another surprise for you. Go look under the bed. There's a big box under there. Bring it out here."

Anne dashed off as instructed, and nearly stepped on half a dozen paws in her rush to get back. In her hands was a large cream-colored box with a big red bow wrapped around it.

"Take a look inside," Henry prompted.

Anne ripped off the bow with one hand and the lid with the other, sending them to opposite corners of the room. She shredded through the tissue paper to reveal a beautiful pastel blue gown with rhinestone accents and matching shoes.

Bibbity Bobbity Boo. Anne's eyes popped out of her head, followed by the all too familiar squeal of delight he had grown so fond of hearing. More like Bibbity Bobbity Broke, he joked. He didn't mind at all. Her love was worth all the gold on earth, Elvis once sang. He would give everything he had if it would end her nightmares, he vowed.

"That's only part of the surprise. Go put that on, we have another special place to go to."

She didn't ask where, but raced to the bedroom to change. Everything with four legs and a tail gave her a wide berth. Henry slipped into a pair of slacks and a button-down shirt. He emerged from the bathroom moments before Anne reappeared from the bedroom. Webster has yet to come up with a word that could adequately describe the vision that stood before him. Stunning, beautiful, radiant—nope—not even close. Breathtaking would have to do for the moment. She beamed with joy and happiness and spun around for Henry to see. Henry clicked his heels together, bowed and extended his hand. Anne took his arm and he escorted her to the car.

"Where are we going?"

"You'll see. It's another surprise."

"Will I fly again? Will I breathe under water?"

"In that dress? Seriously?"

"Will I see animals? Will I see flowers?" She kept peppering him with questions to which he responded on each, "You'll see."

Finally, they arrived at their destination, the Arthur Murray Dance Studio. "You're going to dance like a princess," Henry said opening the door.

Anne ran into the studio, her smile wide and arms out performing a pirouette. "Dance!"

They were greeted by their instructor, a tall slender Hispanic man named Sidney with caramel skin and bright eyes. Sidney showed them how to walk first, learning to move in sync with each other. Anne had a little trouble following Henry's lead, and they took turns stepping on each other's feet at first, laughing each time they did. But then they found their groove. Sidney took turns replacing one or the other to make sure they were feeling their way with each other in the movements and direction.

Sidney told Anne to put her hand on Henry's arm, and Henry to put his arm on her back. He instructed them to hold their arms out together while he restarted the music. Henry stepped forward with his left foot—Anne stepped back with her right. They followed with a perfect smooth box step. Soon the music found its way into their souls, drawing them together as if they were one. Nothing and no one else mattered.

They found their rhythm with the tempo of the music and with each other. Henry gazed into Anne's blue eyes, falling into the world that was Anne. Never in his life had he imagined he would meet so wonderful a creature, let alone be loved by one. She was everything to him now. The dance steps became second nature to him, his girl in his arms.

* * *

She was a Princess in her own movie! Anne clung to Henry with everything inside her, feeling his strong arm surrounding her, guiding her across the floor. Sidney kept telling her to look up and to the left, like a Princess, but all she could do was look into Henry's eyes. She was drawn into them, wanting to climb into his very soul, to join with him as their bodies did. His hand folded on her back like it was an extension of her, their joined hands melded into one. She was floating among the clouds again, dancing on air. She was the Princess in a blue dress dancing with her tall handsome Prince. No fairy tale could come close to theirs, no love could be as fierce and deep.

She did not want to stop. But soon, the clock struck midnight, or one hour in their case. Their time was up so they thanked Sidney and left the studio, holding hands and staring into each other's eyes, oblivious to the way out. Sidney smiled and guided them to the door.

* * *

Anne was still full of energy wanting more. Henry decided he would take her to a nightclub so that she could experience the fast life that clubs offered. It was loud, packed, and wild, but she loved it, writhing with the other party-goers on the dance floor. They took a break for food; then she was back, screaming with the rest of the patrons, causing Henry's ear to buzz.

Around one in the morning, Henry had had enough. "Let's go home," he yelled in her ear.

"Okay," she yelled back. They made their way through the packed club and out into the cool night air, where the only sounds were the traffic on Tamiami Trail and the crickets in the bushes. Henry stood for a moment, enjoying the peace, and breathing in the night air to clear his head.

On their way to the car, he noticed two men in dark clothes lurking by his vehicle. There was third man behind the wheel of a black SUV, engine running, parked in front of his car, blocking it in.

"Hey! What the hell?" he shouted as loud as his raw throat would permit. The men spotted them, turning in their direction. The SUV kept pace. Faced with the option of fight or flight, Henry would choose fight every time, but he had Anne's safety to worry about. He thrust his right arm in front of Anne to halt her progress, keeping his eyes fixed on the menacing trio. "Anne, Sweetheart, go back inside and ask the big guy at the door to call 9-1-1 and then stay by his side—"

Before Henry could finish his instructions, a group of young party-goers bursting from the club, laughing and carrying on. No longer alone, the mysterious pair jumped inside the SUV and sped off, leaving behind the smell of burnt rubber and a plethora of unanswered questions.

"What the hell was that all about?" Henry exclaimed, walking to the car. He turned to Anne, "Are you okay? Did those guys frighten you?"

"I am okay, but what did those men want?"

"I wish I knew. Let's not hang around here and find out, in case they circle back."

Henry held the door for Anne, closing it behind her. On his walk around to the driver's side, he scanned the parking lot and surrounding area for anything or anyone suspicious. There was no way of knowing if there were any more of those creeps, and he wasn't about to be caught off guard. Behind the wheel, Henry immediately fired up the engine, slammed the gear shift into drive and stomped on the gas pedal. He swerved a little, putting on his seat belt, and nearly clipped one of the party-goers bent over puking up her spleen. Hell of a way to pay someone back who, inadvertently, may have saved your life. He kept a close eye on the rear view mirror on the ride home, disturbed by what had happened at the club. Combined with the weird shadows in his room at night and the dogs' odd behavior barking at imaginary intruders, something didn't feel right.

Saphan rips off my beautiful wings and throws them to his sons. The black dragons fight each other to be the first to tear into and devour them. My back throbs with indescribable agony. My screams delight my captors. I can only mourn watching my wings torn apart and consumed.

The large black dragon stands on his hind legs and roars while his sons feast, the force of his roar shaking the ground beneath me. My golden blood runs into the iridescent membrane, washing out all the beautiful colors reflected in my wings. My back bleeds from the deep wounds, to wash the ground with the tears falling from my eyes. I am forced to watch my flesh torn into pieces and consumed by the gloating dragons, afraid of what more he will do to me....

18. DR. JACKSON

Monday, June 29

On Monday, they went to see Dr. John Jackson, an older Southern gentleman who had taken care of Henry's parents before they died. Dr. Jackson would help them without insurance or an ID card for Anne.

They were shown in to the exam room by his nurse, Katie, who greeted them with a smile. "Good Morning, Henry! Nice to see you again. This must be Anne. Come on right over here and sit down, sweetie." She patted the examination table. Anne hopped up.

Katie took her blood pressure, noting the results on the chart. "120 over 80, that's good." She took Anne's temperature. "Temperature is normal. Is she on any medications? Are there any issues that you are aware of?"

"No on both," Henry answered. "She seems fine."

"Are we doing a full exam today?"

"I guess so," Henry answered. "I want to make sure she is checked out from head to toe."

"Okay," Katie pulled out the paper gown doctors provide that never seem to cover enough. "Anne, take off all of your clothes and put the gown on open in the front." She laid out the necessary medical instruments, then left the room. Anne disrobed, donning the paper gown as instructed.

A few minutes later, Dr. Jackson entered with Katie close at his heels. "Mornin' Henry. And this apple blossom must be Anne. Good mornin' little lady. Pleased to make your acquaintance," he said with a slight bow. "Let's have a look see at you then." He listened to her heart and lungs, then performed a physical examination of her body. He spent a few minutes examining the birthmarks on her back. "Interesting," he commented. "I've never seen birthmarks so even. Hmmm."

"But they are birthmarks, not scars?" Henry asked.

"Yep, strawberry birthmarks. Nothing to worry about." Dr. Jackson said.

"Lie down now, honey," he instructed. "So, we are going to do a pelvic exam today?"

"Yes. I want to know if there is any indication that something happened to her, any signs of past abuse or injuries," Henry said.

Dr. Jackson pulled out the stirrups and told Anne to put her feet on the cold steel. "This might feel a bit uncomfortable," he warned. Anne winced a bit, but remained still during the examination.

"Well," he said removing his gloves. "I checked her out from her bonnet to her bunions and everything appears to be right as rain as near as I can tell. I don't see any indication of abuse or injury, either physical or sexual, although I do see indications of recent sexual activity." He looked up at Henry. "I reckon y'all had something to do with that?"

"Yes," Henry confessed, his face turning red.

Dr. Jackson stood up and wrote on the chart. "I would like to do a complete blood workup and an electrolyte panel, a skeletal survey and certainly, a CT scan of her brain, to make sure there are no indications of internal injuries or abnormalities. We can take the blood here today, but y'all have to set up the x-rays and CT Scan. I'll give you an order for it. I won't charge you for today, but can y'all handle the cost for the other tests?"

"Yes," Henry affirmed. "I can handle it." He had quite a bit of money saved up by inheriting his parents' home.

"Okay. Anne, honey, it has been a pleasure. I'll see you soon." He offered his hand to help her sit up. "Katie will be back to get the blood sample."

Katie returned with a bin with tubes and syringes. "This might hurt just a bit," she said inserting the needle into Anne's arm. Anne did not move, but watched the dark red liquid fill several small tubes.

"Okay," the nurse said. "Go ahead and get dressed. I'll be back with your orders."

Anne dressed, examining the Band-Aid and cotton ball taped to the inside of her arm. Katie returned in just a few minutes with a clipboard. "Okay, Doctor wants a full set of x-rays and a CT Scan. Here's a list of places you can go that will take her without insurance, but you'll need to pay cash. Call us after you do to set up a return appointment."

"We will." Henry took the papers.

"Nice to meet you, Anne." Katie shook Anne's hand. "We'll see you soon."

They left the doctor's office and headed home. "What is an x-ray? What is CT Scan?" Anne asked.

"A CT Scan takes a picture of what's inside you. Susan suggested the memory loss may be due to a prior injury. The CT Scan will tell us that. X-rays are where they take pictures of the bones inside of you. I just want to be sure we do everything we can to help you regain your memory and to make sure nothing happened to you."

"I would like to remember," she said. "All I see are the dreams."

"I know. We'll work on that too. Susan said maybe by writing the story, we can get the cause of the nightmares to come out. But we'll only go as fast as you feel you can handle."

"I am good," she said.

"Okay, are you up to working on it some more today?"

"Yes." They remained silent for the remainder of the ride.

Once home, Anne retreated to her own art table to work on her latest painting of the dragons building the Crystal Mountains. The picture depicted three dragons in a circle with the pieces of the crystal floating over their heads, conducting what Anne now knew to be telekinesis. Fortunately, lately her dreams consisted of more and more of the happier day-to-day glimpses into the lives of the golden dragons before the nightmare took over. She slipped on her headphones to listen to a new audio book, *The Princess Bride*, then sprayed down her sheet to resume her painting.

Henry sat at his desk in the studio and turned on his laptop to do some research on memory loss. He flipped through countless web pages and read all he could on the different types of amnesia. Retrograde, Anterograde, Post-Traumatic, Dissociative, Lacunar, Childhood Transient Global, and on and on! He never guessed that there were so many types of amnesia!

Anne had no difficulty remembering things since he met her. In fact, her memory was almost photographic. Her ability to see or hear something once, then remember it was incredible! It was only her past that escaped her. About the only thing she struggled with was mastering the English language. So many words have double meanings and most people speak in contractions or slang. All in all, she was holding her own, even though she would get mixed up or confused once in a while. In a way, it was quite charming.

Until she had her medical test done and they got the results, no one could determine if this was physically or psychologically induced, or possibly both. Henry didn't think her amnesia was caused by a specific incident. He reasoned that a person who had amnesia due to a traumatic event would probably remember something prior to the event. Anne had no memories at all! Or perhaps she did, but somehow her memories had been transformed into this fantasy world of mind-reading dragons and mountains made of crystal. Nowhere could he find any example of anyone forgetting their past life and replacing it with an entirely new one—especially a fictitious one. Assuming he was right, and her dreams were distorted memories, it only served to make her situation more complex and unique.

He found the description of dissociative amnesia interesting because a person could forget his or her entire life. She had not only forgotten her life, she'd forgotten how to talk, walk or even eat, regressing to the level of a newborn! Amnesia that would cause such a severe loss had to be from a significant event. But muscle memory should have remained, bodies working on autopilot for the most part. He was anxious to get Anne tested.

His head hurting from all the research, Henry took a break and played solitaire on the computer to get his mind off the enormity of the task ahead of him. Try as he might to clear his thoughts, that nagging question kept creeping back into his brain like a spider skittering across his synapses... *what if?*

What if he did find out what happened? Could he truly handle it? What if the truth was something so horrific and unspeakable that it was unbearable? Could it destroy both of them if they found out? What if he stopped looking for answers and let her go on with no memories at all? Should he keep this new Anne all to himself, leaving her past behind, vowing to never to look back? Would that condemn the woman he loved to a lifetime of nightmares and unanswered questions? She was bright and intelligent and filled with curiosity. She already wondered what her real name was, when her birthday was, where she came from. He couldn't deny her that. His mind was spinning with the possibilities.

Finally, he'd had enough of the bright screen and closed the laptop, shutting it off. Anne was still engrossed in her paintings, lost in the fantasy of the story. Henry smiled, got up from his chair and touched her on the shoulder. She turned off the audio and took off her headphones.

"I can't work anymore. Do you want to come on a run with me?"

She nodded, putting her brush in the water and the headphones down on the table. They changed into running clothes and shoes and started out running down the street. Henry really didn't have a plan where to go, he just wanted to move. He would, however, keep to the neighborhood streets because it was dark. He knew these streets and neighborhood well, and was running on autopilot.

It was on their way back that Henry noticed the black SUV following them. Something was seriously wrong here. He didn't want to alert Anne, so he decided to go somewhere public and get off the deserted streets. "Let's go to the gas station and get a drink," he told Anne, keeping an eye on the car. They sprinted out onto the main road and ducked into the first building that was well lit, a small convenience store. The SUV followed, turning onto the highway, slowing down past their location, before speeding up where it was swallowed by the night. Henry waited a few minutes to make sure it didn't come back, then guided Anne back through the small streets that led home. Either he was going crazy seeing shadows and cars following them, or there was something nefarious in Anne's past that had caught up with them. Whichever way he looked at it, he had a bad feeling about it.

After my wings are devoured, Saphan orders the black dragons to hold down my beautiful tail. I thrash it back and forth in my pain and anger. Several dragons dig in their long sharp claws, preventing my strong tail from hitting them. Saphan pulls out the three fins from the tip. Then he takes the crystal sword and begins to saw into my flesh where my tail joins my body. I fight with everything I have left to escape the agony, but I cannot move. I beg him to stop, but he continues to saw through my muscles. My vision fades and my strength fails me as the pain overwhelms me. Saphan throws my severed tail to the black dragons who fight over it to feast....

19. MORE TESTS

Tuesday, June 30

Anne went for her x-rays and CT scans the next day. She was more nervous about the CT scan's narrow tube than the open but uncomfortable x-ray machine where the radiographer bent her body in ways it wasn't designed to be bent. The technician and Henry assured her she would not get stuck in there. Henry had her bring along her audio book so she could listen to her stories. She was enjoying the stories with rich characters, adventures and romance.

As she was pushed into the machine, Anne's heart raced. She gripped the side of the table so tightly her fingers turned white. The technician piped in her audio book, helping her relax to the familiar voice of the narrator. The audio calmed her as the machine hummed, probing deep into her body to reveal the secrets it held. Before the chapter was finished, the scan was over. The technician pulled her out and helped her sit up.

"Was it as bad as you thought?" he asked with a smile.

"I was scared at first but then it was okay," she answered. Henry helped her off the table. After she dressed, they stopped at the checkout desk on the way out so Henry could pay the bill.

In the car, Henry asked her if she was okay.

"Yes," she said. "I was afraid at first but my stories made it better."

"Good. Some people have a hard time in the enclosed space. What do you want to do with the rest of our day?"

"I would like to make more paintings. I want to get the pictures in my head on the paper."

"Home it is."

They spent the remainder of their day together in the studio, Anne working on her drawings with her audio books, and Henry working on his illustration listening to the blaring music he called heavy metal. She did not like that music as much as the others. They took comfort in having the other near, while retreating to their private spaces, and interrupted regularly by a nosy feline or attention-starved canine.

Anne noticed something odd. Out of all the visitors that came slobbering her way, Flack was not among them. Anne put her brush down and went to find him. He was lying on his bed whimpering, his eyes sad. She picked him up and cuddled him, cooing softly.

"What's wrong?" Henry came to investigate why Anne left.

"Flack is dying," Anne whispered, rocking the little dog.

Henry stood still. "What do you mean? How do you know?"

"I know. I feel it."

Henry turned around, grabbed the car keys. "Let's go. We're going to the vet now!"

Anne wrapped Flack in his blanket and followed Henry to the car. He helped them get in. Anne cradled Flack. She cuddled both arms around him tightly, petting his little head, love in her eyes.

* * *

Henry tried to hold back his tears as they arrived at the vet's office, pulling into the parking space a bit too fast. He jumped out and rushed Anne and Flack into the reception area.

"Mr. Williford, how can I help you?" the nice lady behind the counter asked.

"He is dying," Anne said.

"Let's get you right in to exam room number 3. I'll let Dr. Lewis know and pull Flack's chart." She ushered them into a small exam room and shut the door.

Within two minutes, Dr. Lewis rushed into the room. "Hello Henry, what seems to be the problem?" He had Flack's chart in his hand.

"Anne believes he's dying," Henry said.

"Anne," Dr. Lewis said examining the little dog, who was having difficulty breathing. "Why do you think he's dying?"

"I know he is. I feel it."

Dr. Lewis listened to Flack's heart, felt his abdomen and nodded. "There is a chance you may be correct, but I need to run a few tests to confirm. I can call you and let you know what I find out, or do you want to wait?"

"We'll wait," Henry said, his arms around Anne. They both sat down on the bench in front of the examination table while Dr. Lewis took Flack away.

"How are you doing, sweetheart?" Henry rubbed Anne's back, knowing that if he was having such a difficult time dealing with another death, Anne must be too.

"I am fine," she said calmly. "Flack is going to be happy in his new home."

Henry assumed this was Anne's way of dealing with the loss. Perhaps she was in denial and was seeing the dog going to a better place, rather than facing the fact that the dog would be gone forever. But he wasn't going to break her bubble even if he didn't believe it. Maybe she couldn't face Flack's death because she would be reminded of the death she saw in her nightmares. He had to let her deal with this in her own way.

After an eternity, Dr. Lewis finally returned, without Flack. "You were right," he said gravely. "Flack passed while we were doing the echocardiogram. His little heart gave out. He was ready to go. I am so sorry for your loss. He was one tough little pup."

Henry's efforts to keep the tears in failed. They escaped from his eyes, making their way down his cheeks. He brushed the tears away and extended his other hand to Dr. Lewis. "Thank you, sir, for trying."

Dr. Lewis offered them a box of Kleenex. Anne was not crying, instead she had a peaceful look on her face and a small smile on her lips.

"What do you want to do with him? I can offer cremation services, if you like."

"Thank you," Henry said, his voice cracking. "But I'll take him home and bury him in the back yard, where his brothers can still be near to him."

Dr. Lewis nodded and went to retrieve the body.

Henry put his hand on Anne's shoulder. "Are you sure you're okay?"

"I am okay," she put her hand on his. "I am happy for Flack. I see him running now with the other dogs in the bright place. Do not cry, Henry. This is a happy time for him. He no longer needs his cart, his legs are fine."

Henry had to use the Kleenex. Anne's statement made the tears come on stronger. He was glad she was doing okay because he didn't think he could be strong enough if she lost it too.

Dr. Lewis brought back a cardboard carrying box with Flack's body inside. Henry nodded silently and took it. The receptionist offered her condolences, and told him they'd bill him instead of dealing with payment at that moment.

Back home, Henry performed the sad task of digging the tiny grave with trembling hands and eyes blurred with tears. He buried his brave companion in the yard near the back fence, with all the other animals in attendance to say their goodbyes. He marked the grave with a large slab of granite he took from the front of the house. Flack's little wheelchair was buried with him.

While his sons gorge on my tail, Saphan covers me with his massive body. "I warned you what would happen when you refused me." Under his onslaught, I shriek. The weight of his enormous form crushes me. "You were always mine." His voice is not in my head anymore but fills my ears with painful vibrations.

"Please..." I try to move away.

"You belong to me for all time now and I will enjoy every moment of your suffering." His body tears me inside. He bites my back and shoulders, tearing skin and muscle, and swallowing. He sears the wounds with his hot fiery breath. The agony is unbearable from his attack, the other black dragons dancing around us in a circle, watching with glee in their red eyes. The more I try to get out from under him, the harder he bites. The other dragons laugh. I can only hope he kills me soon and makes the pain stop...

20. RESULTS ARE IN

Wednesday, July 1

Anne was sitting with Henry in the studio working on their book when the phone rang. It was Katie from Dr. Jackson's office. Anne moved closer to Henry so she could hear.

"Hi Henry and Anne, we got the test results back. Dr. Jackson wants to see you both to talk about them. Can you come in tomorrow about three?"

"Sure," Henry said. "We'll be there. Thanks!" He ended the call and turned to Anne. "Dr. Jackson has your test results back. Hopefully, we can find some answers."

"That is good," she replied. She was anxious about what was going on inside her. She did not understand why she could not remember anything before Henry found her, or why she had the same dreams night after night. She felt uneasiness in her stomach after the call, hoping Dr. Jackson would have answers.

That night, Anne's nightmares were more intense than they'd been in days.

"Anne!" Henry's voice pulled her from the dark, quieting her screams in the dim bedroom. "Anne, wake up! It's okay," he whispered holding her. "It's okay. You're with me. There are no dragons. You're safe. It seems like the nightmares have been getting worse these last few nights. I wonder if you should talk to Susan."

"I will do what you think best." She snuggled deeper into his arms, her wet cheek dampening the hair on his chest. The bed grew crowded as several of their companions joined them.

"I'll call her tomorrow and set something up after we see Dr. Jackson."

Anne held on to him until she finally fell back asleep.

* * *

Henry stayed awake for a long time, staring into the dark room, his heart breaking for the woman in his arms. He could only imagine what she was going through each time the nightmares came. It wasn't just the nightmares though. How could anyone deal with losing an entire life? How would he react if it was him? He'd probably be a lot worse off than Anne. Despite the unknown horrors in her past, she always had a smile and a positive outlook on everything. She never let anything get her down. He snuggled closer to her, kissing her head, wishing her troubles away.

He thought he might have fallen back asleep and was also dreaming when a dark shadow figure move quickly across the room, then disappeared. This seemed to be happening a lot lately. Maybe the house was haunted. As he drifted off to sleep, his last thought was, *Who you gonna call?*

I lie in darkness too weak to do anything but wait for the black dragons to take me to Saphan again. My back and neck are torn open from his long teeth. My beautiful wings are gone. My strong tail is gone. I will never again fly over the Crystal Mountains into the silver sky. I will never see Kenta, my friends, or my father. I will never play with the little dragons on the water while we chase the silver fish. I will never rest again at the bottom of the green oceans, the water cool against my skin. I will never see the white sun again. I will never know love....

21. ANSWERS

Thursday, July 2

Henry awoke with a pounding headache. His body was telling him to stay in bed, but there were animals to be fed and answers to be faced. He ignored his body's protest and forced his weary bones out of bed and headed to the kitchen. He was thrilled to find that Anne had already fed the animals. A wave of sadness rippled through his heart remembering Flack was no longer among them.

"Thanks for feeding the hoard," he said, sitting at the table.

"You needed more sleep," Anne replied, placing a steaming cup of coffee in front of him.

"Oh, and thanks for this too! I thought I smelled Dark Roast, but was afraid I was only dreaming." Henry grabbed her hand and kissed it before she could get away. One of the best things he'd taught her was how to make coffee in the morning. He took a big slurp of the dark brew, and life returned with the hot liquid coursing through his system.

"I thought we might go to the beach today since we don't have to see Dr. Jackson until three. Would you like that?"

She smiled. "Yes!"

Anne loved the beach, and the outing might serve as a distraction, keeping both their minds off the pending doctor appointment and the results.

Anne was adventurous with her newly learned kitchen skills, and treated Henry to a delicious breakfast of scrambled eggs, toast, coffee, and orange juice. She picked up most of it just by watching him, although she was nervous around the flames of the gas stove at first. When a girl dreams every night of herself and everyone she loves being incinerated, being around fire was, understandably, upsetting. But she handled it well, and Henry was proud of how brave she was.

After breakfast, they divided up the tasks of preparing for a trip to the beach. Henry packed the blanket, beach towels, and suntan lotion before filling the cooler with ice and bottled water. Anne packed a bag of chips, grapes, and whole wheat chicken wraps she'd made all by herself. The only thing left to do was to jump into their bathing suits: a hot pink bikini with matching floppy hat for Anne, and swim trunks patterned after the American Flag for Henry. Once dressed, they headed out to Venice Beach.

The beach was already crowded by the time they arrived. They cautiously tipped-toed around the tourists, as if maneuvering a mine field, until they found a quiet spot. Henry spread out the blanket and in moments, they were lathered up with sunscreen and racing each other to the water. Henry didn't hold back this time. At a full gallop, he scooped up Anne in his arms and tossed her in. Anne squealed in shock and disappeared beneath the surface, only to emerge a moment later with her hands cupped, dowsing Henry in playful retaliation. They laughed and giggled, chasing each other amongst the waves, splashing, grabbing, and tickling along the way. Finally, they headed to their spot to enjoy the sun and relax.

* * *

Anne followed Henry back to the blanket where he put on his sunglasses and stretched out his lean muscular frame, tucking one arm under his head. She lay on her back, donning her beach hat, and tilted forward, casting a speckled shadow across her face.

Listening to the heartbeat of the ocean waves upon the shore, Anne's thoughts swept away with the current to the distant land in her dreams. She imagined herself lying on the top shelf of her home in the Crystal Mountains. The Florida sun was replaced by the white sun in the sky of the golden dragons, and it was Kenta, not Henry, by her side. Since her own memories abandoned her, maybe she could borrow someone else's for a while, even if they were only make believe. Comforted, Anne slipped into a dreamless sleep.

* * *

After a bit, Henry noticed Anne had nodded off. He woke her up by stroking her cheek with the back of his hand. "Hey, Sleeping Beauty, if you don't turn over soon, you're going to go from medium well to extra crispy."

"Huh?" Anne replied, confused.

"You'll get sunburned. Remember, we talked about this?"

"Yes, I remember. Why didn't you say that instead of me getting more crispy?"

"You're right, I should have been more specific," Henry tried not to laugh. "Turn over, I'll put some suntan lotion on you." Anne rolled onto her stomach, rearranged her hat, and rested her head on her arms. Henry squeezed a generous amount of coconut oil onto his hands, then started to rub it on her back, spending extra time examining her birthmarks. Anne tensed up at first when the cool liquid touched her hot skin, then her muscles relaxed under his touch.

"Your birthmarks are fascinating," Henry said tracing the outline of each.

"I do not know. I have never seen them," Anne said.

Henry stopped his movements, surprised. He took a picture of her back with his phone and showed it to her.

"Do you feel the extra joint in your back?" he asked.

She put the phone down and tried to turn her head to see her back. She shook her head. "I do not feel anything different. Do not other people have this joint?"

Henry pressed her back under her shoulder blades feeling the bony protrusion of her anomaly under his fingers. "Not that I've ever heard." He kissed her back. "You are unique."

"I am unique." She smiled and laid her head down on her arms.

At one point, Henry unfastened the strap to her bikini, exposing her back and part of her breast to the warmth of the sun and his caress, causing Anne to gasp and bite her lower lip. He slowly worked his way from her breast to her sides and down her back to the base of her spine, slipping his fingertips under the edge of her bikini bottom. When he applied oil to her upper thighs. Anne began to moan and tremble, her hips grinding ever so slightly into the hot sand.

"Is everything alright?" a clueless Henry inquired. One could almost hear the needle scratch across the record as the music stopped. He knelt, his hands held up in front of him like a surgeon preparing to operate.

Anne turned and looked at him with wide eyes and a furrowed brow, making a low pleading groan in her throat, unable to speak.

"What's the mat—? Oh, *oh*!" Henry looked down, feeling foolish. "Um, sorry about that. I didn't think." He had a stupid smile on his face. Anne rolled her eyes and took some deep breaths.

Henry's mind had been occupied with the pending appointment with Dr. Jackson, but his body followed its own lead. "I'll make it up to you tonight, I promise." He sat back, wiping his hands on his suit. "Why don't we have something to eat?" Anxious to put this incident behind them, Henry was as clumsy as a boy with his prom date refastening Anne's bikini top—partially because of his oily hands, but mostly, because his own body had responded in kind. He had 'Venice Beach Barbie' all oiled up and raring to go, and there wasn't a damn thing he could do about it at the moment. He now understood why sometimes mistakes were referred to as "boners." Only

Henry could turn a simple outing to the beach into a trip down the erotic highway without trying, or even being aware.

Henry took their lunch from the basket. He couldn't shake the feeling he'd just been caught, like his parents had walked in on him and his girl. He felt every eye on the beach staring at him. It was all his imagination of course, but he couldn't make eye contact with anyone. Halfway through eating her wrap, Anne reached over and gave Henry a reassuring kiss on the cheek. Then she hauled off and slugged him in the arm.

"I deserve that one, I admit that," Henry said humbly.

"Are things like this why Heidi calls you dufus?"

"Yeah, pretty much."

"Okay, dufus."

* * *

As soon as they finished eating, Henry told Anne it was time to go. She packed up the food while Henry gathered their belongings. They didn't bother washing the sand off their feet. Henry drove home barefoot.

Once home, they put the food away, and tossed their towels and swim suits into the laundry basket. They showered together, but not before Anne made Henry make good on his promise. He was happy to comply.

On the way to Dr. Jackson's office on Jacaranda Boulevard, Anne's trepidation of what they would hear crept back into her stomach. There had to be something wrong with her that caused her loss of memory. She hoped she would know something more today, anything.

Katie greeted them with a smile, then led them to the examination room. "He'll be right with y'all," she said, depositing Anne's chart in the basket outside the room. A few minutes later, Dr. Jackson came in, chart in hand, and shook both of their hands.

"Howdy, nice to see you folks this fine day." He smiled. "I reckon y'all want to hear the results of Anne's tests."

They both took a deep breath.

"And..." he hesitated, scanning the charts, "everything is hunky dory."

Anne and Henry looked at each other, mouths open.

"In fact," Dr. Jackson continued with incredulity in his voice, "I didn't find anything out of kilter. She's in perfect health. Her blood levels are exactly where they ought to be, her pap is right as rain. The CT Scan was perfect. Other than the anomaly the hospital found on her shoulder blades, the skeletal scan was normal. I can't find an explanation for the extra joints but they don't seem to hamper her at all. I've never seen anyone in such perfect health before. There's just nothing physically wrong with her that would explain the memory loss or the nightmares. She's fit as a fiddle."

"What do we do now?" Henry asked.

"Well, I can't find a medical reason for her condition. Perhaps y'all should consider a psychological one. Might be good for Anne to have a chat with Dr. Rayback."

"I was going to call her this afternoon once we talked to you," Henry said. "We'll try that and see what she has to say."

"I'm sorry I didn't find an easy solution," Dr. Jackson took Anne's hand. "As far as the memory loss, there isn't much I can do for you. I can give you something to help you sleep. Do you want something for that?"

"No," Anne said. "I am scared, but I need to see what happens in my dreams. I do not want to lose them."

"Let me know what Dr. Rayback has to say," Dr. Jackson stood. "Hopefully we can get to the bottom of what's going on. If anything changes, call me. Otherwise, I'll see you in six months to check her progress." Before he left, he said, "I have very much enjoyed meeting you Anne. You're a refreshing breath of air from my usual patients."

On the way to the car, Henry called Susan's office and made an appointment with her for Monday. Somewhere, they would find the answer to her past.

I do not know how long I have endured the torment of Saphan and his black dragons. They mock me, tossing the burned hides of my kind before me, to remind me I am alone. I cannot even cry anymore. I do not have the strength. My father, my guardian, even the little ones, are consumed by the fires brought by the black dragons. I grieve each one, enduring the constant abuse from my father's brother. Each time he takes me, he gorges on my flesh, leaving my back raw. Finished with each attack, I am thrown into the darkness to cry alone. I wait until I can finally be released by death. I have nothing left but memories and anguish. It is so dark where I am, so lonely....

22. TALE OF THE PRINCESS DRAGON

Friday, July 3

Anne and Henry enjoyed writing their book together. Henry took out his laptop to continue where they'd left off, while Anne gathered her paintings.

Once upon a time, there was a kingdom of dragons, the Thraekenya. They lived on a crystal mountain in a far off land, surrounded by a green ocean with a white sun in the sky. The dragons were a beautiful gold, each with different colored wings; blue, green, orange, yellow, and white.

The Thraekenya were ruled over by two brothers, Aesmay and Saphan. Aesmay, the older brother, was King and Saphan, his Captain. Aesmay and Saphan had iridescent wings that reflected all the colors of the Thraekenya.

The Thraekenya lived in beautiful lairs made from the crystals of the mountains. They were happy, flying high over the mountains and swimming in the green ocean where they dove to catch silver fish. They lay on the shelves of their lairs and soaked up the warmth of the white sun. At night, the sky was lit by two bright moons circling in the sky overhead.

Aesmay had a daughter named Aeya. Her wings were the prettiest of all of the dragons, and shimmered with traces of all the colors that moved over her iridescent wings like sunlight on water. Aeya fell in love with a dragon named Kenta. But Saphan secretly loved Aeya and wanted her to be with him. Every time he saw Aeya and Kenta together, he grew angrier.

One day, Saphan told Aesmay he wanted Aeya to be with him. Aesmay said Aeya could not be with him because she had chosen another. Saphan decided he did not want Aesmay to tell him what to do, so he came to Aesmay, lying on the highest shelf, and told the King he would not obey his commands anymore.

Aesmay was sad that his brother was angry, but because he was King, he could not let Saphan disobey him. He told Saphan if he did not obey the King's orders, he would have to leave the Kingdom. Saphan refused to obey.

Aesmay banished Saphan and those of his army who were loyal to him. He sent them to the other side of the world where black mountains spouting fire towered over dark waters. Aesmay put up a wall between the two worlds, so Saphan and his followers could not return to live with the Thraekenya.

After Saphan and his followers left, Aesmay was unhappy. He asked Aeya and Kenta to help him rule the Thraekenya. Aeya and Kenta helped Aesmay by judging the disagreements between the other dragons. Aesmay lay on his shelf and thought of his brother whom he had banished.

Saphan and his followers went to live on the other side of the world. The more they thought about how angry they were, they began to change. They started to walk on their hind legs and their feet grew long. Their beautiful wings grew gray. Their eyes turned red. Most of all, their beautiful golden skin turned black with hard scales. They called themselves Tannen. They ate black rocks from the mountain and learned to create fire in their breaths.

One day, the shield above the Crystal Mountains was torn and Saphan and his followers came out of the sky with fire spewing from their mouths. Saphan went to where Aesmay lay and took a piece of the crystal mountain that he had hewn with his claws. He killed Aesmay. The other Thraekenya were scattered when the Tannen attacked with the hot fire.

"Okay," Henry said after they agreed on the story to this point. "Where do we go from here? We don't want to have everyone killed and you don't remember anything after this."

"We need a happy ending," Anne agreed. "All princesses should have a happy ending."

"Okay, let's say Kenta escapes the attack and comes back to rescue Aeya. Like in your princess movies."

Anne smiled and nodded. "I'd like that."

Henry turned back to the laptop. "So Kenta escaped..." he typed.

Kenta escaped by hiding deep in the ocean when Aeya was taken by Saphan and his army to the Black Mountains.

Aeya was sad about the death of her father and missed Kenta. Saphan told her she must be his queen and rule over the Tannen. He treated her cruelly and kept her locked up in the center of the mountain where he had dug a deep tunnel with his claws.

Kenta gathered up the Thraekenya who were scattered and brought them back to the top of the Crystal Mountain. They buried Aesmay deep in the sand under the water and mourned him for three days. After the time of mourning their King, Kenta went to look for Aeya. He searched all of the Crystal Mountains and everywhere in the green water. He finally knew he would have to go to the Black Mountains to look for Aeya because that was where Saphan must be holding her.

Kenta created a long sword out of the crystal in the mountain and took down the barrier between the sides of the world. He flew off in search of Saphan and Aeya, his love.

He flew for a long time. The world start to dim as he crossed over to the Black Mountains. The water grew darker and the mountains lost the shine of the crystals. He was getting closer to where Aeya was being held.

"Not bad so far," Henry observed. "I think this will be a good story."

"Is that an act of true love, what Kenta is doing?" Anne asked.

"Well," Henry said. "I guess that *is* love. He was willing to put his life on the line to go and save his princess. So what happens next?"

"He must find her...."

Kenta flew until his wings ached. Finally, he reached the dark mountain where Saphan hid. Kenta landed on the top of the mountain and called for Saphan to face him.

Saphan and the Tannen rose from the tunnels and surrounded him. They brought Aeya up with them, and Kenta's heart froze at how sad she was.

"Saphan," Kenta called. "Let Aeya go. Let us settle this between us."

Saphan laughed. "Why would I let her go? She is so beautiful. She will be my Queen. How can you stop me?"

Kenta was afraid, but he could not leave his princess. He rose up on his hind legs so that he could look Saphan in the eyes and said, "I will never let her be your Queen. I love her."

All the Tannen laughed and circled around Kenta. Aeya cried out to her love. Kenta prayed to the Creator of All to give him strength. He held up his crystal sword. His mighty wings flapped hard to keep him balanced on his hind legs but he was determined to meet his enemy on an equal level.

"This is getting exciting," Henry commented. "I'm really enjoying writing this story with you."

"Me too," Anne agreed. "Now what do we do?"

"They fight...."

Kenta swung his sword at Saphan, only to be met with a flash of light when Saphan's black crystal sword connected with his. He swung again and again, each time, only to meet Saphan's countermoves. They fought for a long time, growling and slashing each other with swords and their claws.

Aeya wept as her love fought Saphan.

Finally, Saphan could fight no longer. He grabbed Aeya by her long neck and put his sword against it. "Stop, or I will kill her!" He threatened.

Kenta stopped his advance. "No!" He cried. "I will not let any harm come to her." He threw down his sword and bowed before Saphan. He loved Aeya so much that he would offer his own life to save hers.

Suddenly, a bright light shot out from the dark clouds overhead. The rays of the white sun pierced the darkness and burned the Tannen. "

What magic is this!" cried Saphan. Smoke rose from his skin.

A loud voice was heard on the rays of white light. "Because Kenta was willing to give his life for Aeya, I will fight for him," the Creator of All roared. Saphan and the rest of the Tannen crawled back into their tunnels and left Kenta and Aeya alone. They never bothered the Thraekenya again.

Kenta and Aeya flew home to the Crystal Mountains. Because her father was dead, Aeya became the Queen of the Thraekenya and Kenta became her King. The dragons could once more fly across the sky, swim in the water and lie on their shelves. Queen Aeya and Kenta lived happily ever after.

"The End!" Henry typed the words. "Now you have to give it a title, and pick which drawings go with the story. Do you want my help with that?"

"No, it is good for me to do the paintings," she replied. "It helps me making the dragons. What is a title?"

"What we call the book."

"I like fairy tales. Can we call it *Tale of the Princess Dragon*?"

"*Tale of the Princess Dragon* it is." Henry smiled and put the title on the story. "Okey doke," he said. "The illustrations are all yours. I'll contact Elliott and see if he can shop for publishers. I'l send him the manuscript to get some feedback. Just tell me what text you want on each piece."

As Anne sorted through her finished pieces to determine which ones she could use and which ones she still needed to do, the meaning of an act of true love, like the one they wrote about in their story, latched onto her heart and did not let go. She wanted to know more about this kind of love. Was this what she felt for Henry? Had she ever felt this way before? She couldn't remember. Why was it so hard?

The black dragons come and drag me to Saphan again.

"You know I hurt you because you would not choose me on your own," he hisses at me. "You are alone and will always be alone." He begins his assault. "And you are mine forever to do with as I please." When he does not taunt me, the other dragons take up his words, laughing at me.

He has taken away all that I love. I am weak as much from despair as from the torture. There is no one to help me. All I can do is hope death will bring relief....

23. FOURTH OF JULY

Saturday, July 4

Henry and Anne arrived at James and Heidi's house around ten in the morning on the Fourth of July. They joined the others, who were already poolside. Henry handed a copy of *Tale of the Princess Dragon* to Heidi and waited while she read it.

"This is wonderful!" Heidi exclaimed. They sat around the pool watching the kids swim. "I can't wait to see the illustrations!"

"Let me see, let me see!" Robbie grabbed at the papers, dripping water.

"Stop that, Robbie!" she yelled. "You're wet! You'll ruin the paper! Sit here next to me and I'll read it to you. Nattie, wanna hear a story?"

Nattie was already out of the pool following her brother. She climbed up into her mother's lap, plugging her thumb in her mouth. She wrapped herself in her beach towel and laid her head on Heidi's chest. Robbie curled up against her on the side of the lounge chair. Heidi read them the story, supplying different voices for each character. Even James was intrigued, standing behind her as she read, her voice transporting all of them into the strange and beautiful world created by Henry and Anne.

James stood up from where he was leaning on the back of the chair. "I have to say, that's pretty good! What's your next step? And, please, Henry, let me negotiate any contract."

"Well," Henry replied. "First, of course I want you in on any negotiations. I've asked Elliott to check out some publishers to see if anyone is interested. If we get an offer, I'll have you check it out. In the meantime, Anne has a lot of work to do to finish the illustrations. She wants to do them all herself, and I'm okay with that."

Anne nodded. "I see the pictures in my head. It is easy to paint them."

James looked at her with concern. "Have you talked with Dr. Jackson yet about the test results?"

"Yes," Henry said. "There's nothing physically wrong with her that would explain the memory loss or the nightmares. I've made another appointment to see Susan."

"I haven't found any more information on a fire in the area where someone has gone missing," James offered. "I've got a friend in Sarasota County looking into it. I also checked with someone in the Coast Guard for a fire on a boat, but nothing popped."

Heidi put Nattie down and handed the printed manuscript back to Henry, who returned it to the briefcase next to his chair. "We'll find out something, I'm sure, Sweetie," she reassured Anne. "In the meantime, you're all ours!"

Robbie was bored. He hopped down off his mothers' lap and jumped in the pool splashing all of the adults. Little Nattie adjusted the small swimming floats around her tiny arms and followed Robbie in.

"Well," Heidi said water dripping off her head, "I guess it's swim time!"

"I couldn't agree more!" Henry stood up. He offered one hand to his sister, the other to Anne and tilted his chin towards James. "You comin'?"

"Wouldn't miss it for the world!" He grabbed his wife's free hand.

"Okay then, everyone, on three! One...two...three, *group cannon balllll!*" Henry screamed. The four of them charged the pool, leapt into the air, and came splashing down in a curled up pile of arms and legs. Water sprayed out in every direction, followed by a huge wave. Nattie squealed and laughed and grabbed onto Robbie for dear life. The children were swept away in the ensuing tsunami and washed up on the steps leading into the pool.

"That was awesome, Uncle Henry, *do it again!*" Robbie pleaded.

"No, no," cough, cough, gasped Heidi, "once is more than enough, thank you. I think I swallowed half of the pool."

"Awe mom!" Robbie lamented.

"C'mon, Robbie, let's show 'em how it's done. Do you think we can make an even bigger one?" Uncle Henry came to the rescue.

"Yeah!"

Cannon balls were continually launched into the pool until it was time for James to start the steaks and other assorted goodies, since the coals were ready and glowing red. Heidi and Anne went to the kitchen to retrieve the meat for the fire. Henry made sure the kids stayed out of the way.

* * *

In the kitchen, Anne noticed a pitcher of brightly colored liquid with cherries and pineapple floating on top. Thirsty and curious, she asked Heidi, "Can I taste please?" she asked.

"Sure," Heidi said. "Help yourself."

Anne took a hurricane glass sitting on the counter and filled it to the rim. She took a small sip at first, smacked her lips, smiled, and took a few more. "I like it." She finished off the glass and poured another.

"Whoa, easy girl. Jim gets his rum from a client in Jamaica. That stuff'll knock you on your ass," Heidi warned.

Anne wasn't exactly sure what Heidi meant, and for some reason she didn't care either. She was experiencing a tingly feeling all over her body, and was in an inexplicably wonderful mood. She drank the second glass and refilled it again before following Heidi out with the plate of food for the barbecue, with the pitcher in hand.

* * *

Henry sipped his beer and watched his brother-in-law prepare for his role as pit master. James stood at the ready with spatula and tongs, donning a 007 LICENSE TO GRILL novelty apron. A brush and a bowl of marinade waited on the table by the outdoor kitchen. James took the first steak off the plate and threw it on the fire. Flames jumped and the meat sizzled deliciously.

"This stuff will knock your ass on," Anne proclaimed, taking another sip from her third glass of Piña Colada.

"Anne, honey," Henry sat up. "What the hell are you doing? You're not used to drinking."

"Did you know Jim gets this from a Jamaica? Whatever a Jamaica is? It tastes really good." She put the glass to her lips and guzzled it down, followed by a long, "BBRRRRRRRAAAAAAAAAPPPPP!" She held her hand to her lips with a look of surprise that turned into a giggle.

"Let her have as much as she wants," James called from the grill. "She's an adult."

"But she's not used to drinking," Heidi said. "She has no idea how this will affect her."

Anne steadied her glass, then refilled it, spilling some on her hand. "I can choose," she said defiantly.

Henry shook his head in disbelief, struggling with his next decision. "Alright, but this is the last glass. I'm cutting you off." He took the nearly empty pitcher away from her. "I'll just keep an eye on you and make sure you don't hurt yourself."

Heidi shrugged. "Your problem if she pukes. I'm not cleaning it up." She went back into the house to bring out plates and silverware. James had just plated the first of the grilled meat and placed it on the patio table when Heidi returned.

"Dig in!"

Heidi prepared a couple of hot dogs with potato chips, and sat the kids down to eat their dinner. Henry snared a large steak and sausage, a huge mound of potato salad and a roasted and buttered corn-on-the-cob. Anne had chicken, corn, and a third as much potato salad as Henry. Heidi and James finished off the steaks. After dinner, Heidi brought out cupcakes with red, white, and blue frosting for dessert.

Anne stood up to go to the bathroom then fell over onto Henry's chair.

"Whoa there, girl!" Henry caught her before she hurt herself. "You've had a bit too much to drink, young lady! I was afraid of this."

"I need...to peeeeeeeeeeee!" She drew out the word holding on to Henry.

"She's wasted," James said, laughing.

Mercifully, the kids were too preoccupied to notice, sticking out their multicolored tongues at each other and laughing.

Henry put his arms around Anne's waist. "I'll help her. Heidi, do you want to come along?"

"Oh, no, thank you. I told you if she blows chunks, it's your problem. I haven't held another girl's hair back while she called Ralph on the porcelain phone since...well, never mind when. Just don't get any on my new rug."

"She's not going to hurl, she just has to take a leak." He hoped.

"First time for everything," James commented.

Was this the first time she'd gotten drunk, Henry wondered. Had she ever used drugs? Wouldn't that have shown in her test results? Would he ever know?

Thankfully, the trip to the bathroom was uneventful, despite the fact that Henry had to guide Anne onto the seat. By the time they rejoined the group, it was time to pack everyone up to head out to see the fireworks. Henry debated taking Anne straight home to sleep it off, but she begged and pleaded because she was so looking forward to seeing fireworks for the first time. Not surprisingly, he gave into her, and they all climbed, or staggered, into James's SUV and headed to the beach nearest the Venice Jetty, which offered a spectacular view of the display.

At the beach, Anne lost her balance getting out of the car and fell back onto the side of the vehicle. "I feel thunny," she said, her speech slurring.

"You look thunny," Henry answered. "Come on." He put his arm around her waist, helping her to walk. "I've got you. James, can you get the chairs while I help Anne?"

"Sure, why not," James grumbled.

"Hey, you're the one who said, 'let her have all she wants,' remember?" Henry reminded him in a mocking tone.

"Yeah, yeah, I remember."

"Here, let me have the cooler. I can hold her up with one arm; she's just a little unsteady."

There was a little bit of beach left where they could all spread out. The sun lit up the sky with beautiful hues of blue and orange, flaming the clouds as it made its way down into the horizon. The crowded beach let creation know its appreciation with an enthusiastic round of applause, a fitting opening act to the fireworks show.

"Where did the sun go?" Anne shouted. "Did it go swimming?"

"You've seen a sunset before," Henry said, smiling. "The sun doesn't really go into the water, it just looks like that. Sit down and enjoy the fireworks." He guided her to a beach chair and sat her down.

She did, just in time for the show to begin. The fireworks were set off on a boat several yards from the shore. The blossoms of fiery beauty reflected over the surface of the water. Anne cried out at the first one. "Flowers in the sky!" She stood unsteadily and pointed.

Henry made her sit back down. "There's going to be more," he said firmly. "Stay in your chair."

As the exploding blooms filled the sky, and "ooohhs" and "aaahhhhs" came from the audience, Anne howled with delight at each display, clapping her hands, calling out the colors of the blasts. The children joined her, and all three hollered at the display. The people nearest them responded with not so nice looks. Henry explained to them that it was her first time and that she'd had a bit too much to drink. It didn't help. And frankly, he really didn't care if they didn't like it. He was just being nice.

The finale came with multiple fireworks filling the night sky with light, color and thunder. Everyone on the beach made noise now, drowning out Anne and the kids. The complainers near them had moved away, so Henry let her scream as loud as she wanted.

With the sky now dark but for trailing lines of smoke and the smell of sulfur, the crowd flowed to the parking lot and the mass of cars. Henry, Anne, Heidi, James and the kids stayed behind a few minutes until the web of traffic was not as tangled, before heading to the SUV.

By the time they got back to the house, Anne and the children had passed out. James scooped up Robbie, and Heidi took Nattie. Henry helped Anne out of the car, but she couldn't stand up. The rum and the excitement of the show had taken their toll on her, forcing Henry to pick her up with an audible groan. With Anne slung over his shoulder like a sack of potatoes, Henry had an awkward time bending to kiss his sister goodnight. "This has been a Fourth of July I won't soon forget. Thanks for everything." Henry took one of Anne's arms dangling in midair and helped her wave goodbye.

Back at his car, Henry propped Anne up against the passenger side and opened the door. Anne's head hung down and her hair covered her face. She rolled her head back and forth in a futile effort to stand up straight. Henry poured her into the seat, buckled her up, and lowered the seat so she could lie down. She sang a nonsensical tune to herself and kept her eyes closed.

Henry got Anne home, taking her right to bed. She was still humming her tune.

"Huuhhhh...Henry...." Anne said, her eyes half open. "I fly in the sky... you fly too?"

"Yes, I fly too, but not as high as you are at the moment." He pulled the blanket up to her neck. "Go to sleep." He kissed her on the forehead.

"I sleep," she slurred into a light snore.

Henry retreated to the bathroom, brushed his teeth and splashed water on his face and head, letting it linger there to drip back into the sink. He watched the cares of the day disappear down the drain. By the time he joined Anne in bed, she was already in the throes of another nightmare. He held her as he did every night, but this time Anne stayed asleep. He doubted very much if she would remember this dream, or even how she got home and into bed.

Anne finally settled down. Henry rolled over to his side of the bed. Just before shutting his eyes, he saw that damn shadow dart across the room again. He sat up with a start, his head spinning. He was worried about what he'd been seeing lately. Was he getting paranoid, seeing shadows in his room and mysterious cars following him? Or was there good reason to be concerned? Maybe he needed to talk to Susan too, so she could help him sort it all out. Finally, the beer and the late hour took their toll. He lay back down and fell into a deep sleep as soon as his head hit the pillow.

* * *

The mysterious black shadow oozed out of the corner and crept closer to the helpless couple, stopping at the foot of the bed. Slowly, it expanded and solidified into a huge grotesque, not quite human-like form with glowing red eyes. Despite its mass, it moved silently, sliding up along the side of the bed, stopping by Anne's head. Anne's breath turned to fog as the temperature in the room dropped dramatically. Leaning over her, its forked tongue whispered through jagged teeth into her shell-like ear. "*Soooooon!*"

I lie bleeding after my daily assault. But this time Saphan is not pleased.

"I grow bored of you. Take her to the black mountain and throw her into the fire," he orders. The other dragons lift me to carry me to the fire. "She will be an offering to the Master in celebration of his victory."

I wonder who this Master is as I am dragged away. I try to fight with what little strength I have, and beg him not to throw me into the fire, but he does not hear me over his own laughter....

24. THE MORNING AFTER

Sunday, July 5

Anne fought the demons in the night, screaming and dragging herself, the sheets, and blankets onto the floor. Henry jumped up and ran around the bed. Either the nightmare from earlier in the evening had returned, or she was just now sober enough to fully react to it. They were soon joined by a parade of concerned pets streaming into the room and surrounding them, sniffing and licking Anne wherever they could once she was still.

Anne woke up on the floor, disoriented and tangled in the sheets. She put her hands on her head and moaned, obviously suffering from a pounding headache. Henry brought her a bottle of water and handed her a couple of aspirin. "Take these and drink some water."

She managed to get most of the water down, although some spilled on her breasts, one of which had popped out of the bikini top she still wore.

"Come on." Henry helped her to her feet, fixing her wardrobe malfunction along the way. Still shaky, she was able to stand on her own. "I'll make you some breakfast." He put one arm around her waist. She put her arm around his neck and laid her head on his shoulder.

They started to walk a few feet when Anne stopped and promptly threw up all over Henry. Then she started to cry.

Henry stood for a long moment blinking in surprise. It had all happened so fast and unexpectedly, it took a few seconds for his brain to process. Then the odor of vomit wafted up his nose. *That's disgusting!* He turned his attention to Anne.

"Sweetheart, it's okay, don't cry," Henry said, reassuring her, guiding her back to the bed to sit, trying not to hug and redistribute the mess. He squatted in front of her and grabbed a nearby wastebasket. He was mid-sentence explaining what it was for when Anne blasted him with a second volley straight to the face. Anne's crying went off the chart and Charlie and Sam jumped up and started licking him.

"*Go...get! Damn it!*" Henry yelled.

"*Wahhhhh!*" Anne's crying soared up an octave.

Perfect! Henry grabbed a towel from the hamper and started to clean up the vomit on his face and bare chest. Then he wiped up the vomit on the floor, competing with the dogs. Finally, he had things cleaned up enough he could tend to Anne. She had fallen back onto the bed sobbing, tired, and weak.

"Anne? Honey? How are you doing?"

Her only reply was a long somber groan.

"Come on, we need to get you cleaned up." Henry escorted her to the bathroom. He had her rinse her mouth and splash water on her face, holding a cold wet washcloth to the back of her neck.

"Do you remember if you've ever felt like this before?" he asked.

"*Nooo!* And I never want to feel like this ever again." She winced at her own voice.

"Didn't think so. Brush your teeth and we'll jump in the shower."

Under the steamy waters, Henry could feel his pores opening and the morning's mishap circling the drain. Anne was still among the walking dead. She leaned against him letting him wash her as best he could.

"That'll make you feel better." Henry helped her out of the shower, wrapped a towel around her and sat her back on the bed. He toweled himself dry and slipped into a pair of running shorts and a muscle shirt. Anne found the strength to drag a comb through her hair while Henry retrieved a pair of pink shorts and T-shirt for her to wear.

They made their way to the kitchen where Henry gave Charlie, Sam, and the rest of the menagerie a more suitable breakfast than blown chunks. He gave Anne some herbal tea and dry toast to settle her queasy stomach. He made himself a strong cup of coffee and ate a stale powdered doughnut which, up until now, had been forgotten in a bag tucked in the back of the cupboard.

Anne started to feel a little better, the color coming back into her face as she sipped her tea and nibbled her toast.

"I think we'll just stay in today," he said. "You need a day of rest."

"What is rest?"

"Doing nothing. A day where we don't have to go anywhere or do any work. We'll just hang out with the animals."

They finished their breakfast and Henry cleaned up. Anne stayed in her seat for a while petting each critter who came to say good morning. Henry opened the doggy door so the animals could go outside into the bright Florida morning sun.

After the morning chores were done, they went into the living room and sat on the sofa, turning on the television. The set came on to a church service where a Pastor was in the middle of a sermon.

"Do you know," the Pastor said leaning on the pulpit on his forearm, the other hand pointed at the audience. "Even if you were the only person on this earth who would ever believe in him, Jesus would still have gone to the cross for you? You mean that much to him. Jesus chose to suffer the pain he knew he would endure because we were all sinners. We didn't even know him yet, and still he chose to go to death on Calvary for us. He made the sacrifice.

"We need to be reminded why that sacrifice was made. You cannot earn your way into Heaven. All your good deeds are as filthy rags to him. You cannot buy your way into Heaven. God created gold, man created greed and lusted after it. Jesus is the only way to be with the Father in Heaven. Therefore, a sacrifice had to be made to make that way happen. Sacrifice would not be a sacrifice if someone could earn it."

Henry picked up the remote to change the channel but Anne put her hand on it. "No, please, I want to hear."

Henry grimaced, but set the remote down. He'd heard it all before and had believed it until God turned His back on him. But Anne sat on the edge of the sofa concentrating on the words of the man in the impeccable black suit with perfect hair.

Didn't they all look like that, Henry thought sarcastically.

"When we look at Jesus's example, what we should learn from it is that we should be willing to make sacrifices in our lives for people we haven't even met yet. Maybe it's giving a little more of our money to support a charity."

Henry rolled his eyes. *It's always about the money.*

"Maybe it's giving more of our time to help the homeless at a shelter, or a young mother who's been abused. The simple definition of sacrifice is giving up something you want to keep, even if it hurts to do so. Parents know this better than anyone. How many evenings and weekends have you sacrificed to support your son or daughter's recital or soccer game? How many of you have worked a second job, or put off buying a new car to pay for your child's college? Parents make these sacrifices out of love with no guarantee their child will someday play at Carnegie Hall, or sign some huge sports contract.

"Our men in uniform know about sacrifice. How many men have died to keep our nation free? They made the ultimate sacrifice for people they didn't know. Men and women today in the armed forces, police officers, firefighters–they all sacrifice for people they don't know. They may never hear a 'thank you' or 'job well done' but every day, they make that choice.

"God gave us his only Son. Handed him over to the Pharisees and stood by and watched as they beat, mocked, and eventually killed him in one of the worst ways possible. God the Father gave up his only Son's life so that one day you would become one of his children as well. He gave us all free will. He looks to the day when you will use that gift of free will to willingly accept Jesus's sacrifice and be forgiven." He stood up and walked in front of the thin wooden pulpit with the raised cross on the stand.

"As God made a sacrifice, he calls us to follow him. Sacrifice is giving up something for someone else, even if they don't deserve it or even know about it. Even if no one knows about it! We certainly didn't know about God's sacrifice when it was made. And we certainly don't deserve it. Paul tells us in Ephesians, Chapter 5, verses 1 and 2, to be 'imitators of God, as beloved children; and walk in love, just as Christ also loved you and gave Himself up for us, an offering and a sacrifice to God as a fragrant aroma.'"

The Pastor walked back behind the pulpit and closed his Bible. "So the next time you see someone in need, don't worry about the cost, or what glory you may obtain by doing something about it. Be willing to make the sacrifice just as Christ made the ultimate sacrifice just for you. Then you will truly know God's love, just for you." Music started to play in the background, the camera panning over the audience. Henry began to feel very uncomfortable; memories of a faith long buried rising to the surface of his heart.

Anne got off the sofa and sat on the floor in front of the television, focused on the words of the Pastor.

"Everyone, please bow your heads. Have you accepted the sacrifice of Jesus?" He continued. "Have you acknowledged the sacrifice he made hanging on the cross, beaten and humiliated, to the point of his death, just so that you may have eternal life? The beauty of His sacrifice is that because He made it, you don't have to. All you have to do is accept that sacrifice and ask Him to come into your heart as your Lord and Savior. As the choir sings 'Just as I am,' I'll be waiting in front of the stage here, with our trusted assistants alongside me, waiting for you to come forward and acknowledge that you accepted that sacrifice. Everyone, keep your heads down. Don't be afraid. Come on down."

One by one, people rose from the audience and came to the stage where the people waiting there laid hands on the heads of those who came forward, their own heads bowed and mouths moving. The music kept playing. More came to the stage, hands in front of them, heads bowed. Anne stood up and walked up to the television, her hand outstretched, then touched the screen.

Henry turned his head away, his mouth clenched, his breath forced. He'd made that walk before. It didn't mean anything! When he needed God, or Jesus, or whoever, no one was there! It took everything in him not to change the channel and find a nice action movie, or see if the game had started yet.

But he saw how Anne was responding.

He left the room under the pretense of needing the bathroom. He didn't want to say something in anger that he would regret.

Henry stayed in the bathroom a few minutes fighting the anger; the specters of his losses haunting him like the demons in Anne's nightmares. He took several deep breaths, willing himself to let go until his heart slowed to a normal beat and his breathing became easier.

When he returned to the living room, the program had ended, the credits rolling on the screen. Anne still stood in front of the television.

"Tell me about Jesus," she asked.

Henry closed his eyes and sighed.

"I'll see if Pastor Jennings can meet with you. He's the Pastor from my parents' church, South Bay Baptist. He can better explain things than I can."

"Okay," she said nodding, coming back to sit on the sofa.

After that, Henry took control of the remote and found a good action movie where lots of things blew up, making him feel much better. There is real healing in big fiery explosions, he thought wryly. They watched another movie starring that wonderful Austrian bodybuilder, where more things blew up. They ordered Chinese food for dinner and didn't leave the house at all.

Henry put the morning out of his mind.

As the black dragons drag me down to the tunnels, I feel the heat of the fire near the center. I wonder if the pain of the blaze will be better than the pain of my agony. All I can do is look forward to the release that death will bring. I must accept my fate. I am powerless to do anything to stop it. But I am afraid of what I will feel when the fire touches my skin. I have suffered so much pain. Can I endure much more? I can only hope it will be quick. The black dragons lift me and throw me into the fire. I wait to feel the hot flames consume what is left of me, wishing with everything inside me that I could be somewhere else, someone else...

25. ANNE MEETS DR. RAYBACK

Monday, July 6

Anne sat on the sofa in Susan Rayback's office while Susan typed notes on her laptop. Henry sat beside her, his arm around her shoulders.

"Anne," Susan said. "Let's start with what you remember before you met Henry."

"I do not remember anything," Anne shook her head. "There is nothing before Henry."

"Interesting," Susan typed on her laptop. "Henry thinks you may have been on a boat that caught fire; that maybe you fell into the ocean. How does that make you feel?"

Anne shrugged her shoulders. "It may be but I do not remember a boat. I do not remember the fire, but I feel it."

"I understand the nightmares are getting worse. Can you tell me what's happening?"

Anne blinked her eyes rapidly against the forming tears, her hands trembling.

"It's okay, Anne. Take your time. You don't have to tell me if you don't want to."

They all sat quietly for several minutes letting Anne take time to compose her thoughts. Finally, in a little voice, she spoke. "The black dragons come and kill all of the golden ones. I see my...father?...die at my feet. Then the dragons take me away to the Black Mountains where...." She stopped.

"Anne," Henry offered. "You don't have to talk about it if it's too difficult."

"Give her time, Henry," Susan suggested. "I'll only charge you for the hour, but we can take as long as we need. Anne, take a deep breath in through your nose and let it out through your mouth."

Anne did.

"Again."

Anne took a few more deep breaths until the trembling stopped.

"Take your time," Susan encouraged her.

Anne nodded. "I am taken to the Black Mountains where Saphan...cuts off my wings...then my tail...." She struggled to get the words out. "Then...he takes me...."

"What do you mean 'takes you?'" Henry's brows furrowed. He seemed upset by her words. She didn't want to make him angry, but they wanted her to talk about the dreams. She took his hand and held tightly.

"He...has intercourse with me...not like we do...he is hurting me...I do not want to...."

"Anne, you don't have to say any more," Henry said in a low voice. His muscles tightened in the arm around her.

She closed her eyes and shook her head sharply. "No, I must...."

Susan took her other hand. "It's okay Anne. There's no one here who can hurt you. You're safe with me and Henry. No one is going to hurt you anymore."

Anne held on to both Henry and Susan's hands. She continued. "He takes me and bites me, tearing out my skin....eating me...the others laugh." She began weeping, letting go of the hands holding hers and burrowing herself in Henry's chest.

Susan sat back, drawing a deep breath. "I think what she went through was more than a fire on a boat. It sounds like maybe she witnessed someone close to her being killed before she was viciously assaulted. You're sure there were no reports of something like this from the police department?"

Henry shook his head. "Nothing that matches her description or hasn't already been solved. If this happened, it was never reported to anyone so far as I've heard." He continued to hold onto Anne, stroking her back. "I never imagined it was as bad as this."

"One thing I don't understand is..." he hesitated a moment, "she is, or was a virgin when I met her. And Dr. Jackson examined her completely and said she is in perfect health with no signs of prior abuse or injury. How could she have been sexually assaulted? Wouldn't there be physical evidence of that?"

"Well," Susan responded. "Sexual assault is not always vaginal, but I would think Dr. Jackson would have found some scarring in any case." Susan noted this on her laptop. "Also, dreams of rape don't always mean a physical attack. It may be something totally unrelated to the actual act, such as when one feels betrayed or abused or humiliated. We have no way of knowing if the attack in her dreams is from an actual incident or something else."

Susan tapped a finger on her desk a moment before adding, "We may have an idea what caused her memory loss but we still need to understand why these events manifest in dreams of dragons. It may be the dragons attacking her in the dream world are the memories of her trauma trying to get through. I'll continue my research. In the meantime, Anne, are the drawings helping you?"

Anne had ceased weeping and now only sniffled, her eyes red and swollen. "Yes, I think I can talk about it now because I have drawn the dragons."

"Okay," Susan continued. "Keep up with your drawings. If you feel at any time though that the pictures are making you feel worse, try to focus on lighter subjects, like the animals."

"I can do that," Anne agreed.

"Henry, take pictures of her drawings and paintings and email them to me. They could be very helpful."

"I will."

"Also, I'd like to set up some sessions with you, maybe once a week while you are creating your paintings to see if we can uncover any of those lost memories. Your memory may even come back on its own." She took Anne's hand. "We'll do all we can do to help you get back your life."

They stood up and Susan reached out, taking Anne in her arms and hugging her. "It's going to be okay, Anne," she said, smiling. "We'll find out who you really are. I promise."

"Thank you," Henry said, hugging Susan next. "I can't tell you how much this means."

"Let's set up a time for next week. Wednesday at ten?"

Henry nodded, pulling out his check book to pay for the session. "We'll be here."

Susan put her hand on the checkbook. "No, Henry. It's okay. There's no charge."

"Thanks."

* * *

They were silent on the drive home. Henry pondered what the secrets revealed in the session meant; the answer to the dilemma that was Anne was still unsolved. He was getting angry when she told them about her dreams. How could he not? It took everything inside him to keep it bottled up. But he was there for Anne, not for his own feelings. The rage that grew at the possibilities her story implied tied his stomach into knots. Yet there were no scars or evidence of a physical assault. What had been done to this girl to utterly deprive her of memory, yet leave no visible scars? Was that kind of torture even possible?

Henry was so lost in thought, he didn't notice the black sedan follow them home.

* * *

I wait to feel the heat of the inferno take my life and end my woe. I wish with all my heart to escape the flames, to go to another place. If only it were possible!

The fire surrounds me but does not touch me! I do not know what is happening. The flames fade away until I am surrounded by complete darkness. There is nothing but the darkness. I do not feel pain anymore, I do not feel anything. I am prisoner to the dark surrounding me, pulling me further in. Is this what it is to finally die? Am I finally free?

Where am I? What am I? Why can't I feel anything? Am I alive? Am I breathing? Do I even exist? There is nothing before the blackness that swirls around me and I do not know if it will ever end. How did I get here? What is happening to me!

26. PASTOR JENNINGS

Tuesday, July 7

Anne finally finished her paintings and together they put the text on each panel. Henry packaged up the drawings as carefully as he could, and sent them to Elliott, who would shop around for a publisher, or publish it through his company. It felt good to finish the project and they were both quite happy with the final result.

"Now that we've finished the book," Henry asked. "What are you going to work on?"

Anne shrugged. "I do not know. I think I would like to learn more about what I heard. About Jesus."

"I'll give Pastor Jennings a call."

"I would like that," Anne said.

A few hours later they sat in the office of Pastor Ron Jennings of South Bay Baptist Church. His thinning blonde hair was graying at the temples. He had a remarkable smile that put one at ease. He was unusually fit for a man of the cloth, and stood six feet with Paul Newman blue eyes.

"Hello Henry." He extended his hand. "Good to see you again. It's been a while." Henry smiled nervously. He hadn't set foot in the church since his father's funeral.

Pastor Jennings turned to Anne. "You must be Anne. How can I help you?"

"Anne saw a church service on TV where they had an altar call and has some questions."

"I think I might be able to help. Won't you sit down?" Pastor Jennings smiled at Anne. "What are your questions?"

"Tell me about Jesus," she began.

Pastor Jennings nodded. "Jesus is the Son of God. We believe Jesus became the ultimate sacrifice to pay for all of our sins. Another way to look at it is to realize God is a perfect being. Because man is sinful, he cannot have communion with a perfect God. But God loved us so much that he sent his own Son to be a sacrifice, to bridge the way for man to commune directly with Him. That sacrifice was Jesus. Do you understand so far?"

"What is love?" Anne asked. "And what is sacrifice?"

"Well!" Pastor Jennings steepled his fingers in front of him. "That is a very big question. There are many different kinds of love, and the term means different things to different people. For example, I can say 'I love chocolate cake,' or 'I love to dance.' That's not really love but we use that term to express how we feel about certain objects or foods, or things we enjoy doing.

"The love you would feel for Henry is *eros* love. It's the passionate love between a man and a woman, expressed in a physical way. That's where people get confused. They say they are 'falling in love.' Eros is more physical than other types of love, but is not by itself true love.

"True love, or unconditional love, called *agape*, is the love God has for all of us. The Bible tells us 'There is no greater love than this; that a man lay down his life for another.' Agape love means sacrifice, or putting the needs of someone else above your own. This is the love that led Jesus to willingly die on the cross for our sins. But I like how the Apostle John explains love. 'God loved us so much that he sent his only Son to die for our sins.' That is what true love, or the highest form of love, means. Do you understand?"

"I do not know," Anne said hesitantly.

"How do you feel when you are with Henry?"

She looked at Henry with longing in her eyes. "I do not want to be away from him. I hurt in here," she pointed to her chest, "when he is away from me." Henry took her hand to encourage her. "Everywhere inside me needs him."

"When we," she glanced at Henry, "make love?"

Henry blushed, embarrassed to be discussing his sexual relationship in front of the Pastor, but nodded for her to continue. This was for her benefit, after all, not his.

"When we make love," she continued, "I only know him. Nothing else is around me. I tickle inside and I feel heat burning in me when I am with him. We are like one body." She held out her hands, palms up, shaking her head. "I do not know the words to tell you what I feel."

Pastor Jennings smiled and nodded. "You're doing fine, Anne. That's a very good example of Eros love." He looked at Henry over his glasses. "You and I will need to have a discussion about this another time, my friend." Henry fidgeted in his seat, the red on his face growing brighter.

Pastor Jennings turned back to Anne. "I'm glad you have Henry and his family. But it is the agape love we all need. When you're willing to surrender everything you have and everything you want, even to the point of giving up your life for someone else...*that* is true love. That's sacrifice. It doesn't depend on what someone looks like, who he is, or even what he does. It's truly from your own heart. This is the kind of love only God can give."

He took out his Bible and opened it. "Let me read something to you that might help explain love. Paul writes about love in his first letter to the Corinthians, in Chapter 13:

"Though I speak with the tongues of men and of angels, but have not love, I have become sounding brass or a clanging cymbal. And though I have the gift of prophecy, and understand all mysteries and all knowledge, and though I have all faith, so that I could remove mountains, but have not love, I am nothing. And though I bestow all my goods to feed the poor, and though I give my body to be burned, but have not love, it profits me nothing.

"Love suffers long and is kind; love does not envy; love does not parade itself, is not puffed up; does not behave rudely, does not seek its own, is not provoked, thinks no evil; does not rejoice in iniquity, but rejoices in the truth; bears all things, believes all things, hopes all things, endures all things. Love never fails."

Pastor Jennings stared for a few moments at the printed words before lifting his eyes to Anne. "When we think about what Jesus did by going to the cross to die, that is the epitome of both love and sacrifice. God loves us so much, he sacrificed his own Son so that we could be with Him. God loved his Son, but knew Jesus had to die for us to be able to come to the Father. And Jesus willingly submitted himself to become that sacrifice, knowing what it would cost him. That is the ultimate act of true love."

He closed the book and smiled at Anne. "I hope this has helped you."

"I want to know that love," she said. "I want to know Jesus."

"You can know him right here, right now."

Anne nodded. "What do I do?"

"Let me pray with you," Pastor Jennings took her hands.

Henry closed his eyes as the pastor led Anne in the sinner's prayer— but not to pray. It was more to keep the anger behind the shades of his eyelids. How could Anne fall for this stuff? *Faith in God only leads to disappointment.* If God was really there, he sure had a screwed up way of showing it! God had abandoned Henry, and Henry was happy to return the favor.

Anne looked up. "Thank you, Pastor. I feel like I have known him before."

Pastor Jennings put his hand on her shoulder. "That's great! Jesus lives in your heart now."

Anne shook her head. "Yes, but it is more than that. I know him from somewhere else."

Pastor Jennings chuckled. "It can seem like that for new believers. You have a strong faith, Anne."

Henry rose and extended his hand to Anne to help her up. Pastor Jennings walked them to the door. "Come see me any time you want to talk more about it." To Henry, he said, "Take good care of her, my friend. I look forward to talking with you soon."

Henry gave the Pastor an uneasy smile. He wasn't looking forward to that at all.

A bright flash of light replaces the black void and a voice softly speaks.

"Hello my child, it is time for you to fulfill your destiny." The voice is soothing, driving the fear away.

"Who are you? Why can't I see you or touch you? How am I hearing you?"

"You are in-between. I am here to guide you to a new beginning."

"New beginning? I do not understand."

"You will, in time. Do you remember who you are or where you came from?"

"No. I cannot remember."

"That is because your true destiny awaits. Hush. Sleep now. When you awake you will be renewed. It is time...."

The voice fades and the nothingness returns.

* * *

I sense the body I now have but cannot see it. I cannot see anything. Cool liquid surrounds me. I am pushed by the cool liquid until I feel something firm under me. Light begins to filter through the darkness and shapes appear around me. Something approaches me.

"Heh ... hello. Miss, are you okay?"

27. THE BOOK IS PUBLISHED

Wednesday, July 8

"We're going to be published!" Henry waved a letter over his head. "Elliot's company is going to publish the book. They'll be sending a contract."

Anne had been working on a still life of the shells she had collected. "I am very glad to hear that." She looked up and smiled.

"You did it, girl!" He hugged her and kissed the top of her head. "Guess I better call James and let him know we're going to need him after all." He punched in James' number on his phone.

Anne dipped her brush into the cerulean blue glob of watercolor paint to use in the shadows of the shells. She listened to Henry explain the letter to James. She wasn't sure what it would mean to have her dreams printed in a book. The act of drawing out the dreams, although it didn't stop them, made them less intense. But now she would be sharing them with many people.

Like Henry, she did not know why her dreams were about dragons. She wanted to find out what had happened to her and more importantly, who she really was. Did she have a family like Heidi and James? Why couldn't she remember anything about her childhood? The dreams were so real, so vivid, even to the point of knowing the names of the dragons in her nightmare world. Would she ever stop having nightmares? How could anyone forget so much in one world and remember so much in another? Did she really suffer such a trauma to take away her entire life? Why couldn't she remember?

Henry got off the phone. "Let's go out and celebrate. I'm taking you to a movie and dinner at the pier. Come on, let's get cleaned up!"

"I would like that," Anne said, putting her brush in the jar of water. After a quick shower, she put on a white sundress with small flowers on it and white sandals. Henry chose black slacks and a button-down black shirt with black loafers.

Henry told her they were going to go see a science fiction film about an astronaut who crashes on another world and meets a race of strange glowing aliens. He told her the story about how the astronaut searches for a way back to his home world where he has a wife and two children.

They watched the movie play out. On the new world, he fell in love with one of the alien women, who became pregnant with his child. When his shipmates found him years later, he had to choose between his family on his home world and his new glowing bride and hybrid child. He chose to stay but was forced to fight his old comrades, who refused to leave without him. In the midst of the struggle, he killed his best friend from the ship. He prevailed over the crew of the starship and returned to his home, only to find that during the fight, his alien child had been struck by falling debris when their home was hit by a laser cannon, and died.

As the final scene played out, Anne wept for the astronaut and his family. Henry held her, whispering it was only a movie and not real, although he too had tears in his eyes. They watched the credits roll up the screen as the rest of the audience filed out of the theater. Henry picked up the empty tub of popcorn and their cup. "Let's get something to eat and after that, we'll go watch the sunset."

Henry parked by the beach and they walked to the seafood restaurant. Several people lined the pier fishing for sharks. Anne and Henry enjoyed a garden salad, fresh crab legs, a baked potato with a side of broccoli, and hot chocolate chip cookies with ice cream for dessert. Anne rolled her eyes, relishing each decadent bite of warm sweet chewy dough and cold melting ice cream on top.

After dinner, they returned to the beach, took off their shoes and sat on the sand with the crowd of onlookers waiting to see the beauty of a Florida sunset sinking into the water. The sun slowly made its way to its watery grave, painting the clouds above the water with bright orange and yellow flames on a cerulean blue canvas. The sky gradually deepened in hue until the orange orb of the sun dipped into the dark blue ocean. Anne saw the scene as an artist, wanting to capture it in watercolor. Everyone clapped at the spectacle of nature, finally folding up their beach chairs to leave. Henry and Anne stayed on the beach as the dark of night took its turn on the sky.

"Did you like the movie?" Henry asked Anne. They sat in the sand, pushing up piles of it with their toes.

"It was beautiful," she replied. "I would love to go to that place."

"It's not real, Anne," he corrected her. "It's make-believe. Like your princess movies."

The stars in the night sky began to reveal themselves, a million lights twinkling on one by one. Anne gazed up at them. "Are there other places like that?"

Henry lay back on the sand. "I believe there are other worlds. We *can't* be the only one. In this whole universe, there *must* be other worlds where there's life. Our planet is like a piece of sand on the shore of the grand beach that is the universe. It's humbling to think of how small our world really is when you think about the billions of stars and planets up there."

Anne lay back with him, both of them ignoring the sand that crept into their clothes. "I know in here," she pointed to her chest, "there are other places we cannot see. Maybe a world like my dreams is out there."

"Maybe," Henry mused. "I have to think there are so many possibilities of life, more than we can imagine. It's arrogant to think we're the only life forms in the entire universe."

"Someday, I would like to see them all." Anne gazed at the sky, the stars sparkling in her wishful eyes.

"Me too. I have to think there is so much more we can experience and learn from other worlds. Can you imagine what they would look like?"

They lay on the sand watching more stars come out, the surf enchanting them to lose themselves in imaginary journeys to exotic and alien lands. The rest of the crowd of sunset aficionados left. The beach became theirs.

* * *

Sometime later, Henry stretched his arms over his head and sighed. "Probably time we should head home." He turned to her, his head up, leaning on his elbow and gazed upon her lying on the sand, smiling at him. He wanted nothing more than to love her right there in the open on the sandy beach. He leaned down and kissed her passionately. Anne responded by running her fingers through his hair before wrapping her arms around him and pulling him close.

There was something about the danger of being discovered on the beach in the middle of the night that made it that much more exciting. The moon blushed as they gave into their passion, forgetting where they were or who might see. It was one of those special moments two lovers alone in the universe share, just the two of them; time and the earth held still so the moment was theirs alone. The moon rose higher behind them, carving a path of light across the ocean, bathing them in the glow of true love.

Afterward, they relaxed on the moonlit beach, beyond which lay a black wall. Henry guessed it was well past midnight. "We need to go," he said. He stood up, brushed what sand he could from his clothes, then reached out to help her stand. She brushed sand from her dress, her sandals in her hand.

Shoes off, they crossed the dark sands to find their way to the car in the moonlight. Henry saw the gleam of the hood a few yards ahead and guided her to the wooden walkway over the wild grass, to the sand-covered black asphalt of the parking lot.

28. ATTACK!

As they approached their car, Henry saw four men in black standing near it, and a black sedan parked next to it that looked disturbingly familiar. He slowly held out his hand for Anne to stop and pushed her behind him, whispering in the hope only she would hear, "These are the guys who've been chasing us. We need to get away." It was too late; they had been spotted.

The shorter man, with blond hair sticking out of the black knit hat, rounded the car to Henry and Anne. "Quite a show you two put on. Care to share some of that?" He sneered at Anne. "Hey, little lady. We've got someone who wants to meet you."

Henry dropped his shoes and assumed a fighting stance. "Run!" he shouted. Anne turned and ran as fast as she could.

"Get her!" Blondie yelled. Two of the men bolted after Anne while Blondie leapt at Henry. Henry connected with Blondie's chin, knocking him into the car, spun and struck the other man's face with the back of his fist. Anne's scream distracted him, allowing Blondie to land a blow on Henry's left cheek.

Henry recovered just in time to block the other guy's fist hammering toward him. He shot his right arm up, striking him square in the nose, breaking cartilage and sending him squealing to the asphalt. Blondie landed a blow to Henry's lower back. He spun to face his attacker, on time to see the black SUV drive up with two more uninvited guests to the party.

Henry had keep the odds against him to a minimum. His Navy training was rusty, but not that rusty. He punched Blondie in the solar plexus, doubling him over. As blondie hit the ground with a thud, one of the newcomers grabbed Henry from behind, wrapping his arm around Henry's neck, and squeezed. *Damn he's fast, maybe I'm rustier than I thought.* Using his arm as leverage, Henry kicked Gut-puncher in the chest, knocking him back. But New Guy's partner connected a left hook to Henry's jaw, followed with a punch to his kidneys, causing him to fall. He shot back to his feet, threw three quick right jabs at New Guy, then pivoted for a side kick to his partner.

Blondie rejoined the fray; all three surrounding Henry. *This is not where I want to be!* Tactically, this was the worst case scenario, not being able to keep all of his opponents in his field of vision. The trio punched and kicked from all sides.

Henry blocked as best he could—until he felt the sting of a blade slice his side. He never saw it coming and had no idea who stabbed him.

Henry's first thought when he looked down at his shirt was that he was bleeding. The blade was cold, piercing his side. He noted, as a detached observer, it hurt, but not as much it should. The stabbing was surreal, as if he watched someone else grapple with the four attackers. Well, two really, because Tall Guy with the broken nose was too consumed by his own pain to keep up his part of the attack, and one of the newcomers rolled on the ground after a hard kick to his groin.

The two who went after Anne came back without her. Despite his own predicament, facing six pissed-off attackers and weak with a stab wound, Henry felt a great relief. It would be worth it if Anne got away.

One fist slammed into his cheek and another to his stomach, crumpling him to the asphalt. His body was going into shock. He huddled in a fetal position, arms around his midsection, as the attackers kicking him over and over.

Suddenly, a siren pierced the air and the flash of lights from a Venice PD squad car lit the night. By some miracle, someone must have witnessed the fray and called 9-1-1. The four who were still able to walk grabbed the other two, shoved them into the vehicles, and sped off moments before the squad car arrived. Two patrolmen jumped from the car and rushed to Henry.

"Sir," a male officer shouted, his hand on Henry's shoulder. "Are you alright?"

"I've been stabbed." Henry grunted, rolling to his back, clutching his abdomen. The other officer was on her radio calling for an ambulance.

"My girlfriend," Henry gasped. "Two of them ran off...after her, that way." He indicated north from the pier with his bloody hand. "They came back without her...I don't know where she is." He found it hard to breathe, let alone talk.

The female officer retrieved a first aid kit from the car. Her partner held on to Henry's side, hands pressed to the wound trying to stop the bleeding.

"I'll look for her," the female officer said, handing off the first aid kit. "What's her name? What does she look like?"

"Anne. Her name is Anne. Blond hair, white dress...." Henry stopped, a spasm of pain taking his breath.

"Thanks," she said, turning north to run down Harbor Drive, a flashlight in her hand, shouting Anne's name.

"We'll find her, Sir." The man pressed the pad to the wound. "I'm Harrison. My partner is Officer Wilson. Can you tell me your name?"

"Henry Williford." Henry strained for his wallet.

Officer Harrison reached into Henry's pocket and pulled out the black leather tri-fold. "I got it, Mr. Williford." He pulled out Henry's driver's license.

"Can you tell me what happened?" Harrison kept Henry talking and awake.

"We...were on the beach late...came back to the car...black sedan...."

"Take your time."

"Four guys waiting...told Anne run...two of 'em...chased her. I held my own...against the other two...second car...two more. Till...one stabbed me." Henry tried to laugh but it hurt too much. "Should've seen the other guys!"

The ambulance arrived and the paramedics tumbled out, running with their bag to help.

"Stab wound, lower right quadrant of abdomen," Harrison called out.

One of the paramedics, a woman with blonde hair tied back, knelt over Henry, checking his vitals. Satisfied he was breathing on his own, she shined a light in his eyes. "Sir, I'm a paramedic. I'm going to take care of you. Can you tell me your name?"

"Henry Williford."

"Hi, Henry, I'm Jill. Henry, can you tell me where you are?"

"In a stupid parking lot...bleeding like a stuck pig...while my girlfriend is...alone in the dark...where I should be...out there...looking for her," Henry gasped. "Venice. Florida."

"You're in no shape to help anyone at the moment. The officers will find your girlfriend. What's her name?"

"Anne." Henry's replies grew weaker by the moment.

"Okay, Henry, stay with me. Are you hurt anywhere else? Any other injuries I should know about?"

"No...I don't think so. Unless you think...numerous kicks and punches to my head...face...vital organs...counts?"

"You're doing fine, Henry. My partner, Garcia, is here and we're going to put you on a backboard, then onto the gurney."

The other paramedic pulled up a gurney. "Okay, Henry," Jill said. "We're going to put you on the gurney and get you to the hospital. On three."

Henry waved his right hand grimacing in pain. "Can't leave...Anne... need to find Anne...is she okay?"

Jill called in as soon as Henry was secure. "Thirty two-year-old white male, single stab wound lower right quadrant of the abdomen, multiple contusions. Breathing and alert but in shock due to loss of blood. I'm going to start an I.V. and administer oxygen. Patient name, Henry Williford." She added a few more pads over the wound and taped it down with medical tape.

Jill looked at Officer Harrison. "Someone's looking for Anne?" She put a blanket over Henry.

Harrison nodded. "He says she ran off north down Harbor Road. My partner is looking for her."

"We've got to go, Henry," Jill said. "The officers will find Anne." The paramedics lifted the gurney into the ambulance.

"No, please." Henry grabbed her arm. "Need to find her."

"Sir," she answered urgently. "You're in shock and losing a lot of blood. How would Anne feel if we found her and lost you? They'll find her and bring her to the hospital as soon as they do."

Officer Harrison stepped into the ambulance. "We'll stay here until we find her and bring her to you. You have my word."

Henry reluctantly nodded, closed his eyes and lay back. Jill relayed his status to the hospital. "Let them find her," he prayed to a God he no longer believed in, but now wanted with all of his heart to be there.

* * *

Anne ran as fast as she could, catching her two would-be assailants flatfooted. She had a tremendous lead on them in her race toward a bend in Harbor Drive that led to a thickly wooded area of palm trees and tall beach grass. She disappeared into the night, darting left and right so she wouldn't leave a clear path for them to follow. She leapt over a small sand dune and curled up in a shallow section, hoping her white dress and blonde hair would blend in with the white sand of the beach. Her heart beat wildly in her chest. Seconds ticked like hours as she waited breathlessly to see if her ruse would work.

For a long time her pursuers were nowhere in sight. She began to think she'd eluded them, until she heard their voices and heavy breathing.

"Where...the hell...did she...go?" The heavier of the two men gasped, sucking in air and holding his side.

"Man, we're going to be in deep trouble with the Master if we don't bring her back," his partner replied. "We better split up. You go left, I'll go right; keep each other in sight so she doesn't slip past us."

The thugs split up, the mouth breather heading toward Anne. She couldn't see him, but she could hear him rustling through the tall grass, crunching dead twigs and sand as he trudged ever closer. Anne was on the verge of panic at his approach, *crunch, crunch, crunch.* In moments he would be upon her, *crunch, crunch, crunch*. If she bolted she would give herself away! *Crunch, crunch, crun...*

"Damn it, *look*!" The mouth breather shouted. "Cops are coming. Squad car!" He pointed behind them. "Coming down the hill!"

"Crap! Let's get the hell out. Better empty handed than apprehended."

"The Master doesn't tolerate mistakes," Mouth Breather warned.

They took off back to the parking lot, missing her hiding place.

Anne lay on the ground shaking, frozen by fear. She was sick to her stomach realizing Henry was alone against those evil men. But she was too afraid to go back. She lay shivering until the light from the pending dawn started to brighten the dark and a voice called her name.

"Anne, this is Officer Wilson of the Venice Police Department. I'm here to help you! Henry told me to find you!"

Anne peeked over the edge of the sand to see a woman. Recognizing the uniform, she crawled out over the top of her hiding place. "I'm here!" Anne shouted, waving her arms.

The officer pointed her flashlight in Anne's direction, blinding her. "Are you Anne?"

"Yes, I am Anne."

"Are you alright? Are you hurt?"

"Just tired, cold, and thirsty. Where is Henry?"

"Henry is at the hospital, exactly where I suggest we take you and have you checked out. I don't think he'll rest for a moment until he knows you're alright." Officer Wilson spoke into the mic on her shoulder. "Officer Wilson to dispatch."

"Dispatch to Wilson, over."

"I have the girl, repeat I've found the girl, Anne, missing at Venice Beach, over."

"Roger that, do you need medical backup?"

"Negative, she is ambulatory and appears cognizant. I will transport her to the hospital in my unit and take her statement after she's been medically cleared. Wilson out."

"10-4. Dispatch to Wilson, out."

"Why is Henry at the hospital?" Anne asked nervously.

"Same reason you're going, to get checked out. He did suffer a single stab wound during the fight, but the paramedics were on the scene right afterward and he's in good hands."

"Henry!" Anne sobbed.

Officer Wilson sat with her in the back of the squad car while Harrison called Dispatch to advise they were en route to the hospital. "Can you tell me what happened?" she asked.

"We went to the beach and stayed on the sand a long time staring at the stars," Anne began. "We were almost back to our car when Henry saw another car we had seen before with men waiting for us. They said someone wanted to meet me, and Henry told me to run. I ran and two of the men chased me into the trees. I heard them talking and one of them saw your police car coming and they ran. I was too afraid to go back."

"You're very lucky. Someone from Public Works was nearby cleaning the Visitor Center and called it in. Did you hear any names?"

"No, but one did say something about 'The Master' not being pleased."

"What did they look like?"

"One man was brown like you, and one man had hair like mine but short. I do not remember what the others looked like, but they had black pants and black shirts and black hats on their heads."

"Okay," Officer Wilson said. "You're doing great, Anne. We'll be at the hospital soon. I'll have you sign a statement after you've been medically cleared. First, let's get you looked at and then reunite you with Henry."

Anne sat silent, tears flowing down her cheek. Why would anybody want to 'meet' her? She desperately wanted answers about her past, but not if it would cause Henry harm...or worse.

29. AT THE HOSPITAL

When the ambulance arrived at the hospital, Henry was in stable but weak condition. The paramedics rolled the gurney in to the waiting arms of the emergency room staff. They rushed him to the trauma unit and within seconds, had cut off his clothes, covering him with a white sheet. Like buzzing bees, nurses surrounded him, starting an IV, hooking him up to monitors and placing an oxygen mask over his face.

Dr. John Turner introduced himself and examined the wound to determine the extent of the damage. Henry was awake and able to answer questions about his medical history and to sign forms. As they itemized and cataloged his personal effects, he persuaded a nurse to call his sister. The poor girl nearly dropped the phone from Heidi's high-pitched shriek. Henry would not be surprised if Heidi arrived at the hospital before the nurse hung up.

The nurse told him a Venice police cruiser had just pulled up to the ER entrance. Anne had been found and was safe. Tears formed in his eyes. He finally relaxed, a weight off his shoulders. He silently thanked God, in case there was some small chance He really was there and had actually answered his prayer.

They wheeled Anne in, reuniting the young couple. The entire ER buzzed with the story and was rooting for the two. Anne saw Henry wired up, a blood stained bandage on his abdomen. She jumped from her wheelchair and ran to him, sobbing with joy. Henry tried to hold her, tearing off his oxygen mask to kiss her. The nurse's station erupted with applause and someone took a picture on a cell phone.

Henry's nurse closed the curtain, "Let's give them a moment."

Suddenly, someone else ripped the curtain open, yelling, "Moment my ass! What the hell happened, Henry!"

Heidi had arrived!

She stood with a look on her face Henry had seen a million times: concern, mixed with love, tempered with anger, that said, "I can't wait until you get through this so I can kill you myself." She wore a mismatched pair of flip flops, baggy shorts, and her pajama top. Her hair was a mess. Henry wasn't sure if she had driven or flown on a broom.

In a weak voice, he said, "Long story; no mood, nor do I have the strength. Take care of Anne while I'm in surgery."

Anne looked at Heidi, tears in her eyes, dirt and sand in her hair and on her dress, and scratches on her face and legs. She pulled Anne into her arms, crying, and slipped into mother mode. She kissed Henry. "I'm sorry. I'm here for you both. I just freaked out when the nurse called...said you'd been stabbed...police. I was terrified. Rest, Henry. I won't leave Anne's side."

Henry kissed her back. "Thanks, Sis, I owe you one."

"Sshh, you don't owe me anything. This isn't a favor; it's family pulling together in a crisis. You relax now. Rest and save your strength. And do what the doctors and nurses say or I'll have them give you an ice water enema."

Henry winced from the pain trying to laugh at her teasing. *She was teasing, right?*

"He'll be okay, Anne," Heidi smiled. "They're going to take good care of him. It's time to take care of you now. You need to get back in the wheelchair and go with the nurse and let them have a look at you. I'll be right here."

Anne kissed Henry one last time and reluctantly obeyed. The nurse put the mask back on Henry's face. They waved to each other as she was wheeled backwards to her own examination room. The technicians came to take Henry to his CT Scan while Heidi followed Anne.

* * *

"What happened?" Heidi finally had the opportunity to ask once they had Anne settled in her examination room.

"We were on our way home from the beach near the pier when men came out and came after me." Anne' eyes were red and puffy from crying, but she seemed steadier now they were at the hospital. "Henry told me to run and I did, but two of them ran after me. I ran as fast as I could and hid." She looked up at Heidi. "I left Henry alone with the others!"

"It's what he wanted you to do, Anne. It's his job to protect you. He wouldn't have wanted it any other way. If you hadn't run, you'd be a captive of those men, and Henry would probably still be here with a stab wound worrying about you."

Anne shook her head. "I was too afraid to go back. I left him alone!"

"Anne," Heidi said, gently but firmly. "You couldn't have done anything to help. You did what you had to do to protect yourself. Don't feel bad about it."

"I will try."

"You have to be strong for Henry. He would feel terrible if he knew you were feeling guilty. How many were there?"

"There were four when I ran. I do not know what happened after that. I do know that one man said they wanted me for 'the Master.'"

"The Master," Heidi asked. "Who the hell is that?"

"Probably some kind of drug lord or something." Officer Wilson looked up from her report. "Mr. Williford was able to give us a description of the vehicles so we've put out a BOLO for them. If you can think of anything else, Anne, please let me know."

"I will. Thank you," Anne said.

Moments later a nurse walked in and had Anne put on a hospital gown. After taking her vitals, she got Anne a basin of hot water and soap. Anne felt better freshening up a little. Heidi brushed the beach out of her hair. The ER doctor came in as they were finishing up. He gave her a clean bill of health, instructing the nurse to prepare her release.

Anne and Heidi returned to Henry's room and waited.

A few minutes later, the technicians brought Henry back. "All done!" the young man in blue scrubs said. "The doctor will see you once he gets the results."

Henry was propped up with pillows behind him and reached out to Anne. "Hi, honey," he said in a weak voice. "Are you okay?"

She took his hand. "I am okay. I am sorry I did not come back. I could not help you. I was too afraid!"

Henry slowly shook his head. "It's my job to protect you, not yours to protect me. I'll always be there to protect you. Besides, I had it all under control."

"How do you feel?" Heidi straightened his pillows for him.

"Like a million bucks," he boasted. "After taxes." Heidi could see he didn't want to let Anne know how much he really hurt. But she knew her brother. She saw the pain on his face. He laid his head back and closed his eyes as if willing the pain away.

The nurse came back to check Henry's vital signs. "We're still waiting for the results of the CT Scan."

They sat quietly, each lost in thought and worry as the minutes ticked by. Henry had fallen asleep. The blood loss, combined with a healthy dose of morphine, gave him some badly needed rest. Heidi kept an eye on both Anne and Henry, watching the young woman struggle with guilt.

Finally, Dr. Turner returned. "Well, Mr. Williford," Dr. Turner said, waking Henry up. "You are one lucky fellow. The knife seems to have missed any major organs, although it did just nick your small intestine.

We're going to take you to surgery to stop the internal bleeding and then close the wound up, but I don't think you'll need any major repair. After that, you'll be admitted for a couple of days, just to make sure the stitches hold and nothing else develops. In cases like this, the biggest risk is infection."

"Thank you," Henry said groggily and nodded. He took Anne's hand. "Anne, when the surgery is over, you can't go back to the house. It's not safe. Heidi, can she stay with you for a few days?"

"Of course," Heidi said.

"Just make sure you have Jim stop by the house and feed the animals."

"No, I need to be with them. I will be okay," Anne protested.

"You can't stay there alone and without protection," Henry insisted.

"James taught me how to use his shotgun, Henry," Heidi interjected. "You forget, I'm often alone with two kids when he's away on business. He made sure I can hold my own if the unthinkable ever happens. I'll stay with Anne. We'll keep Charlie close and the gun loaded and ready."

"We'll have a patrol car near the house," Officer Harrison added. "Our best chance of catching these guys is if they make another attempt. With the description you gave us of the vehicles and your attackers, we plan on keeping an eye on your house anyway."

Henry nodded. Heidi knew he felt uneasy using Anne and her as bait, putting them in harm's way, but Heidi would do anything for him, including putting herself in the line of fire. Despite her sometimes rough treatment of him, Heidi loved her brother fiercely.

Soon, a young female orderly with big brown eyes came into the room. "Okay Mr. Williford. I'm going to take you to surgery now."

Anne and Heidi kissed him one last time. "We'll be here when you get back," Heidi said. She took Anne to get some breakfast before they began their vigil in the waiting room.

Three hours passed before the doctor came with the news the operation had gone smoothly. Shortly after, a nurse escorted them to Henry's room. He was loopy from the anesthesia and didn't say much. The smile on his face said it all.

Heidi was proud of how brave Anne was, holding back tears bursting to get out. Anne kissed him gently on the cheek, as if he were made of glass and might shatter at any moment. Henry had taken quite a beating in addition to being stabbed. Heidi kissed him too, whispering that she was going to take Anne home so she could rest. She turned to look back before she left. Henry was already asleep.

On the ride home, Heidi called James. Anne had been up all night. The physical and emotional ordeal was taking its toll on her. Heidi instructed

James to meet them at Henry's house and bring the shotgun and a box of ammo. James's parents had returned from their trip to North Carolina in time to take the kids to Orlando for the week.

He was waiting for them when they pulled up. "I'm so glad you're here," James said, looking relieved. "The police stopped by. It was all I could do to explain why I was here with a loaded shotgun. Fortunately, they checked with the hospital and both of us are on Henry's emergency call list." He looked at Anne, "You poor thing, you've been through the ringer." Anne weakly returned his hug. "I've checked the perimeter of the house and the shed out back. There's no sign anyone's been around or broken in. Just to be safe, once we're inside, you two stay put while I check out the house."

Once inside, Anne dropped into the chair nearest the front door. She smiled as Charlie and his four-legged gang rushed up to greet her. A few moments later, James reappeared to announce the all clear. "I have serious reservations leaving you guys alone with someone after Anne. Promise me you won't open the door for anyone and to call 9-1-1 if anything suspicious at all happens."

"We promise," Heidi said. She needed James to be okay with leaving them. Heidi would stay with Anne as long as she needed to.

"I'm leaving now. The kids are with my folks for a few days and I'll be working from home. Call if you need anything and I'll rush right over." James kissed them both goodbye.

Heidi immediately turned her attention to Anne. "You need to get out of that dress and into a shower. Go wash out those scratches." Heidi pushed her to the bedroom. "I'll look after the animals."

* * *

In the bedroom, Anne took off her dress. Stepping into the hot water of the shower, she let it run down her body, washing away the last dirt, Henry's blood, and her tears. She replayed the scene over and over in her mind, the guilt of her escape at Henry's expense relentlessly pummeling her. The reason she did not go back was because she was afraid, not because Henry told her to run. Right or wrong, in her heart, she had failed him.

Anne climbed into bed that night afraid and ashamed. Maybe she didn't know what true love really was. She hadn't been willing to make the sacrifice to save Henry. She began to doubt her feelings for Henry. How could she have left him like that? After all he had done for her, she hadn't stayed to help him and he'd been hurt as a result. She cried, her tears taunting her that she had failed the one she thought she loved. Could she really love if she couldn't make the right choices; make the sacrifices love called for? Maybe this was who she really was. The thought scared her.

That night, Heidi, Charlie, and the shotgun curled up on an air mattress next to Anne's bed. She didn't dream of black dragons because she lay awake reliving the attack and the taunts of "The Master" wanting her. Was the past she so desperately wanted to uncover catching up to her? If so, why didn't she remember any of it, of them, of him? Maybe it would be better not to remember anything at all.

30. THIEF IN THE NIGHT

Saturday, July 18

It was ten days after the attack. Henry was enjoying some time alone at home. After three days in the hospital and a week at home with Anne and Heidi taking care of his every need, he was all pampered out. They followed him everywhere he went, treating him like an invalid, insisting on opening every door, fetching food from the fridge, retrieving the remote and changing the channels—everyone knows you never get between a man and the TV remote! It could disrupt the balance of the space time continuum or worse.

He was relishing his break from recuperation so he could have a few hours to actually recuperate. He sent Anne with Heidi to a home shopping party Heidi had been invited to long ago. She protested and refused at first, but he'd finally gotten her to agree.

He ambled to the refrigerator to grab a can of soda, as beer and pain meds didn't mix, then made his way to the sofa to watch a horror movie about a knife wielding killer on the loose in a small town—something he didn't think would help Anne's nightmares go away. Probably also not the best movie to watch after what happened, but he liked horror movies.

The phone rang.

"Good Afternoon, Detective Ortega!" Henry said, grabbing it. "I hope this means you have good news!"

"I'm sorry, Henry. Our research didn't yield any results. But I wanted to talk about what happened to you. Officer Wilson told me about the attack."

"Yeah, that's a game changer for sure. The fact they specifically targeted Anne tells me they're connected to her, and not in a good way."

"That brings me to the other possibility," Detective Ortega suggested. "I'm concerned with your report of the attackers talking about taking Anne to 'the Master.' Is that what they said?"

"Yeah." Henry frowned remembering Blondie's words. "I have no idea what they meant by that."

"Well, there's another possibility. Anne may have been involved in something darker than we thought."

"What do you mean?" Henry's stomach cramped with trepidation, making the wound hurt more.

"There's a possibility she may have been a victim of human trafficking. That would explain a lot of things, like why there are no records of a boat fire or missing person's report. These guys don't file reports with the Harbor Patrol or Coast Guard. They aggressively avoid them. It could also explain why she dreams of fires, attacks and murder, and who this 'Master' may be. If your girl has been bought and paid for, maybe some rival cartel tried to abduct her, and something went horribly wrong. You better believe they'll stop at nothing to fulfill their contract. I've tried to find any explanation for what could have happened and when you add everything up, this seems like a very possible scenario."

Henry felt like he'd been kicked in the gut. The thought of Anne being sold on the black market tore at his sanity. "If any part of what you're saying is true, Ed, you better hope you find these assholes before I do." Henry was shaking, his pulse pounding in his ears.

"Calm down, Henry, I'm sorry I brought this up," Detective Ortega apologized. "But I have to consider all possibilities. Don't go off and do anything rash, especially in your condition. It's just one of many possible scenarios. We have no other leads and this recent event has me concerned. I'm going to do some more digging and see if I can find any known traffickers who go by the name of 'Master.' In the meantime, Henry, be careful. This is a dangerous situation."

"Thanks, Ed," Henry said. "I'll take all necessary precautions. Let me know if you find out anything more." He sank back on the sofa, regretting letting Anne out of his sight. Was he selfish, putting his own needs before her safety? If anything happened to her now, he would never forgive himself.

His mind absorbed what Detective Ortega told him. Even though he didn't want to face it, the explanation had to be considered. It would explain so much. The trauma she'd gone through must have been severe, to wipe her memory away. The nagging question that haunted him since he first met Anne rang out loud as a church bell in his ears. *What could have possibly happened to her to cause her to regress to a newborn, yet leave no physical evidence of injuries or sexual assault?* The answer Detective Ortega suggested tore at his heart like a lion tears through its helpless prey. It just didn't make any sense. Or maybe it made too much sense.

Henry relived what Anne revealed about her dreams at Susan's office, the horror of being brutally raped multiple times; her body mutilated before being cast into the fire. He felt conflicting urges to cry for her, or go out and kill someone. To run outside and scream at the universe for the pain inflicted on this girl who meant everything to him. He would face a thousand thugs with a thousand knives if he could take away what had been done to her!

He put in a DVD, picked up his drink and put his feet on the coffee table, sliding it away to accommodate his long legs. He was dressed only in his running shorts, going commando. He had to get his mind off the call or he would go insane. He hoped the movie would do the trick.

Halfway through the movie, Henry started to doze off. The dogs' barking snapped him back to reality. *Uh oh, something's up.* Slowly, Henry got to his feet, his muscles still stiff, his wounds nagging. He paused the movie and headed to the bedroom for his gun. "What is it, Charlie, what's going on?" he whispered.

Charlie whined, circling between Henry and the back door, clearly agitated by something.

Henry retrieved his pistol, then cautiously cracked open the door to peek outside. There was nobody there, but that didn't mean there was nothing dangerous lurking about. The dogs pushed their way out.

"Heel," he commanded. Charlie stayed glued to his hip on their walk around the house. The dog was alert, sniffing the ground around them.

After they made a complete circuit and found nothing, Henry took the dogs inside. The animals stayed near the door whining, pacing back and forth, reluctant to leave the kitchen. Even the cats were agitated and scattered to find good hiding places.

Henry headed back into the living room. Before he reached the sofa, a black shadow crashed on top of him, whisking him away into oblivion.

31. THE WAREHOUSE

Henry woke to intense pain in his side. He looked down to see he was naked and bleeding. His bandages had been ripped off and the wound viciously reopened. His arms were stretched above and to the sides, gripped by heavy metal shackles that cut into his wrists. He was strung between two poles, his legs spread with metal restraints at his ankles. The blood from the gash in his side ran down his body, pooling on top of the metal restraint. He seemed to be an old abandoned warehouse. Other than two dim hanging lights with hooded metal shades above him, the rest of the room was dark.

Two men sat on a rusty metal desk.

Henry felt a knot in the pit of his stomach. They were the men who had attacked them at the beach, dressed as they had been that night, in black jeans with black long sleeve shirts, leather gloves and black knit caps on their heads. Henry imagined white circles painted on their shirts reading THUG 1 and THUG 2. The tall guy sat on the edge of the desk. Blondie sat in a metal chair. Both had bandages over their noses. Henry smiled at his handiwork. *Let me down from here, Jerkoffs, and I'll make a broken nose the least of your problems.*

"Where the hell am I?" he croaked, finding his throat dry and raw. He heard a reply but it didn't come from either of the men.

Rather, from behind him came a deep growling voice that didn't quite sound human. "You are my guest, Mr. Williford."

"Wh-who the hell are you?" Henry struggled against the chains but they were too taut to get any movement.

"Let's just say we have a mutual... acquaintance," the voice rumbled.

Henry was finding it hard to breathe stretched out as he was. "Wh... What...do...you want...with Anne? You...leave...her...the hell... alone. I'll kill you...I swear!"

Blondie stood up and punched Henry's stab wound. Henry squeezed his eyes against agonizing pain.

The voice oozed over the room like rancid honey. "Patience, my friend. You'll know soon enough. Stan."

The black man looked up.

"Make the call."

Stan took Henry's cellphone. He punched in a number and moments later his voice oozed out. "Hello, Anne. We met the other night but you were rude and ran off, remember?"

Henry's heart froze. "Leave her...the hell... alone!" He struggled against the wrist shackles. "Leave her alone!"

The voice from behind chuckled. "Don't worry. She's an old friend. She'll be surprised to see me again."

"I don't know why you...assholes are doing this...I don't care. Do what you want...with me, just leave her...out of it."

Stan and the other man laughed.

The voice from behind spoke. "She is the reason you are here. I could care less about you. Stan, go ahead."

Stan held the phone to his ear. Henry could hear Anne screaming into the phone. "Who is this? What do you want?"

"Calm down, sweetie," Stan said. "We've got your boy here. If you want to see him alive again, get into the black car waiting outside. We know where you are. Come alone. Don't tell Heidi you're leaving." There was a pause as Anne spoke but Henry couldn't make out what she was saying. Then Stan put the phone up to Henry. "Tell her you're fine, lover boy. She just wants to hear your voice."

Henry shouted, "Don't come here, Anne! Call the police! Don't worry about m—" Blondie punched him, causing the wound to gush fresh blood. Henry couldn't even double over in response, as the chains cut into his flesh and restrained him. He rolled his eyes. The room turned red from the pain.

"Come alone and don't say anything to anybody if you want to find him alive. Be a good girl. Get into the black car and everything will be fine," Stan's voice smiled. He ended the call and spoke to the voice in the dark. "She's on her way." Stan threw Henry's phone on the floor and stomped it, crushing it.

"No," Henry whispered. "Anne, no."

The voice in the dark drew closer. Hot air brushed the skin on Henry's back. He turned his head to see the face of the voice in the dark. "What do you...want with us?"

"All in good time, my friend," it said. "All will be revealed in good time. Stan, Ed, let's make our guest comfortable while we wait for my Lady."

As Henry hung between the poles like a fly laced in a spider's web, he tried to figure out who the mystery voice was. Was this the man from Anne's past? Were these people the traffickers Detective Ortega warned him about? Was this ass-wipe the 'Master' Thug 1 and Thug 2 were yammering about the other night?

He only had a moment to contemplate the possibilities before Stan and Ed started beating him with wooden strips. They took turns hitting him in the back, legs and side. He was grateful they left the stab wound alone for the time being. He could take the beating elsewhere, letting his muscles absorb the blows, but the tender area around the wound burned. He closed his eyes, bit his lip, and tensed his body in anticipation of each blow. *Have your fun while you can, boys.* Henry tried to keep his courage up. *Payback's gonna be a bitch when I get loose.*

He didn't know how long it would take Anne to get to where they were. After a half an hour of beating him, Stan and Ed stopped, breathing heavily from their labors. Henry relaxed a little, bowing his head at the respite.

"Oh no!" The mysterious voice feigned distaste. "Our painting is uneven! As an artist, Mr. Williford, I'm sure you want your work to be balanced. Boys, you need to make sure that your 'brush strokes' are evenly distributed on our canvas. We must present a complete picture for my Lady to help her understand the situation."

Stan and Ed sighed, took a drink of water, cracked their necks, and began beating their human canvas again with renewed vigor. This time they didn't hold back. Henry tried not to cry out. He didn't want to give them the satisfaction. But the blows to his wound and groin were too painful. He was soon covered in horizontal red welts, some bleeding, with the flow of blood from his side intersecting the welts with dark red lines.

"Beautiful, isn't it?" the voice drawled. "I'm sure you couldn't do better yourself, Mr. Williford. My only regret is that we ruined that beautiful dragon tattoo. Oh well, couldn't be helped." The voice sounded closer now. "Maybe I should call you Henry, seeing as we are now friends. I hope you enjoyed our play time," the voice continued. "The main event will be so much more fun! We have to show my Lady only the best."

Henry's chin was on his chest. He struggled to breathe, between being stretched out and the beating. He slowly lifted his head and partially opening his swollen eyes. "I...told you…. Leave...her...alone...or...I swear..." was all he managed to get out.

"Henry," the voice admonished. "You are in no position to make threats." The voice moved behind him. "You thought you could love her, didn't you."

"I…do love her."

The voice cackled with what might have been laughter. "Did you really think you could have what was mine? You could never be worthy of a creature like her. Your arrogance will cost you dearly."

Mine? Detective Ortega was right! Human traffickers! Real fear began to seep into his heart. *Anne! What have they done to you?*

"We have a full evening planned for both of you," the voice purred. "We're just getting started. So why don't you sit back, well, hang back in your case, and enjoy the show!"

Henry heard a car pulling up and the doors closing. Anne was here!

* * *

An hour earlier, Anne had been enjoying her outing with Heidi until she got a call she thought was from Henry. It was one of her attackers from the other night. Her legs gave out and she fell into a chair. Panic washed over her. She struggled to remain calm and not alert anyone at the party to the seriousness of the situation. Henry was in trouble and she wasn't going to run this time. She would follow the instructions to the letter and trust God to help them get through this.

Hanging up, she headed to the front door. The car was waiting. She didn't answer any questions from Heidi or their host, briefly glancing at Heidi before she left, her fearful eyes conveying a message. The back door on the passenger side opened and a voice in the darkness spoke. "Get in." Two men sat in the back, dressed in black jeans, shirts and knit caps.

One pointed a gun at her. "Sit still and be quiet," he ordered her. "Give me your phone." A moment later he threw it out the window of the speeding car. "Make one sound and I'll put a bullet in that pretty face of yours, understand?" Anne opened her mouth to speak but caught herself before she said anything. She nodded, fighting back the torrent of tears trying to get out. She felt sick to her stomach.

Anne couldn't understand why someone would do this to her and Henry. She closed her eyes, remembering what she had learned about faith, and held her hands together, trying to form the right words to ask the God she had come to trust to protect her and Henry. She prayed for the strength to face whatever was waiting for her.

She couldn't see where they were heading through the blackened windows. A divider hid the driver in the blackness of the interior. They rode in silence. The man holding the gun smiled, then shoved it inside Anne's blouse, ripping off some of the buttons. His eyes drank in her exposed flesh. He pulled the gun out, leering at her like a juicy steak about to be devoured.

Finally, they reached their destination. The shorter one held the door for her, helping her out of the car. Her legs felt like jelly. Her chest hurt. She had to force herself to take the next few steps into an old, dark building.

The smell of rotting wood and animal feces assaulted her senses. Gravel and dead leaves crunched beneath her feet with every step growing heavier and heavier. Anne wished she was home having one of her nightmares. Horrible as they were, they paled in comparison to her current reality. At least with nightmares, she would wake up safe in her lover's arms.

Anne's throat tightened at the sight of Henry, bound in heavy chains and strung up so tight his limbs were almost pulled from their sockets. Blood pooled beneath him. He had been beaten so badly, she thought he was dead.

"*No!*" She screamed and ran towards her love only to be knocked to the ground in front of him. She was dragged to her feet and held in vice-like grips, tears streaming down her face. "*Why?*" Anne pleaded. Henry's eyes flashed open and blinked. A raspy, angry groan escaped his parched lips.

A deep growling voice thundered in the darkness.

"Now, now, my dear," the voice oozed with glee. "Not so fast. I have been waiting for this moment for a very long time."

"Who are you!" she cried struggling against her captors.

"Don't you know?" the voice said. "Don't you remember?" A towering shape lumbered out of the shadows into the dim light. He stood before her, over seven feet high, skin covered in scales the color of India ink. His nostrils flared at the end of a short snout, revealing a mouth of pointed teeth. A ridge of bony spikes outlined his face, mouth, and eyes tapering off at the tip of his pointed ears. His powerful chest and massive arms seemed diminished beneath the enormous black wings which folded against his back. His glowing red eyes were human in shape but had no pupils.

The creature walked up to Anne, grabbing her chin in his clawed hand. His forked tongue licking his lips. "Hello Aeya, how about a kiss for your beloved Uncle Saphan?"

Anne's head spun. Her legs folded under her and she would have fallen if not for the two thugs who held her arms. She couldn't breathe, couldn't see and couldn't move. There before her stood Saphan!

How could he be real! He was only in her nightmares! A manifestation of her imagination! But there he stood in front of her, changed from the hellish figure in her dreams, but it was him just the same. It was him. He was real! She felt the heat from his breath. The room grew dark and her vision blurred. She could not comprehend what was happening.

"Get my Lady a chair," Saphan hissed.

A metal chair slammed hard against the back of her knees forcing her to sit. She wanted to scream but couldn't muster a sound from her open mouth. Sharp, intense pain filled her chest. Each pulse of her rapidly beating heart magnified throughout her body. All the fear of her nightmares, combined with the shock at seeing Henry beaten and bleeding, converged on her like an avalanche of emotion, burying her in terror so intense her body shut off. She passed out, slipping into blackness.

32. CHOICES

"Wake up, my dear," the voice of evil commanded. "Do not spoil my game. Open your eyes, Aeya. Open your eyes or I will slit your lover's throat."

Anne forced her tear-filled eyes to open. She lay on her back, naked, on a metal desk, her hands bound in front of her. Saphan knelt on the floor looking into her eyes, his red eyes burning into her soul.

"Aeya," he said, smiling, then stood up. "Imagine my surprise when I discovered you were still alive after I ordered you thrown into the fire." He walked around the table to stand near her head. "When my Tannen told me there was no sign of your burnt body in the fire, I knew something wasn't right. I was so angry I slayed them all, one by one. It took me a long time to find you and understand what happened."

"Let me tell you a story, my Lady." Saphan walked around the desk. "After Aesmay defeated me and banished me to the Black Mountains, I wanted to die. I hated him and I hated you! All I wanted was revenge on my dear brother and his offspring.

"That's when my Master found me cursing all of you in the darkness. He promised me the strength to defeat my enemy if I would swear my allegiance and serve him. I gladly accepted and surrendered myself to his will. In exchange, my Master gave me the power of fire and the strength to defeat Aesmay."

Saphan looked up at the ceiling, his eyes closed, breathing heavily, his fists clenching and unclenching. "Aesmay was such a fool! He thought we were sent to guide the Thraekenya. He never understood we were meant to *rule* them! I can't tell you how delicious it felt plunging my crystal knife into his foolish heart. To feel his pathetic life leave him at my hands and flow around my feet made my heart soar."

Saphan leaned over Anne, his hot and foul breath burning her cheek. "Then taking you was the most stimulating and thrilling crown to my revenge. My only regret was he didn't last long enough to see it. To watch me take his precious and forbidden daughter would have been priceless! How tasty your flesh was, how...vulnerable...your body was under me! But, the gift from my Master comes at great price and only you can give me back what was paid."

Anne forced herself to look into his face through eyes blurred with tears. "What can I give you? I do not have anything!"

He kissed Anne's forehead. "You have Aesmay's powers, my dear! You have the power to change your appearance, which is what I want." Saphan walked down the side of the desk, dragging his claws down her body, leaving long deep cuts on her skin. "You chose our true appearance, probably thinking you could hide among the humans, blending in with them."

"I did not choose," Anne whispered. "I do not know what happened to me."

"What?" Saphan appeared stunned. "How could you not know—wait! That so-called 'Great Creator' of yours must have interceded. That would explain how you escaped the volcano. Well, I am not as fortunate as you, my sweet. Because I cast my lot with my Master. He enhanced the body the Creator gave me into something far more enjoyable. Apparently, though, that is the reason I couldn't completely transform and am now caught between Tannen and Aeyohem. This was the cost I paid to gain my victory."

"I still do not understand what you want from me and Henry?"

"Henry? Henry was the key, my dear. He served two purposes."

"What purpose?" Anne cried.

"First, without Henry how would I ever have been able to get you to accept my…invitation? Besides, he volunteered the moment he chose to play, what do they call them on this world—oh yes, hero—and foil our attempts to collect you."

"And the other reason?"

"That should be the most obvious of all, my Lady." Saphan snapped open one powerful wing, punching Henry hard in his mid-section. Henry screamed in pain. "It was so much *fun*!"

Saphan and his men roared with laughter.

Anne wept. "What do you *want* with me?"

Saphan's demeanor became deadly serious. Flapping his massive wings, he hovered over the terrified girl, inches above her body. Saphan gripped her head, cupping her face in his clawed hands. "You have the ability to give me back my power, my sweet."

Anne looked up at him trembling. "I do not understand," she said, gagging from the stench of his fowl breath.

Saphan took one hand and pointed a sharp claw at Anne's chest. "You have Aesmay's heart." He dug his claw deep into her chest, ignoring her screams of pain. "Aesmay's heart is power and when I have it, I will be restored to my former magnificence. There are so many new mates I can take on this world, and I do want to look my best."

"Leave her alone!" Henry spit.

"Shut him up," Saphan ordered his servants. "I have no more use for his words."

Stan shoved a dirty rag in Henry's mouth and sealed it with duct tape.

"But," Saphan continued, "here is my dilemma. For me to gain your power, I cannot simply take it from you, or we wouldn't be having this conversation. No, my dear, you must give it to me willingly. You see, you have Aesmay's authority because he gave it to you. You must make a choice."

Anne shook her head. "I don't know what I have or how to give it to you."

"Lucky for you, I do. This is the choice you have. In order for me to have your power, you must surrender your heart to me, your physical heart. You will give yourself to me freely, unlike the last time. Then I will rip out your heart and consume it. But before I do, know that what you suffered before will be nothing compared to what you will suffer now." He patted her cheek. "I know, I know. What kind of choice is that? Only a fool would make it...unless properly motivated."

He extended the longest claw on his left hand in front of Anne's face. With a wink, Saphan soared over to Henry and stood next to him, extending his right hand behind Henry's back, as if in friendship. "The choice, my dear, is that if you do not give me what I require, you will watch Henry die a slow, painful death. I will rip him apart piece by delicious piece."

At that moment, he plunged his claw deep into the knife wound on Henry's side and twisted it back and forth, expanding the wound, a fresh spurt of blood spewing from the gash. Henry screamed into the gag, straining fervently at the restraints in his attempt to escape the pain.

Saphan removed his claw, licking off Henry's blood. "The choice is yours, my Lady. Give your heart to me or Henry will suffer everything you endured in your dragon form. You do remember what that was like, don't you? And Aeya, I do mean...*everything*! Then, after I'm done with him, he will *burn*. So, Aeya, what will it be, your life or your love?"

Anne wept bitterly. Somehow this was all real, but how could that be? How could Saphan force her to make such a choice? How could she endure the terrifying ordeal of Saphan's assault and torture? Could she live and watch Henry suffer them instead, then to die such a horrible death?

She fought to breathe, her lungs burning with fear. Her heart pounded against her sternum. She couldn't move, her muscles lost all control. Terror worked its way through her body. Her nightmares were real!

The realization made her sick. She turned on her side and vomited over the desk until nothing was left inside. This couldn't be real! She drew her knees up to her chest, sobbing into the ropes around her wrists, her hands to her face. She had asked God to help! How could He let this happen? She felt abandoned, like her nightmare in the cave, waiting for Saphan's minions to take her to him again. Despair overwhelmed her, clouding her vision and her mind.

Saphan was losing his patience. He walked over to Henry and dug his claw into the open wound, slowly dragging his claw across Henry's abdomen, slicing through skin and muscle, as if gutting a fish. Henry's intestines threatened to break through the wall of his abdomen at any moment. Henry screamed through his gag and wept, tears running down his cheeks and onto the tape around his mouth.

"Take the gag out, Eddie. Let Mr. Williford convince her."

Eddie ripped off the tape and pulled the oily rag out.

Henry gasped for breath. "Anne...please! Don't...Don't let him...take you! I can't...let you suffer...again. Please!"

"Enough!" Saphan waved his hand. "Put it back in."

Ed stuffed the rag back into Henry's mouth and put fresh tape over it. Henry thrashed against his chains cutting his wrists and ankles deeper, the belly wound expanding. The dark puddle under him grew.

"Aeya," Saphan sighed. "How long do you think Henry will last if I take him now? I'd much rather have you, and I think deep down inside you would too. In his condition, he wouldn't last five minutes under one of...my size. Make the right choice! Right now, even if I try to kill you, you can transform and escape to live again in another realm, like you did before. Henry can't. He will simply suffer. Then *die*! Then you will leave me no choice but to bring Heidi and the children over to play and start this all over again. *Choose*!" Saphan walked behind Henry, lifted his head up by his hair and started licking his face.

Anne's body seized and her sight went black. She heard a voice saying, "Do not be afraid. I am here. I will give you the strength to endure. I am here with you."

She knew then what she had to do; an act of true love, a sacrifice. She could and would make that choice. Her body relaxed. The finality of her fate was sealed. She understood what it meant to truly love someone, because her love for Henry overcame the intense fear, even in the face of her own death. The greatest gift she could give Henry was her life so that he could live. She was ready to make the sacrifice for love. Her cries quieted and her heart stilled. Although she was fearful of the pain and torment she would suffer, she felt peace, knowing she had chosen love, that love would sustain her through the upcoming ordeal.

She rolled back to face Saphan, who pressed to Henry's back, whispering in Henry's ear. Henry moaned behind the gag, his wet eyes shut tight against the anticipated assault.

Anne stared at him with defiance in her sapphire eyes. "I give you all of me, my heart and my body to do with as you will. But you must promise that Henry will live."

Saphan nodded. "You have my word. Henry will live." Saphan backed away. "Bring him down. My Lady has chosen. Bind up the wounds. Take him to the main road."

"You must take him to a hospital or home to his sister. She's a nurse, a...a healer. He needs help." Anne pleaded.

"And risk capture? I think not. He should make it to town by sunrise. By then, our little party will be over and we'll be long gone. He'll be fine," Saphan reassured.

The men loosened Henry's chains, his body collapsing on the floor with a loud thud. While the others unlocked the shackles, Stan asked, "What should I bind the wounds with Master?"

"I don't care. Use the duct tape."

Stan gathered whatever he could to help patch the Master's handiwork, including Henry's shorts. He held the garments over the wound while Ed wrapped duct tape around Henry's abdomen, bracing the wall against the breach. As soon as they pulled him to his feet, Henry tried to wrestle his way out of their grasp to reach Anne, but was too weak to sustain the fight. "No, Anne! Please...don't do this! Please! I love you!"

"I have to do this," Anne whispered, tears streaming down her cheeks. She kept her eyes on him, wanting to remember his face when she endured what had to be. "I love you too, Henry, so very much! Go home to Heidi, James and the kids. Live a good life and don't forget me. This is my gift of true love, my sacrifice for my love for you."

"Get him out of here," Saphan waved his hand dismissing Henry.

"Please," Henry fought to stay. "Let me stay with her!"

"As much as I love an audience, I already have one. My willing servants are ready to play the game with me. You have your life, Mr. Williford. Aeya is mine. Take him far from here and leave him where he can find help."

"No!" Henry shouted. "No!" Weakened by the loss of blood and the beating, he could not fight Saphan's men. They dragged him away from her sight. Anne closed her eyes, keeping his face in her mind.

Anne could only lie on the desk, silently crying out to God to watch over Henry, and to give her the strength to endure what was to come. She did not know what would happen if she died this time. She didn't understand what

Saphan had told her about her ability to transform her body and travel to another realm. Whatever was going to happen could not be changed.

Anne squeezed her eyes and waited for the first strike, the tears that would never stop until her death washing into her hair and spilling onto the desk. Saphan positioned himself in front of her and roared like a hundred lions standing over her, the sound hurting her ears and rattling the walls of the building.

33. GOING BACK

As Henry was being dragged out of the warehouse, an exchange between Saphan and one of his goons made his blood freeze.

"Sir," Stan said. "Do you think it's wise to drop him off on the main road? If he gets picked up by a passing car, or worse, a cop, he'll give up our position in a heartbeat."

Saphan backhanded Stan to the ground knocking out several teeth. "Question me again and I'll tear out your spine!" the dragon-man hissed. "I promised my Lady he would live. I never said for how long. Keep him alive long enough to fulfill my end of the bargain. Then take him out on the back roads and dump him where no one will find him. The local wildlife will take care of the rest."

Henry tried to scream, to warn Anne of Saphan's betrayal, but the scaly fist hit the side of his head sending him into blackness.

He woke up on the floor of the black sedan, his hands bound behind him. He didn't know how long the car had been traveling. Henry did his best to track what direction they turned, but his head was pounding too badly. They were not in a populated area. There was no other traffic and the road was bumpy. If they were going to put a bullet in the back of his head, they would have done it long before now.

Finally, the car stopped. Two of Saphan's sycophants dragged him out and dumped him on the side of the road. They were in a heavily wooded area with no lights visible from any towns or cities. The men got back into the car and drove off, leaving Henry bound, naked, and weak. He had a choice, either he could try to find help, or try to get back to where Anne was, wherever that was. It really was an easy choice after all. He could not leave her. Once he made it to his feet, he took off in the direction the sedan went.

Although the pain in his stomach was excruciating, the duct tape binding actually seemed to help. It was pitch black in the middle of the night. The stars shining overhead gave him some hope. He ran through a mental map of the area he believed he was in, based on the time it took for Anne to get there from the time they called her, estimating they were maybe sixty miles from Venice. That could put them somewhere between Venice and Arcadia, Florida, possibly in the Myakka River State Park. Henry didn't remember any warehouses around there. So it had to be beyond the Park. The roads they traveled on were mostly rough, and the fact that there was no traffic around also made him believe they were in an unincorporated area.

He tried not to despair as he ran, thinking of the hopelessness of finding her in time. But he had to try. He could not go back to his life without her, finally admitting he was truly in love with her, the kind of love that would last beyond the grave. If he could just stay alive until he got to her, he would tell her. A weaker man would have succumbed to the wound to his stomach, but his powerful physique held him together.

After he lost sight of the red taillights of the sedan, he decided to keep to the gravel road he was on until it intersected with a paved road. He reviewed the mental notes he had taken on his ride here. The last turn they made before leaving the paved road was left, so they had to go to the right to go back the way they came. That was the direction he headed.

Henry's entire body ached from his ordeal and his wounds still bled. His throat was raw and his left eye partially swollen shut. Still, he ran for what seemed like hours. He was not worried about the roads as much as he was on alert for signs of alligators. Saphan was right; the Florida wildlife could easily "take care" of him.

At one point, he passed a road sign that had been run over by someone long ago, leaving a jagged metal stump where the post used to be. He used the sharp edge to cut through the tape binding his hands. With his hands free, he could now use them to support his stomach and help hold himself together.

Once he heard the sounds of cars on a highway somewhere to his left. He kept off the main roads because that was consistent with the feel of the sedan on his way to the area where they forced him out of the car. Also, a naked bleeding man running around wouldn't be allowed to roam free for very long. If he were seen, he would undoubtedly be picked up by the police who would take him to a hospital and away from Anne. He couldn't risk that, even if the police would act in his best interests. There was no time! He had to find her before Saphan took her heart. Besides, no one would believe him.

He kept running, imploring the heavens above that he would find Anne still alive. The farther he went with no sign of the place he believed they were keeping Anne, the more he needed to rely on a forgotten faith.

"God, if you're... there," he managed between gulps of air. "Keep her alive...I...love...her...." He hadn't prayed in a long time. But each time he fell to his knees, he called out to God for the strength to get up and keep going.

The farther he ran, the stronger his pleas grew.

He tripped over a branch and fell face first into the ground. He lay there for a few minutes, unable to get up. The pain in his stomach was unbearable. He rolled over on to his side and listened to the voices in the night.

You'll never make it.

She's already dead.

You'll die out here and they won't find your body for months.

Don't believe in God again, he'll let you down like he always has.

Henry fought against the despair and the pain, tears washing trails down his mud-stained face. Hope was as dark as the night around him. It would be so easy just to stay on the ground and close his eyes. Maybe it would be better to just die here…

It was useless. He would never get to Anne in time. Even if he did, what could he do against a dragon man and six armed men?

"God," he cried. "Why do you hate me so much? Why did you turn against me?" Henry lay sobbing into the mud.

Get up! There is hope.

He heard something else....

Henry pushed aside the desolation. He had to get up. He had to get to Anne. *Shut up!* He cried out to stop the taunting voices. With everything in him, he rolled over and made it to his knees. He willed his broken body to obey. *Get up!*

He saw a puddle of rainwater near where he had fallen and drank his fill, splashing water on his face. The water gave him enough strength to get back on his feet. He started running again, pushed by his love for the golden haired woman and some unseen force holding him up. Maybe God was watching out for him after all. Maybe God really did love him, even when he couldn't see it. It was a miracle he was still alive and able to move at all, let alone run. With every step forward, he was finding his way back to his Heavenly Father.

"Father, I know I've turned my back on you. But I need you now. God, how I need you! Help me to get to her. Let her still be alive!" The further he ran, the easier Henry found it to pray.

His vision at times became blurry and he pushed himself on only by sheer will, fighting off his body's threats to throw him into shock and shut down. The only thing keeping him going was the adrenaline rush caused by his intense desire to get to Anne. He prayed he was still traveling in the right direction.

Henry tapped into the connection he had developed with Anne. Somehow, he sensed she was still alive, and her life force was pulling him toward her. *I'm coming, Sweetheart, just stay alive and I will find you.* The gravel crunched under his bare feet with each stride. The sky above started to lighten with the dawn.

Finally, he saw a building fifteen or twenty yards ahead. It was surrounded by a dense overgrowth of trees and bushes. There was a rusted metal-sided building with dock doors on one side.

In the front was a parking lot with broken asphalt where wild grass and weeds burst through. Three black cars were parked in front, the sedan in which he and Anne rode and two SUVs. A faded and peeling sign read Miller's Boats.

Two of Saphan's goons, Carl and Ed, leaned on the sedan smoking, wearing only their black jeans. Henry ducked into the bushes and squatted.

"That was something else!" Carl exclaimed.

"Tell me about it," Ed agreed. "That was some weird shit. I mean, that was...*weird*."

"Yeah, like we was vampires or something."

Carl shrugged. "I guess." He shuddered. "I feel like I'm in a horror movie. Be glad when this assignment is over. I'm still covered with blood."

"You think that asshole boyfriend of hers might have found his way to the main road and called for help?"

"No way! Even if his guts didn't pop as soon as we dumped him, the gators'll get him before he finds help. You saw all the blood on the floor and the beating we gave him. He's either already dead, or passed out and soon will be."

Henry squatted behind the bushes between the needle palms and high grass feeling his blood boiling, realizing they were talking about Anne. But he had to be smart. He was naked, unarmed and very weak. All it would take is one punch to his gut and he'd be done. They both carried AR-15 high-powered rifles on their backs and 9mm Glocks on their belts. Henry picked up a chunk of the asphalt about the size of a football. He silently made his way through the trees and behind the vehicle. He waited for his chance. There was no way these guys would have dreamed he'd find his way back here, which gave him the much needed element of surprise.

Carl put out his cigarette, hefted his rifle to settle more comfortably on his back and turned to head back into the warehouse. "Guess we better get back. I wonder how far the Master has gone."

"Be right with you," Ed said. "I want to enjoy this smoke as much as I enjoyed the Master's playtime. I'm sure the Master isn't done yet."

Carl entered the building. Henry saw his chance. He lifted the piece of pavement above his head with both hands, snuck up behind Ed and brought it down with all his strength. Ed crumbled like a rag doll at his feet. Henry took a deep breath that hurt. He pulled the rifle off Ed's shoulder and took the handgun out of his belt. Then he slowly opened the door to enter the building, dreading what he might find.

The place was dark except for the end of the building where the two hanging lamps barely illuminated the area where they were held. Henry saw Carl and the four other goons standing in front of the metal desk, laughing and cheering. Henry didn't have time to dwell on them. He had to get to Anne. He could not see beyond them to where she was. He stayed along the dock side of the building and crept up to the scene.

What he saw took his breath away, freezing his heart and causing his stomach to seize up into a tight ball of pain extending down his legs. Saphan bent over Anne's prone figure, his teeth tearing at her shoulder. Large black wings spread above him, beating in time with his exertions. Henry watched in horror as Saphan threw back his head, Anne's flesh bloody in his mouth. He made one last violent thrust, then gave a bloodcurdling yell. He straightened, Anne's blood dripping off his huge frame.

But it was Anne that made Henry's knees weak. She'd been bitten, torn, and beaten everywhere. Three of her fingers were gone. Her long golden hair had been ripped out and lay in heaps around her head. Her arms, stomach, legs—all were mutilated with bites and the gashes of teeth. Blood spilled onto the floor in a wide puddle. She was alive though, her head to the side staring into the dark with eyes open, red with tears.

"*Noooo!*" Henry screamed, running to where Anne was.

Carl was the only one who still had a weapon. The others had left their guns on the floor with the rest of their clothes. Henry shot him in the chest first before he had time to aim. The other cowards dove to the floor to retrieve their guns in a feeble attempt to return fire, but were not fast enough. Henry peppered the area where they lay with fire, not sure if the bullets found their mark. He turned the automatic rifle on Saphan and held the trigger down.

Saphan laughed as the bullets bounced off his scaly skin. "That won't work on me, Mr. Williford." He thumped his chest with his fist. "Skin as hard as dragon scales you see. Wait a minute. I'm almost done here. I'll play with you after." With that, he thrust his clawed hand deep into Anne's chest, and pulled out her still-beating heart. She gasped as her body lifted with her heart. Once the heart was severed, she fell back to the desk with a wet slap, sending splatters of blood in a macabre fountain around her.

Henry screamed with everything inside him, tearing his throat and his vocal cords, and ran to Anne, only to meet head-on the hardened fist of Saphan. Henry collapsed in defeat, crushed by the knowledge he was too late. Anne, the love of his life, was dead. Saphan held Anne's heart up, his roar thundering in Henry's ears. Then he feasted on his prize.

34. HEAVEN

Light... I am surrounded by a bright light that shines warm around me, brighter even than the white sun of my home. I lie on a soft bed with satin pillows under my head. The light comes from a man standing by me dressed in a white robe that blinds me in its brilliance. I cannot see his face clearly but hear his voice. "Welcome, Anne."

"Where am I?"

"You are in my home." The man touches my cheek with his hand.

"Saphan took my heart!" I am afraid to know the answer but ask the question anyway. "Am I dead?"

"No." He smiles with such a soft smile. "You are merely in transition."

"What is happening to me?"

He holds my hand. "Saphan was wrong. He cannot take your power by taking your heart because, even though you gave it to him willingly, it was done with love for Henry."

"I do not understand." I try to sit up and he helps me.

"Anne, Aesmay and Saphan were created not as you remember them. They were the Aeyohem, the First Born, but chose to take the form of the Thraekenya when they inherited the world of the golden dragons. You are not from the dragon realm, but came directly from Aesmay's heart out of his love. You were not hatched from an egg but created in the form you are now. This is your true self.

"Only by love can this gift be given. It cannot be transferred or taken by any other means. You know Aesmay and Saphan were forbidden to mate, but Aesmay never told you why. The Aeyohem are pure and without sin. If they mate or sin in any way, they break their vow to me and become one of the Fallen, stripped of their transformative power and condemned to eternal fire. Saphan chose to disobey his vow and has become one of the Fallen."

"But as for Aesmay, after many years of faithful service to me and to the golden dragons of the Thraekenya, Aesmay came to me and pleaded for a child. He offered his Aeyohem heart in exchange for a dragon heart and a mortal life. I agreed, and used his heart to create you. When Aesmay gave his heart to create you, he willingly gave you all of his authority and power

to control the appearance of your body and to travel between the many realms of Aeyoronis. You too are one of the Aeyohem. This is the power Saphan lost in his fall, and the power he wanted restored to him but can never have."

"It was I who transformed you from Aeyohem to Thraekenya and sent you back to the Thraekenya. Aesmay would tell you the truth about who you really were and where you came from someday, but he wanted to wait until the twilight of his years before revealing your ability to transform and visit other realms. He could not bear the thought of losing you, he loved you that much. He died before he had the opportunity. Because you did not know you were Aeyohem and the vow on your heart came from Aesmay who never broke it, you alone of the Aeyohem are forgiven."

"That is why, when you were cast into the fire and wished you could be somewhere else, someone else, you were transported to the in-between place where I transformed you. That is why you did not know what it meant to be human. I have always had a plan for you, Aeya, for your future and your hope. And it has been that you be with Henry in your true form. Henry's finding you was no accident. It was by design. You were meant to be together."

I look at my body, which looks so much like my human body, but glowing with a translucent light under my skin. I have large white wings behind me that unfold into a beautiful display of iridescent feathers. My body feels strong and powerful, as if I can lift up the sky.

The man places his hand on my cheek. "Besides, Saphan cannot take what has already been surrendered. You gave your heart to me."

Suddenly, I am flooded with memories of my life as the Thraekenya called Aeya, daughter of Aesmay, and I know it is all real. My heart leaps in my chest at the revelation of my entire existence unfolding. But when I remember the destruction of my world, my heart hurts. I feel the death of each of the Thraekenya. "Why did they have to die?" I look up with tears in my eyes.

"Do not cry, little one." The man wipes away my tears. "When Aesmay surrendered his authority to you, dominion over the Thraekenya was given to Saphan to do as he willed. Aesmay knew that by giving his heart to you, he surrendered his own life to Saphan. But your suffering was the pain of birth that brought you into a new life with Henry and with me."

"What happens to me now?"

"I will give you the power to defeat your enemy. Return and avenge my children, your family. But then, because you are unique among your kind, having lived as a human without knowing your true form, you must choose your destiny. If you want to remain in this form, you will live forever with me in my home here, where you may be sent to other worlds to bring the good news to those realms, retaining the power you now have. There is much work to be done and many worlds that need to hear about me. However, you will never be with Henry again.

"If you choose to stay with Henry, you do so by my law. You will become human, subject to all the frailties of man, including your allotment to die. You will no longer be able to change your form or travel to the realms of Aeyoronis on your own. Someday, you will die and return here to be with me forever. But there are also greater works I have planned for you and Henry.

"Also, my child, I have a gift for you. Because I know what you have suffered and lost, I give you back all the memories of your kind regardless of your choice, but I take away all the pain you have endured."

"Why would you do this for me?"

"Because I have been waiting for you since the time you were first created, child of the First Born. I have always loved you, Aeya." He kisses my forehead.

With His kiss, all the pain and sorrow of my torture, exile, and death wash away like the sand under the waves of the beach. My spirit soars and I weep with infinite joy, the fear carried so long in my heart evaporating. I feel a peace deeper than the oceans cover me, and I know in my heart that everything will be alright now; there will be no more nightmares. And I finally know what true love really is.

The man takes my hand. "Do not worry about Henry. Give him the gift you have received with a kiss. Tell him who you are. All will be as it should be. And know that even when you may face difficult times ahead, I will always be with you here." He points to my heart.

I cry and hug him. "Thank you, but I do not even know your name."

"Yes, you do." He smiles as the light begins to fade away.

I do know him. I have always known him.

35. FINAL BATTLE

Henry crouched on the floor of the warehouse, his head in his hands. Tears flowed from his broken heart. He was too late to save Anne who lay lifeless on the old metal desk, her heart consumed by Saphan. He knew he was also going to die here in this old broken down warehouse. It didn't matter anymore. Anne was gone. His reason for living was gone. He didn't want to face life without her. He just prayed it would be quick.

Saphan swallowed the last of the organ and turned toward Henry. "I gave you the chance to live, you pathetic fool. With my princess gone, I am free from my promise. I am going to enjoy your agony and humiliation. You will be my dessert!"

Henry stood, shaking his head, weapons raised before him. His hope for a quick death wasn't going to happen. "Try and do what you want, Saphan. But I won't go easy. I'm going to take you down with me, you son of a bitch!" He felt like a child kicking the toes of a giant, bracing his legs for a fight he could not possibly win, but also couldn't walk away from.

Saphan approached, smiling. Anne's blood dripped off his teeth. His massive body poised for another attack. Henry swallowed and waited, fingers hovering over the triggers. Saphan reached out his claws to grab his prey.

Suddenly, a bright light blazed from where Anne's devastated body lay. Henry gazed astonished, realizing the light was coming from her remains, increasing in intensity and closing the wounds on her body. Her form began to grow larger and transform. Her torso lengthened into a serpentine shape and her hands and feet grew long and sprouted sharp claws. Her head stretched out, and her eyes became pure white. She grew until her massive form touched the ceiling.

When the transformation was complete, a great golden dragon filled the room. "I am Aeya of the Aeyohem, last of the Thraekenya, and I will avenge my father and my kind."

Saphan spun, crying out in surprise at the sight of Aeya's transformation. "How is this possible? I took your heart! You...you gave me your heart!" He backed away. He attempted to morph into his own dragon form and could not. Terror twisted his face.

The golden dragon queen faced her enemy. "My heart is not my power. You ate my flesh, but the power of the Aeyohem heart is the love that it holds. I have no love for you!" The glowing dragon descended on the black dragon-man, tearing his scaly body to pieces with her sharp teeth and long claws. Saphan struggled to fight her, but locked in his current form, he was no match for the massive golden dragon.

Saphan shrieked in agony and horror. He attempted to shield himself but couldn't escape Aeya's deadly claws. Bright white teeth pulled him apart bit by bit, his eyes remaining wide with fear. With one last stroke, the golden dragon tore out the throat of the once powerful Aeyohem. The severed scraps burst into flames before disintegrating into black dust, until he was decimated and reduced to a pile of putrid black ash. Without a body, a black wisp of shadow fled across the warehouse and out into the night sky, perhaps doomed to remain forever in a non-corporeal existence.

Henry stared in bewilderment watching the woman he loved transform into a mystical dragon creature capable of destroying the powerful demon enemy. He could not wrap his mind around what he was seeing. He must have already died and was in Heaven, or if he was still alive, he must be so in shock he was hallucinating. What he was witnessing was impossible!

When Saphan was no more, Anne's dragon-shape shrank back into a figure that looked like Anne but with glowing skin, and large iridescent feathered wings on her back. She started to walk toward him. "Henry," she called. "It's me, Anne."

"I—iI don't understand," Henry shook his head, his voice coming out almost as a squeak. "I watched you die! Then I saw you turn into a dragon! Now you're an...an angel? What are you?" He backed away until he hit the wall. His head was spinning and his knees were ready to buckle.

"I am Aeya and I am Anne." She held out her hands in supplication. "Aesmay was my father. He wasn't always a dragon. He and Saphan were the Aeyohem, the First Born, with the power to change their appearance and travel to different realms. They chose the form of dragons to guide the Thraekenya.

"My father surrendered his own heart to the Great Creator to bring me into existence, giving me his power to change my form and travel to other realms. I was unaware I had this power, for my father had not yet revealed it to me. When Saphan cursed me and threw me into the fires of the Black Mountain, the Creator intervened, transforming me into the human form you know as Anne. Then He sent me to be with you. That is why you found me like you did, why I had no memories. But now I know who I really am. I am Aeya, one of the Aeyohem, the First Born. What you see before you is who I truly am. But, Henry, my love, I am also Anne, the human woman who loves you with all my heart. Please Henry! Believe me!"

Henry stood staring at her. "You're a dragon!" he cried. "How is that even possible!" He looked at her, shaking his head, his mouth open and his eyes pleading. He sank down onto the floor, his mind and body both in shock. "You're a dragon!" he repeated over and over.

Anne's face softened, her arms out to him. "I don't know how it happened but I know it is true. I died and went to a place where I met a man and He showed me who I really was. He healed me and sent me back to be with you." She began to cry. "I love you! The Creator sent me here to this world so I could be with you! That is why the dragon in your dreams, when your mother died, gave you peace, the dragon you made into the tattoo. Henry, we are meant to be together!" The light from her body dimmed. She assumed her human form, her wings disappearing and the golden gleam of her skin returning to its normal color.

"I love you, Henry."

Henry didn't say anything for a while, remaining on the floor rocking back and forth, his lips pressed together in a tight frown, his arms in front of his face, clenched fists on his head. His heart warred with his intellect. The incredulity of what he had just witnessed struggled with the love for Anne in his heart.

What does anyone feel when faced with the truth, however fantastic it may be, of one's true love? What wins out, love or truth? Is love based on what one is on the outside or what one is inside? Anne was his true love and they were connected. They were meant to be together. Of that he was certain. But was it even possible for him to love such an incredible being? It —she— was Anne, but it was something more!

Henry felt as if the weight of the world was crashing down on him. But the possibility of life without Anne was far more painful than a thousand deaths. To be loved by this miraculous creature was a journey he could not imagine living without. And like Anne before him, suddenly he was filled with peace, the realization that he *did* love Anne, with all of his heart, broke through the shock, giving him clarity and resolve.

Finally, he took a painful breath and pushed himself up from the floor and stood before her. The battle was over. True love won.

"It all makes sense now," he nodded coming toward her. "I know it's crazy but I believe you!" He took her hand, tears flowing down his face. "Anne or Aeya, whoever you are, I love you! I want you with me forever. I don't care what you are. I can't lose you again. I love you more than life!"

With his whole being focused on the woman he loved, he didn't see Ed creep back into the warehouse and crawl behind the metal desk, picking up one of the loose guns. Henry heard the pop of the gun a heartbeat before the bullet slammed into his left side puncturing his lung. The shot threw him back several feet, where he collapsed in a heap on the floor.

Intense pain filled his chest, as if something had exploded inside him. It felt as if all the air had been sucked out of the room. The pain was unlike anything he had suffered to this point, making even his abdomen laceration pale in comparison. He couldn't talk, couldn't move; every breath a painful struggle, as if his lungs were being cut by a thousand knives.

Anne began to change again, the large white wings on her back extending, her skin glowing with a bright light. It was like watching a scene from a movie in slow motion. In her hand she held a fiery sword that created circles of fire in the air. She swung it down to slay the remaining servant of Saphan as he emptied what was left in the gun at her. The fire of her wrath wrapped around him, scorching him. Ed let out a blood curdling scream. The fire covered the bodies of the others who were dead, feeding on them until all that remained were the charred outlines of where they had lain. Their souls were given long ago to the Master; they were sent to reap their reward. Nothing remained of the attackers but ashes, clothes and guns.

Henry opened his mouth to call out to her but could not make any sound. His vision began to fade, the aggregate of the injuries his body sustained finally claiming him, the blood from the chest wound flowing out to join the puddle under the chains, draining him of his last strength. He was bleeding to death. He could feel his heart beat slowing down inside his chest – thump thump....thump...thump. The pain faded, all feeling in his body was gone. Henry felt only a sense of peace and euphoria. This was it. He was dying. He whispered a prayer, "Forgive me." His last thought as he slipped into oblivion was would he see Anne in Heaven.

* * *

With the enemy gone, Anne transformed back into her human form. She ran to Henry lying still in a puddle on the floor, his skin white as her wings. She held him in her arms, his body limp and lifeless. But she was not afraid. She had the assurance in her heart from the Man that everything was going to be alright. Anne knew what to do. She leaned over Henry's battered form and kissed his open lips.

* * *

A glowing golden cocoon of brilliant light encased Henry's body, touching every wound he had sustained, knitting together flesh, muscle, and tissue, shoring up the wall to hold in the breach, erasing the red and blue welts, the healing paintbrush filling them in with a healthy flesh tone. Henry lay peacefully on the floor, the unseen force washing over every part of him.

Finally the cocoon dissipated and Henry awoke filled with joy. He examined his naked form, shocked to discover his wounds healed, every one of them—even the gunshot. He pulled the duct tape off his abdomen to find only a thin pink scar where the slash had opened his belly. Even the injury on his leg was healed. He was strong, the shock from the wounds, the beating and the blood loss replaced by renewed energy, giving him back his life.

Anne smiled with that wonderful face-splitting smile.

At that moment, the child inside Henry stood triumphant on the hill, the flag of victory waving over his head. He'd found his faith again. God was real and had always been there, through his mom's death, his dad's passing, and even Christine's death. Henry was filled with inexplicable joy that erased all the pain he had carried around for so many years. God was real, and Henry would never doubt again! Henry and Anne wept copious tears, holding each other in a tight embrace.

Finally, Henry stood, helping Anne up.

"Where do we go from here?" He asked. "Do you…." he hesitated. "Do you go back to Heaven now? Will I ever see you again?"

She smiled, holding his hand. "No. I am staying here with you. I have made my choice, and I choose you."

"Can you be with me and still be an..." He couldn't get used to the idea of what she really was. "An angel?"

"Aeyohem," she corrected.

"Aeyohem. Isn't that against some kind of code or something?"

She looked down and slowly nodded her head. "It is true I cannot live among the Aeyohem and yet be with you as we have been. But I am unique among my kind because I have lived as a human in ignorance of my true nature. For me to stay with you though, I must give up my life as an Aeyohem and remain in human form, with all of the limits and vulnerabilities, including my allotment to die."

"Would you want to give up that kind of power? To be able to travel to different realms changing how you look? To live forever? For me?" Henry couldn't fathom such a choice.

She looked up at him and smiled her wonderful smile. "Yes!"

36. GOING HOME

Henry searched around the smoldering remains of the attackers, checking the clothes on the floor until he found some car keys. He also grabbed a pair of pants and put them on. They must have been Stan's because they were too long, but at least he was clothed. Even though he was healed, the blood from his injuries covered them both. He wiped off as much as he could with one of the abandoned shirts. Anne retrieved her clothes from a corner near the desk.

Anne resumed her human form, losing the wings and glowing light. Once dressed, they headed outside where they tried all the cars until they found the one the key started. It was the black sedan that had transported them both. "Let's go home," Henry said.

As he pulled onto the main road, he said, "You need to let me do the talking with the police." He was happy to be heading home but dreading having to explain all of this. "I don't think they'd believe us if we told them the truth that you're an angel."

"Why would they not believe us? It is the truth," Anne protested.

"I know, honey. But some people have a hard time believing in angels, demons, and—especially—dragons. I didn't until I saw it with my own eyes. They'll call you delusional or fanatical, or worse, insane, which may earn you a trip to a mental hospital. Some people can't deal with the impossible."

"I do not understand," she frowned. "Nothing is impossible. But I will do as you say."

"Just let me do the talking. My healing will be difficult enough for them to swallow. You coming back from the dead as a shape-shifting angel who ripped apart a dragon demon with your bare teeth, heck, I feel crazy just saying it and I was there. Besides, we now have the makings of a sequel to our book."

"Make our book squeal?"

"No, a sequel." He laughed. "I'll explain later."

Several squad cars were at the house when they pulled up, all with flashing lights. Officers scurried in and out of the house. The black sedan was instantly surrounded by officers with guns drawn, shouting to get out with their hands up. Henry and Anne slowly got out, hands in the air.

"Get down on the ground!" One officer commanded. Henry and Anne both lay down on the grass where officers converged on them, pulling their hands behind their backs and handcuffing them.

Suddenly, Officer Harrison, pushed through the group. "Wait," he yelled. "Those are the victims! Mr. Williford, Anne, are you alright? We've been looking everywhere for you since your sister called in the abduction!" He dropped to one knee to unlock the cuffs, then helped Henry to his feet. Henry was still covered in his own blood despite his efforts to clean up. Another officer released Anne and helped her up. SOmeone called for an ambulance.

"Thanks, I'm okay," Henry said. "We were held at Miller's Boat warehouse off Route 72 near Arcadia. We were both tortured by someone called 'the Master' who wanted to get back at Anne for some old grudge and used me as bait. I was shot in the side and the bullet pierced my lungs. My abdomen was also sliced open but, by the grace of God, I'm fine now. The blood you see is from those injuries."

"That's impossible," a cop named Vaquero chimed in. "If you were shot in the lungs you wouldn't be talking, let alone standing. You'd be dead."

Henry turned and showed him the scar. "I know, I can't explain it. I thought I was dead after the bullet hit me. Believe me, I've never felt such pain in my entire life. But something happened that can only be calleds a miracle because I'm okay now." He showed him the scar on his abdomen, a pink line almost the entire width of his waistline. "This is where they cut me. Officer Harrison can vouch that I didn't have this scar a few days ago."

"He's right," Harrison confirmed. "I was there ten days ago. I was the first responder and administered first aid. He had no cut like that."

Vaquero shook his head in disbelief.

Harrison turned to Anne. "Ae you okay? Did this Master hurt you?"

"Yes," she answered. "But God has healed me also."

"How did you get away?" Harrison asked. "What happened to this Master guy and the others?"

"I'm not sure," Henry replied. "Some kind of explosion took them all out. There were six guys, but there isn't much left to identify them now."

"Sit down," Harrison directed, making Henry sit back on the grass. "The ambulance is on its way. We're taking you both to the hospital."

"How did you get this car?" Vaquero asked. "It's the car your sister reported was involved in the abduction."

"We escaped the warehouse and found the keys in the ignition."

"We'll get a tow truck to take it to impound. We'll need both your prints to eliminate them from the others. Any idea what caused the explosion?"

"No," Henry lied. "We were restrained at the time. Luckily, we were far enough away to avoid being hit. It's strange though. Nothing else burned."

Vaquero didn't look convinced. "Just the same, best if you stay close and be available if we have more questions after we investigate the scene."

Henry nodded.

The ambulance pulled up, siren blaring and lights flashing. The paramedics raced to Henry and checked him for any wound that would have caused the immense amount of blood. Henry assured them he was fine and stood up, getting on the gurney under his own power. For the second time in as many weeks, Henry would take an ambulance ride to the hospital, even though he asserted he was okay.

"You're going too, Ma'am," Vaquero said to Anne. "You both need to be checked out."

The paramedics secured Henry in the ambulance, then helped Anne in, putting a blanket around her shoulders as she sat by Henry and they sped off.

Henry didn't get a chance to see the condition of the house since he was taken, which was probably just as well. When Harrison told him about the damage, he cringed. Dining room chairs had been smashed, books scattered all over the floor, the sofa ripped to shreds, and his beautiful eighty-four-inch plasma television…. Harrison must have thought he he'd suffered enough for one night. Henry's blood left a trail leading from the living room where he'd been attacked to the back door and into the yard.

He was relieved the animals were safe, having been retrieved by James and Heidi. All except Charlie. The brave canine suffered a broken leg. He must have defended his master against the creature that took him. He was at the vet getting extra special care for his heroic efforts. Henry's chest tightened at the news of his faithful companion's injury. He closed his eyes against the tears, so soon after losing Flack.

In the emergency room, they checked Henry and Anne from head to toe. The doctors and nurses were amazed at the healed scars of injuries on Henry that had not there just days ago, apart from the stab wound. Several doctors subjected him to CT Scans, X-rays, and MRIs. They compared the results to the ones from ten days ago, unable to understand how these new injuries had the appearance of injuries healed months ago. No one could believe it.

Anne was also examined thoroughly. All of the results showed no sign of injury or assault, causing some to question her story.

Henry heard later that the police found the warehouse and photographed the scene, taking samples from the pools of blood under the hanging chains, and the desk where Anne had died, confirming it was indeed from Henry and Anne. With the amount of blood left, the experts even more stumped. No one could survive such a massive loss, they insisted.

Yet they were obviously alive. Forensic evidence on the desk indicated biological material from seven distinct individuals in addition to Anne, confirming her story. It was evident something horrible had happened there, and that both Henry and Anne had been gravely injured at some point.

The charred remains of the six human assailants were collected and tested. Their identities were confirmed; however they could not identify one sample that contained human DNA, but something else unrecognizable. The conclusion of the forensic team was that the bodies had been consumed in a manner consistent with spontaneous human combustion, but they could not declare a definitive cause of the fire. Nothing, apart from the six men, had burned. However, it was clear that whatever consumed the bodies was not caused by anything Henry or Anne had done. There were no traces of an accelerant on any of the bodies or at the crime scene.

Henry and Anne were cleared of any culpability in their deaths.

Finally, after hours and tests, one doctor, an older man, Dr. John Geller, one of the chief doctors in the hospital, said with a smile, "I believe you, Mr. Williford. There is no other explanation except to believe this was truly a miracle. We can't do more than God can, so I think you can go home now."

Henry smiled, extending his hand. "Thank you, Dr. Geller."

Heidi and James arrived, having been informed by the police that Henry and Anne had been found. They brought fresh clothes for the couple. Heidi hugged Henry as tight as she could once he was dressed. It was evident she had been crying, but when she saw them, the joy on their faces shining though like freshly scrubbed skin, she smiled.

"Something changed," she said stepping back. "Someday you'll have to tell me what happened."

Henry kissed her forehead, promising, "I will. But there's something I have to do first. Did you pick up what I asked you to get from the house?"

"I did," Heidi replied with a wink, slipping something into Henry's hand.

Henry got down on his knees in front of Anne, in the middle of the emergency room, and with all of the attending doctors, nurses, police and paramedics watching, he uttered words that made Anne's heart soar. "Anne, I know I'm not Prince Charming but, will you marry me?" He held up the ring he'd intended for Christine. It was meant to be worn by his true love and now, it would be. It was Henry's way of casting off the last bitter memory of his past.

"You may not be a prince but...you are charming." Anne paused. "Yes!" she barely got the word out. "Of course I will." The entire emergency room burst out in applause as the couple kissed. Heidi burst into tears, crying so uncontrollably that Jim had to guide her to a chair.

Henry and Anne looked at each other and laughed, saying in unison, "And they lived happily ever after?"

37. EPILOGUE

Anne and Henry were married in a small ceremony in Heidi and James' back yard, with Pastor Jennings conducting the service and some of their new friends from South Bay in attendance. Nattie and Robbie even behaved themselves walking down the aisle as flower girl and ring bearer.

Tale of the Princess Dragon was published and became a huge success, selling over a million copies. After their honeymoon in Hawaii, they traveled around the country for events and book signings.

One day they were at a book store in downtown Chicago for a book signing. The lines of readers at the store reached to the door and into the street with parents and children holding onto their copies of the large picture book. Anne and Henry sat at the table, pens in hand, signing the many copies of the book placed in front of them, taking time to greet and thank each fan.

One young mother had her two children with her, who appeared to be five and ten years of age. She put her open book in front of Anne, smiling with excitement. Anne signed the book, "with love to Crystal." Her reading and writing were now up to par with where she should be and like Henry, she had a great love for books.

Crystal thanked her. She turned to leave the table. "Will there be a sequel?"

Anne smiled and looked at Henry. "You never know! There are so many possibilities out there!"

THE END

About the Authors

Lauretta Kehoe is an avid reader of all types of books, but mostly science fiction and fantasy, seeking in these stories reflections of her Christian faith. Not finding many, she decided to write what she wanted to read.

Michael Kehoe is a professional comedian, actor and screenwriter, who has appeared in movies, television shows, commercials and as his Geriatric Elvis persona at casinos in the Las Vegas area.

Together, Laurie and Michael have published stories in several anthologies. In addition to writing their own books, they work with other authors, including turning movie scripts into novellas for producer, director, and actor Ron Becks.

They are members of the Jerry Jenkins Writer's Guild and Lauretta has studied with Ted Dekker through his "The Creative Way" program and James Patterson's Master Class.

After raising five children in Chicago, Lauretta and Michael moved to Las Vegas, Nevada where they live with their two cats, Thor and Sammy.

Learn more about Lauretta and Michael at: https://laurettakehoe.com/

Also from Gabriel's Horn

Gypsy Heart
the poems of Lilly Gelle
collected and translated by Lauretta Kehoe

Silken Strands
A Novel of the Historic Oneida Community
by Rebecca May Hope

The Blue Bells Chronicles
a tale of time travel, mysteries and miracles, romance and redemption
by Laura Vosika

The Feet Say Run
Hitler's Germany to a desert island: a poignant and humorous journey
by Dan Blum

My Gypsy War Diary
a young boy caught in an ancient family secret, a buried treasure...
by Shawn D. Brink

Look for more at www.gabrielshornpress.com. Learn about new releases and new authors. Join our mailing list there.